Julie Shackman is a f...   ...her
journalist.

She lives in Scotland wi...   ...
little Romanian rescue pu...

julieshackman.co.uk

X x.com/G13Julie
instagram.com/juliegeorginashackman
facebook.com/julie.shackman
BB bookbub.com/authors/julie-shackman

Also by Julie Shackman

JOURNEY TO THE SCOTTISH HIGHLANDS

Scottish Escapes

JULIE SHACKMAN

One More Chapter
a division of HarperCollins*Publishers* Ltd
1 London Bridge Street
London SE1 9GF
www.harpercollins.co.uk

HarperCollins*Publishers*
Macken House, 39/40 Mayor Street Upper,
Dublin 1, D01 C9W8, Ireland

This paperback edition 2026

1

First published in Great Britain in ebook format
by HarperCollins*Publishers* 2026

A catalogue record of this book is available from the British Library

ISBN: 978-0-00-872801-4

Printed and bound in the UK using 100% Renewable Electricity
by CPI Group (UK) Ltd

This book is dedicated to all the dreamers out there, and to anyone who was ever made to feel small, unloved or insignificant. You matter. And you are loved.

Chapter One

I blinked down in disbelief at the critic's stinging words.

My agent, Octavia, always told me to ignore the bad reviews and focus on the good ones, but it was very difficult to do when the six part, glossy TV series I'd just appeared in was being compared to the Titanic.

It was a modern-day drama called *Sinister*, about a journalist and a former conman who teamed up together to try to bring down the corrupt political elite.

I'd been thrilled, after attending a number of auditions, to secure the role of Tammy Conroy, the sister of said former conman.

I'd been sure that this would be the big break I'd been working so hard to achieve over the years.

As if.

I let out a cross between a gasp and a choke as I read the scathing newspaper review.

My flatmate, Jade, spun round to look at me as she rinsed out our teapot at the sink. 'What's up, Daisy?'

I continued to make a series of furious noises. 'This prick who writes for *The London Gazette*. This so-called TV and film critic?'

Jade peered over at the open newspaper which I'd spread across the kitchen table, trying to see what had put me in such a rage.

I snatched up the offending page and flapped it around as though it were alight. The column had its recognisable silhouette of a fox's head, with 'Fox – the critic everyone respects and fears', running along the top of it. How pretentious!

I was so infuriated; I was struggling to make coherent sentences. I gave the newspaper another angry waggle. 'He's just butchered *Sinister*. I mean, really pulled it apart.'

Jade set the teapot down on the draining board and moved over to where I was seething at the kitchen table.

Jade (real name Lady Jacintha Woodstone, only daughter of the Duke and Duchess of Woodstone) owned our gorgeous apartment in Notting Hill.

I'd got talking to Jade eighteen months ago after appearing in a play in a nearby theatre and deciding to join the rest of the cast for a swift drink at a local bar.

Jade, with her pink hair and silver-ringed hands, had been performing her poetry to a group of fascinated art students, and before I knew it, we were chatting at the bar, and she was offering me a room at her place for a reasonable amount of rent. I got the impression, although

Jade never admitted it, that she was rather lonely and craved some companionship.

I almost bit her hand off, and I couldn't get my few belongings packed up fast enough to vacate my dreary one-bedroom bedsit in East London.

Moving into the ice blue and white fronted building with its frilly balcony had been the stuff of dreams after my previous accommodation.

Now, Jade pointed a ringed finger at the newspaper article. 'Is that the critic everyone talks about? Oh, what's his name again? The one who remains anonymous?' She pushed a frustrated hand through her long hair, which reminded me of candy floss.

My jaw clenched. 'Yes, it's him. The twat that calls himself Fox. He's obviously such an idiot; he doesn't want anyone to know who he really is.' I made a growling noise. 'I wish I could land one on him. I really do.'

Jade's mouth twitched. 'Well, good luck with that. Nobody even knows his name, let alone what he looks like.' She sank into the high-backed kitchen chair opposite me and propped her freckled chin on her hand. The stream of silver charm bracelets on her arm jangled. 'Go on then. Put me out of my misery. Read it to me.'

'Ok.' I braced myself. '"The latest offering of a new, six-part TV drama, *Sinister*, promised so much but failed to deliver."'

The blood sizzled in my veins. I snapped my head up from reading. 'Can you believe this? We all acted our arses off! There was a stellar cast, and the number of hours the production team put in was crazy.'

'Take a breath,' advised Jade, 'or you're going to have an aneurysm.' She flicked her hair back. 'Keep reading.'

I gritted my teeth and resumed. '"The cast showed promise, but the script was clunky in parts, absurd in others and so predictable at times, it was embarrassing."' I paused again. 'Poor Lando. He's going to be so disheartened.' Lando Greene was the head script writer and a lovely guy.

I cleared my throat and turned my attention back to the slaughtering review. '"The main protagonist, Cassie Newman, played by Hallie Flint, seemed to spend all her time mooning after former jailbird Eddie Carter (James Millan).

'"Some kudos, however, to Daisy Madden, who satisfactorily portrayed Eddie's troubled sister Tammy, but even she failed to rescue this car crash masquerading as a gritty, modern drama."'

I slapped the paper on the table with the palm of my hand. Shit! That hurt. And I wasn't just talking about my palm. 'Satisfactorily?!' I winced.

'From someone like Fox, that's a compliment,' assured Jade. 'Practically an Oscar nomination.'

My eyes bored into the page. 'There's more, but I can't face reading it; he has a go at the director for trying to be too arty with his shots, and he even compares the soundtrack to a Friday night karaoke session in Islington.'

Jade bit her lip and suppressed a laugh.

'Oh, I'm so glad you're finding this funny.' I shook my

mink-coloured wavy hair in disgust. 'I bet he's never had to trudge to some freezing cold theatre at ridiculous o'clock and queue up for bloody hours for an audition.'

Jade arched one pierced brow. 'No, in all likelihood he probably hasn't. He'll be some posh, upper-class idiot from the Home Counties.'

Now it was my turn to bury an ironic smile.

Jade caught it. 'I know. I know. I'm the pot calling the kettle black.' She turned her head to me. 'Try to forget about it, sweetheart. Move on. Focus on the next acting job.'

I pulled a face. 'I bet there isn't one. Octavia would've been in touch if there had been.' I eyed my silent mobile at my elbow.

Jade offered me an encouraging smile. 'Ok. So, *Sinister* looks like it's not going to set the world alight. Who's to say your next acting gig won't?'

That was one of the many things I admired about Jade. She was always a glass-half-full kind of girl.

I reached across a hand and patted hers. My phone then decided to ping into life with a series of explosive texts from my fellow cast members and some of the production team.

I groaned as it proceeded to ring. It was Lando, the script writer of *Sinister*. He was a sweet guy, but he was prone to theatrical outbursts, and I could only begin to imagine what he was going to say about this scathing review.

With guilt rippling through me, I picked up my phone and declined the call. 'The series scriptwriter,' I explained to a questioning look from Jade across the table. 'I know it must sound mean, but I feel awful enough as it is without mulling over this bloody review again and again.'

Jade stood up, her jewellery clinking and clattering. She nodded over at my phone, which I'd plonked back down on the kitchen table. 'Why don't you give your agent a call? See if there's anything else on the horizon?'

I let out a bark of laughter. 'I doubt that very much.'

'Well, you don't know until you ask.'

Her ringing mobile interrupted our conversation. She plucked it out of her fringed skirt pocket. 'It's mother and father.' She rolled her eyes. 'Won't be a sec.'

I watched her swinging hips vanish out of the kitchen.

I stared down at the dark screen of my mobile. There was more chance of me winning the Nobel Peace Prize than securing more acting work at the moment, but I knew what would happen if I didn't call Octavia. Jade would just nag me until I did. So, what harm would it do to give her a call?

I plucked up my phone and nibbled my bottom lip.

Here I was, twenty-eight years old, born and bred in the Scottish Highland town of Strath Ross, with a BA in acting from Glasgow's Royal Conservatoire of Scotland, living in London and struggling to get the acting break I'd dreamt about since I was a precocious kid. I'd paid my dues on the stage before I'd finally broken into TV, but I wanted to secure more prominent roles in film and television. I loved the ripple of the theatre curtains and the creak of the seats, but my ambition was to get to the next level. I had to. Acting had been all I'd ever wanted to do. It had always felt like part of me.

I'd even taken an online script writing course last year, just to get more of a feel for and understanding of the process, such was my desire to succeed in the industry.

I'd had my darling grandpa, George, and my late grandma, Bea, as a captive audience when I was a kid, making them sit through endless plays I'd written or watch me pretend to be a swan.

Failure for me was not an option. I couldn't ever contemplate the prospect of ending up like my mother, Dee.

She'd been a frustrated singer, got pregnant with me at the tender age of eighteen and decided when I was three months old that she wasn't mother material. She thought Strath Ross had cheated her out of so much, and after I came along, she viewed me in the same way. That was when my wonderful grandparents stepped in and brought me up.

Grandma Bea passed away suddenly when I was thirteen, so it had just been me and Grandpa George for the last fifteen years. I very occasionally saw my mother – she ended up living in Clachan Hill, a town about half an hour away from Strath Ross – but to me, she was just like some odd apparition who would drift in and out of my life when she felt like it, even though I'd made it clear I had nothing to say to her. At least she'd got married two years ago, so that seemed to be preoccupying her more these days. Her new husband was a farmer ten years younger than her called Innes. He was her priority.

As for my erstwhile father, Ritchie Baird, he'd been a

twenty-one-year-old barman in Strath Ross's local pub, The Bat and Cavern.

My grandparents told me my mother had fallen for his twinkly eyes and easy charm. He'd made her laugh. He'd wanted to become an actor and had appeared in a few TV adverts, but he was searching for his big break.

Ha! That was where I got my love of acting.

From what I'd heard the locals say about him, that seemed like the only thing I had in common with him, and that suited me just fine. My mum had been warned by her friends about my dad's restless reputation, but she was too smitten to listen and believed she was the one who could change him.

She fell pregnant with me five months after they started dating. She told him she was expecting, and then he handed his notice in at the pub and took off to London like Dick Whittington, in search of his fortune.

She never saw or heard from him again until his parents had told my grandparents, three years later, that he was working as an estate agent in Chepstow and was engaged to a girl called Liz.

I'd seen a couple of grainy photographs of him. I possessed the same subtle tilt at the end of my nose and similar thick, expressive brows.

But that was where the similarity ended, as far as I was concerned. I would never be like either of my parents, I reassured myself. I wouldn't settle. I would go for my dreams, and ok, if I didn't succeed, at least I wouldn't dine out on what-ifs like my mum did. And I'd been determined to succeed in my chosen career where my dad had failed. Even my maiden name wasn't his. I'd legally changed it when I was old enough from Baird to my grandfather's surname, Madden.

I clutched my phone in my right hand. My acting career wasn't exactly going the way I'd envisaged. I thought about my amazing drama teacher at Forrest Bank High School, Mrs Hazelwood, who'd encouraged me, inspired me and supported me. She'd been in her late twenties, possessed bags of enthusiasm and was determined to bring out the best in her students. I wondered what she'd say to me right now. From the sitting room, I could hear Jade murmuring as she talked to her parents.

Giving my head a wobble, I fetched up Octavia Dawson's phone number.

Her plummy, calming tones slid into my ear after a few rings. She offered a few brief niceties before launching into the newspaper review. 'Not a great write-up about *Sinister*, was it, in *The London Gazette*? Although Fox did describe your performance as satisfactory.'

'Oh yes. I'm welling up right now with gratitude.'

Outside the kitchen window, I could hear the parp of car horns and Notting Hill's mid-morning stirrings from the treelined streets. The stunning Victorian townhouses and the emerald garden squares often made me feel like I'd stepped into a historical novel. The fact that I was now just a stone's throw away from the glittering West End still sent my theatrical heart into a tailspin. It was so frustrating; within touching distance, but right now, with this soul-sucking review glaring up at me in black and white, it seemed further away than ever.

'What else is there for me, Octavia?' I pushed, my lilac painted fingernails tapping the edge of our polished kitchen table.

'You mean any acting roles?'

'No, brain surgery. Of course acting.'

Octavia let out an awkward little laugh. 'To be honest, poppet, there's not really anything I think would suit you at the minute.'

My spine went rigid. The tiny, optimistic flame inside of me, which had been hoping there might be even a crumb of something, snuffed itself out. I knew it. I should never have entertained the thought, even for a microsecond. 'Nothing at all?'

There was an awkward silence. 'If I were you, I'd let Fox's review become tomorrow's chip paper, and then we can revisit what you could be doing next. Oh, someone wants to speak to me. Got to go. Catch up later. Ciao!'

I blinked at my phone as she hung up. I let it clatter back down on the kitchen table.

Great. Just great. Even my agent was reluctant about being associated with me, thanks to that shitty critic and his shitty review.

Oh God. My phone resumed its pinging with more furious texts from other cast and crew members of *Sinister*. They were in turmoil, too, worried about how this Fox piece was going to impact them going forward.

I was still too churned up with anger and feeling sorry

for myself to make them feel better. I'd message them back once I was able to pull myself together.

I had my rent to pay to Jade, and my credit card bill was beginning to resemble a foreign telephone number. I'd received a generous payment for my part in *Sinister*, but living in London had eaten a significant hole in that already. What was left, which hadn't been much, I'd stashed into my savings account. Acting was so precarious, you just never knew if and when the next job would appear, and staying in this picturesque but affluent area meant that everyday living was on the pricey side. My grandparents encouraged me to chase my dreams but advised me that I should have a financial cushion. At the moment, it was more the size of a pin cushion.

I turned over my situation in my head. I had no other option.

I'd give the hospitality agency a call next. Ask them if there were any waitressing gigs going at the moment. That had been my backstop on several occasions when I was struggling to get acting work.

My head jerked up at the sound of Jade's sandals slapping over the kitchen floor towards me. 'How did it go with the Ostrich?'

I pulled a face and laughed, despite my insides feeling like they'd been stomped on. Jade often referred to Octavia that way. 'One of these days, I'll have a Freudian slip and call her that.' I puffed out my cheeks. 'It didn't go well. She said she doesn't have anything new for me right now. She wants the hoo-ha over Fox's review to die down before thinking about putting me forward for something else.'

Jade leant against the sink top and frowned. 'But you were great in it.'

'Not that you're biased or anything.' I sighed. 'It's death by association, I guess. I'll give the hospitality folks a call now. See if there's anything going on there.'

Jade pushed herself away from the sink edge. A satisfied little smile was playing around her mouth. 'I told you that was Mum and Dad on the phone, right?'

'Yes. How are they?'

'Mum's still having fainting fits over my pink hair, and Dad wants to marry me off to the middle son of one of his bridge club mates.' She curled her lip. 'As if that's going to happen.'

She eyed me. 'Anyway, forget about me being a major disappointment to my parents. We know that already.' There was that playful smile again. 'I may have some good news for you.'

My optimism lifted. 'They don't know Guy Ritchie, do they?'

'No. Sorry. But how would you feel about putting your waitressing prowess to good use this Saturday lunchtime? Mum and Dad were just telling me about one of their friends who's throwing a posh birthday cream tea thingy for his missus. They need some extra pairs of hospitality hands and they wondered if you'd be interested?'

'This Saturday?'

'Yep. Just for a few hours.'

I chewed my lip. For just a few hours' shift, I wouldn't receive much but it was still money, and the extra cash would come in handy.

I'd already paid for Marlene's (named after Marlene Dietrich) service and MOT. She was my daffodil yellow, second-hand Volkswagen Beetle. I'd also insisted on sending some money to Grandpa, splashed out on a spa weekend for Jade and me in the Cotswolds last month and treated myself to a lemon Radley bag and a new pair of Ralph Lauren sunglasses. After that little lot, I needed to get my finances back on track.

As if reading my mind, Jade interrupted my thoughts and told me the generous hourly rate I would be paid.

I blinked over at her. At first, I thought I'd misheard her. 'Are you joking?'

'Nope.'

I sat up straighter. 'Bloody hell. Where is this afternoon cream tea? Holyrood Palace?'

'Oh, some pile in Hertfordshire. It's a bit hush-hush. If you say yes, you'll be contacted with all the info.'

I couldn't turn down an hourly rate like that. I'd need a psychological assessment if I did.

Jade stuffed her phone back in her skirt pocket. 'Have a think about it if you need to, but please don't take too long. Sounds like the husband wants to get everything finalised.'

'Are your Mum and Dad going to be there?'

'No. They can't make it. It clashes with some anniversary do they agreed to attend months ago.'

I watched her head towards her room down the hall. 'What are you going to do now?' I called after her.

'Start packing for Somerset.'

I rubbed at my forehead and followed her. 'Of course. Sorry. I forgot you were going to that residential poetry thing for a week.'

'Poetry thing?! It's a poetry workshop, where we delve into our innermost thoughts and feelings and transfer our emotions onto paper.'

I folded my arms and examined her. 'Does your attendance have anything to do with the fact that hottie poetry lecturer with the suede blue eyes is taking the course?'

'How dare you! Yes, ok, it does have a lot to do with Jasper Seaward being there.' She gave a cheeky smile. 'So, still no Jaspers in your life?'

'Ugh! No thanks. Not after the way Leon treated me. Career all the way for me from now on, thank you very much.'

'But that was a couple of years ago now.'

I shrugged. 'There's too many Leons out there for my liking. I'm fine as I am.'

I'd met Leon Sutherland two years ago when we'd appeared together in the cast of a short-lived theatre production in Streatham about a man who falls in love with his cat and marries her.

It was all a bit experimental. (I know, it sounds it.) Leon was the cat owner, and I played Mallory, the cat in question.

He was green-eyed and gorgeous, and he carried the air

of a younger Lenny Kravitz. He was also, as I found out later, ruthlessly ambitious, so you won't be surprised to know that after eighteen months together he realised he could do better than a struggling Scottish actress girlfriend and buggered off. He'd insisted that there was no one else, but two months later, it turned out that he'd been cheating on me with the honey-haired sister of a well-known casting director.

When it came to his career, Leon would've shagged a table leg, if it meant a foot up in the film world. I hadn't known that side of him existed, until then. He'd kept that under wraps from me. I saw the charming, well-read Leon, so when the heartless, ruthless version of him emerged and he deserted me to try and reach the big time, I felt like I'd been with someone I never knew at all. I thought that, as we were both in the same profession, we were there for one another, to support and encourage each other's dreams.

Turns out he viewed me as a temporary distraction.

Last I heard, he'd secured a role in a touring musical theatre production of *Driving Miss Daisy*.

I banished any more thoughts of Leon and followed Jade into her bedroom down the hall, with its framed Sylvia Plath quotes on the walls, hessian rugs and vases of dried flowers sprouting everywhere. My room was next to hers and was filled with retro movie posters, black and white glossy photos of Marilyn Monroe and rows of autobiographies on the shelves. I crossed my arms, as I stood, watching Jade buzz about. 'I've been thinking. I don't fancy rolling around in the flat on my own for a week.

I'm going to drive back up to Strath Ross after working at this function on Saturday. Go and see my grandpa.'

'That sounds like a good idea.' She planted one hand on her hip. 'So, does that mean I can call Mum and Dad back and tell them you're in on this mysterious lunch gig?'

I nodded my head. It was a no brainer.

'Great. I'll ring them back now.' She bathed me in a wide smile. 'Then I can focus on my beauty treatments so I can look my best for Jasper.'

Jade meandered over to her dressing table and hauled out a couple of long, floaty scarves from a drawer. 'All that fresh Scottish air and rolling hills. It'll put some colour back into those bonnie wee cheeks of yours!'

She proceeded to fetch her case from under her bed.

'If that's your best attempt at a Scottish accent, I'd hate to hear your worst.'

She laughed, displaying her small, even, white teeth, as she coiled the scarves up and stashed them inside her case. Then she rummaged in her skirt pocket for her mobile. 'I'll call my parents now and tell them you're in.' She looked up from the screen. 'Just promise me one thing, Daisy.'

'What?'

'You'll give me all the gossip on this Saturday cream tea affair.'

I crossed my heart. 'I promise, although I think you're allowing your imagination to run away with you.' I leant over and absently stroked one of the scarves in her case. 'From previous experience, these things can be rather boring.'

Chapter Two

I checked Google Maps on my phone, which I'd clipped onto one of Marlene's air vents in front of me.

I knew the tea was taking place at a stately home called Carston Manor in the middle of the Hertfordshire countryside, but in order to even glean this information, I'd had to jump through so many proverbial hoops I'm surprised I hadn't sprained an ankle.

Not only had I been asked to provide scanned copies of my driving licence and passport to an encrypted email address, but I'd also had to complete a two-page questionnaire asking everything from whether I was a member of any pressure groups to if I'd ever completed a confidentiality agreement before. (The answer was yes. I'd undertaken hospitality for numerous high-profile events, where the so-called great and the good had been in attendance.)

Once all my information had satisfied the powers that

be, I'd received a secure email reply and two separate passwords I was required to enter in, all so I could access the location and time of this secretive birthday bash.

The Secret Service had nothing on this!

Carston Manor was situated on the outskirts of an English chocolate box village called Little Brook.

The drive there was all winding country lanes, edged with lush, emerald-green hedges. The embankments were dotted with yellow cowslip flowers.

Fields unravelled in a sea of daisies under the powdery blue May sky. Thankfully, last weekend had been the first May Bank Holiday of the year; if it had been this weekend, the journey wouldn't have been so pleasant with traffic to contend with.

A quaint little Gothic church nestled on the other side of the fields, its spire twirling up into the spring sunshine. A road sign coming up on the left-hand side informed me that I was entering Little Brook.

The setting was like a Constable painting, so different from my home town of Strath Ross, which was more like *Wuthering Heights*, with its moody loch and plunging rock faces. There was only one road into Strath Ross, which took you past the stunning and shimmering Loch Crawe. It was like a little secret stashed away on its own, and I loved it.

Refocusing on the road ahead, I negotiated my way through what I presumed was Little Brook's main street.

It consisted mainly of independent shops, their bottle windows brimming with everything from expensive fashion and crockery to jewellery. Willowy, ornate streetlamps craned their necks over the cobbled road. Affluent looking locals drifted up and down the pavement, cheerily waving to one another or slipping into cafes whose awnings rippled gently.

Google Maps directed me through the main thoroughfare, until I saw the meandering traffic behind me disappear in my rear-view mirror in a vanishing trail of BMWs, Mercedes and Land Rovers.

Carston Manor was situated behind a set of imposing black wrought iron gates, well away from the buzz of the high street and down a right-hand lane. Birds were erupting in a variety of song in the surrounding trees. More hedgerows were doing a good job of concealing the grand house from view.

If I angled myself right against the driver side window of my car, I could just make out the odd glimpse of brilliant white stonework.

I eased Marlene up to the closed gates and lowered my driver side window.

An officious male voice barked, 'Name, please,' from a grey and silver intercom system on the right.

'Daisy Madden. I'm here as part of the—'

But he didn't give me time to finish what I was saying.

There was a loud buzzing sound, and the gates slid backwards.

I drove through, my tyres scrunching over the buttery-coloured gravel. The tree-lined avenue opened out.

I let out a long, low whistle as I gazed through the car windscreen. Carston Manor was like something out of a

Disney pop-up book. It was a grand pillared affair with a couple of romantic balconies, a dozen winking mullioned windows and a cherry-coloured panelled door.

A well-built older man, who reminded me of a WWE wrestler, emerged from the right side of the house and directed me to a staff parking area.

I eased in between a battered Mini and a small Transit van and grabbed my giant straw bag from the passenger seat. I'd rolled up my jeans and T-shirt and stuffed them into my bag together with my trainers, in the hope that I could change my outfit at the end of the shift. My packed wheelie case was stashed in the boot.

I didn't fancy driving all the way to Strath Ross looking like Connie from *Fawlty Towers*.

I clambered out and locked up the car. This would be some place to describe to Grandpa when I saw him tomorrow.

The soft May breeze lifted my high ponytail. I straightened the collar of my fitted, pinstriped shirt.

I'd learnt the hard way a few years back that comfortable shoes were everything in this game, so I'd teamed my slim-fitting, black trousers with my pair of charcoal loafers.

No sooner had I started to make my way towards the side door, as instructed in the email I'd received, than a steely-eyed, middle-aged woman appeared.

She too was sporting a very similar outfit to me, but the collar of her shirt was white.

She yanked open the door and encouraged me inside. 'Daisy?'

'Yes, that's me.'

We shook hands.

'I'm Sue Arnold. I'm in charge of the waitressing for this event. Nice to meet you. You come highly recommended.'

I blushed. 'Well, that's very nice to know. Thank you,' I silently thanked Jade and her parents for the glowing report.

Behind Sue's coiffed, highlighted hair, the kitchen was a gleaming chrome and black expanse, with a marble-topped breakfast bar that looked as long as the M6. Copper pots, pans and saucepans were strung up on hooks.

On the breakfast bar was an assortment of platters covered in dome lids and dozens upon dozens of glinting champagne flutes.

I was beginning to get a little worried. There was no sign of any other waiting staff here. Surely it wasn't just us? It really would be like *Fawlty Towers* if it was.

But my doubts were soon put to rest when the kitchen door swung open and four other people dressed just like me emerged. They all looked like students. There were two guys, one in trendy spectacles and the other with a quiff, and two girls: one with a long, swinging blonde plait and the other sporting jam-red lipstick.

Sue rattled through their names, Jason, Kieran, Jasmine and Iris.

'We're expecting around sixty guests,' trilled Sue,

appraising all of us like a sergeant major. 'High profile names. So remember, slick, approachable but phantom-like.'

I think I knew what she was trying to say; we were to serve the guests but not scare them.

She turned to Jason and Kieran. 'Birthday balloons blown up and in the garden room?'

Jason pushed his red spectacles back up his nose. 'Yes. All done.'

Jasmine and Iris offered me friendly smiles.

'Do you know who's coming along today?' Iris hissed out of the corner of her mouth to me. 'I had a look on Google to try and find this place, but…'

Sue swung her neat, blonde hair. 'You'll find out soon enough, but remember. You all signed confidentiality agreements, so unless you want to be sued, I strongly advise the five of you to keep information about today to yourselves. Remember, we act professionally at all times.'

I'd tried to prise information out of Jade about who owned Carston Manor, but she said even she didn't know much. 'It's a couple my parents met last year on a cruise. I think he's something big in the luxury hotel business.'

My attention fell on the lush green trees and hedges past the kitchen windows. Oh well. A few hours running back and forth for people who in all likelihood wouldn't give me the time of day, and then I could jump in Marlene and begin my journey home.

Sue glanced down at her wristwatch. 'Ok, folks. Action stations. The guests are due to begin arriving in about fifteen minutes.'

Beside me, Iris let out a subtle groan. 'Do you think Sue was a company director in a previous life?'

The next fifteen minutes shot past in a flurry of noise from the other side of the kitchen door where we were whizzing around. The babble of conversation and peals of loud laughter rang out from the gathering guests.

Sue had tasked me with pouring bottles of Armand de Brignac champagne into glasses, which I'd stationed on numerous silver trays.

Snippets of guests' conversation bounced through the door towards me.

My hand stilled as I suspended the bottle of champers over another tray of flutes. A couple of the guests' voices echoed in my head.

I was sure I recognised them.

Trying to stem my curiosity and failing, I waited until Sue was occupied with giving orders to Jason and slipped across the kitchen to the door.

I eased it open and peeked through the slim crack.

It was like a who's who of the British acting fraternity, stirred up with a couple of well-known TV presenters. Some were in huddles in the hallway, while others were gliding into the garden room.

'Daisy?'

Oh bugger.

I swung round, plastering a guilty smile on my face.

Sue gave me a look. 'I hope you're not starstruck.'

I shook my ponytail so hard it slapped against my back.

'Nope. Not at all.' That wasn't strictly true, of course, but I guessed that was what she wanted to hear.

'Good, because remember what I said: professional and friendly, but ghost-like. Waitress and then vanish.'

Trying not to envisage myself as Casper the Friendly Ghost, I retrieved the bottle of champagne from the top of the breakfast bar and filled a few more glasses.

Sue nodded her approval at me. 'Right. Off you go then.'

She pushed open the kitchen door, allowing me to angle myself out.

Faces I instantly recognised from stage and screen wavered in front of my eyes. I had to get a grip.

I'd worked at so many events before where there were famous people, but this was on another scale. If Carston Manor were to blow up this afternoon, half of Britain's acting royalty would be wiped out. That must have been why everything was so secret squirrel about who was attending.

I drilled my eyes into the glasses of bubbling, pale gold I was carrying.

It was no good. I had to star spot. I couldn't help myself.

Making my way through the grand hall, I spied Dame Judi Dench, Sir Ian McKellan, Dame Joan Collins and Hannah Waddingham. I wheeled this way and that, proffering the champagne flutes from the tray.

Hannah bloody Waddingham!

Oh God… I loved that woman!

I gripped my tray tighter and headed down the chequered hallway to where the humungous garden room was decked out with row upon row of gigantic silver balloons. The number 60 bobbed in front of the windows.

I glanced back.

Aiden, Iris and Jasmine were bringing up the rear, each with platters of coronation chicken sandwiches, miniature venison pies, caviar crackers, egg mayonnaise with truffle and mustard cress, as well as a tower of crumpets, laden with pale pink smoked salmon and cream cheese.

Sue was taking care of the cakes, which ranged from traditional Victorian style fare to mini sticky toffee puddings, vanilla and passionfruit bites, rich slices of chocolate cake and apricot and almond tarts. Then there were the obligatory flour-dusted fruit, plain, cinnamon, cheese, treacle and coconut scones.

Over by the floating balloons were a couple of TV directors I recognised from the stream of auditions I had attended, engaged in animated conversation. The Saturday sunshine outside was playing hide and seek amongst the trees.

I was smiled at and thanked for the champagne, and not acknowledged at all by only a very small minority.

The atmosphere was jovial and relaxed as we ferried glasses to and from the kitchen and slithered around with the sumptuous food.

In the kitchen, it was a throbbing hive of activity, with clattering crockery and the Armand de Brignac flowing like a river.

My feet were beginning to sting thanks to the endless walking up and down, but I kept reminding myself of the generous paycheque to come, and that I'd soon be jumping into Marlene and making my way back up to Strath Ross to see Grandpa.

I had a fresh tray of bubbling champagne and was weaving in and out of the chattering bodies when two sparkling morganite cufflinks and a hand appeared and took one of the flutes. 'Thank you,' rumbled a male voice. 'I bet you'll be glad to finish after pandering to this lot.'

I looked up.

A pair of dark chocolate eyes were regarding me, framed with black lashes.

They belonged to a tall, well-built man with thick, floppy, blueberry black hair. He was very imposing – and very handsome.

'Yes,' I faltered, trying to gather myself. 'It has been rather non-stop.'

'Well, thank you again for the champagne and for all your hard work.' His voice was deep, with an educated Anglicised accent.

My cheeks pinged with colour. 'You're very welcome.'

I grabbed the opportunity to take another look at him. He had a regal-looking, Grecian nose and a strong jaw, brushed with stubble.

I whirled away, hoping he wouldn't notice my cheeks were now puce. Whoever he was, he'd taken me by surprise.

The endless pouring of champagne was beginning to have an effect on some of the partygoers. Certain voices were growing more and more animated.

I glided around the rest of the garden room, with its panoramic views of the grounds and its sumptuous lemon and tangerine furnishings. I'd gathered up a few abandoned glasses and was about to proffer some more champagne when I noticed out of the corner of my eye three men huddled together over by the open double doors.

The guy in the middle was letting out barks of laughter like a drunk seal.

I moved closer to them, clutching my tray bearing the flutes. I couldn't help but overhear what he was saying. Folks in the Outer Hebrides would've been able to make him out.

'The standard of drama on TV in this country at the moment is appalling. Take that recent disaster, *Sinister*. Jesus! Just dreadful.'

My loafers froze on the polished, blonde wood floor.

'Awful bloody script. Shocking, really, when you take into account the supposed quality of those involved. The girl who played the sister was competent, but that was all.'

The cool, silver tray stilled in my hands.

I knew I should move off. I was working. But it was as if my legs weren't listening to common sense. They refused to move.

I attempted to refocus on the sweeping lawns outside and the tangle of shadows in the sunshine. No. It was no good. My head was already replaying over what he'd just said about *Sinister*. And what he'd just said was exactly what that idiot newspaper critic Fox had written in his column.

It was too much of a coincidence. It must be. It was practically word-for-word. This man, with the cropped red hair and smug grin, must be him. He must be Fox.

It made sense, his attendance at a high profile do like this with so many famous actors.

I gave my head a mental wobble. *Come on, Daisy. Be professional. Just head back to the kitchen. Forget about the prick.*

I tried to take a calming breath and began to tap my way past him. There was a stunning woman in a long, red, floaty dress who seemed to have overheard his booming tones too, because she kept glancing over at him from under her hair.

I thought he might have finished verbally lambasting the TV drama I'd just appeared in. Some hope. His verbal diatribe continued. 'Well, when I say competent, I was rather distracted by those gorgeous legs of hers. I think in all likelihood they got her in there as eye candy for the dads, rather than her acting abilities!'

My hand froze as I reached out to collect a couple of abandoned champagne flutes. Fury burned inside me. What?! The sodding cheek! Nice to know Neanderthal Man was alive and well after all. I thought about how hard I'd worked to get that role. I'd thrown everything I had at it.

I could feel my throat constricting with temper. I told myself not to look over at him, but my eyes disobeyed me. He was ruddy-faced and sniggering into his champagne glass. So pleased with himself.

Warming to his theme, he carried on. 'It's all about inclusion these days, though at the expense of talent.

I suppose they have to get their working-class actor quota up somehow.'

It was like time had screeched to a halt. My breathing caught in my chest in appalled, ragged gasps. I couldn't believe he'd actually turned around and said that. Who the hell did he think he was? What talent or ability did he have? Visions of him crucifying other performers as he sat hunched over his laptop filed through my mind. Did he have any idea what his wounding words could do to people? What effect they could have on their confidence? Their careers?

I was all for free speech and reviews, but Fox was deliberately cruel.

I knew I shouldn't give him another thought, but I couldn't help it. I knew I should just march past him and carry on with what I was doing. Ignore him. Inwardly seethe, recognise him for the ignorant git he was and go take five.

But it was no good.

His self-satisfied grin and boozy, red cheeks were sending my emotions into a frenzy.

Refusing to think about what I was about to do and where, I gripped the loaded tray I was carrying.

Ok. So I was in a posh stately home, surrounded by a lot of very talented people who I'd admired for years. But this man... I was proud of my background and where I came from. It sounded crazy, but his poisonous words felt like a slight against my darling grandparents and anybody else like me, who chased their dreams no matter what. Everyone was entitled to a chance at success.

Acting shouldn't be for the exclusive elite.

Refusing to listen to the warning voice in my head, I found myself putting one dark loafer in front of the other. The guests around me continued to laugh and exchange pleasantries; their champagne glittered pale gold in their glasses and the food was being consumed with appreciative relish.

Before I had a chance to consider what I was doing, I found myself standing in front of him, still holding the tray of champagne. My knuckles were turning white with rage. He was still flanked on either side by his two associates, but all I could see was this braying character, holding court in the middle of them.

I swallowed and jutted out my chin. My voice sounded alien to my ears. It carried a hint of menace. 'Excuse me? Sorry to interrupt. Actually, no, scrub that; I'm not sorry.'

Their conversation drew to a sharp halt.

I could feel three sets of bemused eyes resting on me.

Fox looked me up and down. 'Pardon?'

My hard stare bored into him. My initial feeling of apprehension was gone as I surveyed him from head to toe in his herringbone suit.

'I don't know if you recognise me, but I'm the working-class quota you were just talking about.'

'Sorry?' His freckled brow frowned.

I didn't even try to keep my voice on an even keel.

My words were finding their momentum. 'My name is Daisy Madden. I played Tammy in *Sinister*, remember?'

Fox's thin brows jumped.

Adrenaline accelerated in my chest. 'Do you have any idea the effect your poisonous words can have on someone? You write all this bile in that tawdry newspaper column of yours.'

A ghost of a smirk pulled at his mouth, which riled me even more.

'Well, I can tell you that I'm proud to be working class. I'm also proud to be an actor.'

I tried not to recoil backwards as, still clutching his champagne flute, he took a few sudden steps towards me. 'Looks like you're not doing much acting at the moment, Miss.' His cold, pale eyes raked over me. 'Looks like you're the hired help.'

One of his friends, a man with curly blond hair, grabbed the man's arm. 'Hey. Come on. That's enough.'

But Fox ignored him. He waggled his champagne glass close to my face.

By now, some of the surrounding guests had picked up on the bubbling tension. A few heads turned in our direction.

But I didn't care. I couldn't just ignore what he'd been saying.

The freckle-faced critic dismissed his friend's request to pipe down. Again, he waggled his glass from side to side. 'Be a good girl and top this up for me, would you?'

I could feel curious stares behind me. I looked from the half-empty champagne glass to Fox's sneering face and back again. He gave it another swish and tapped the side of it. 'Refill?'

A slow, tight smile slid across my face. 'Certainly, sir.'

The voice from his right, which belonged to his other friend, also sounded embarrassed. 'Guy. Stop it. You're behaving like an ignoramus.'

But I was too caught up in what I was about to do. Eying his chubby outstretched hand, I accepted his flute and set it down on my tray with a clatter. Temper was racing through me. Dismissing the ramifications of what I was about to do, I put the tray down on top of an occasional table beside me and grabbed one of the fresh glasses of champagne. I spun round, raised it in the air and was about to cascade its contents all over the top of that bullish, red head of his, when a hand appeared out of nowhere and grabbed my wrist. I stared down, incredulous. It was the morganite cufflinks again.

'No. Don't. He's not worth it.'

The intervening man snatched the glass of champagne out of my hand.

'Hey! What did you do that for?'

My voice died.

I was looking up into those deep, dark brown eyes again. But I didn't have time to recover myself. I was aware that the owner of said eyes had thrust the glass back at Fox. He glowered at him. 'Here's your refill.'

Fox took it. 'Thanks, friend.'

Morganite man pushed his face closer to Fox, who took

32

a faltering step backwards. 'I'm not your friend. And I didn't do it for you. I did it for this young lady here.'

I watched, open-mouthed, as the ruddy-faced Fox gulped and dropped his eyes to the polished floor.

But that wasn't the end of the drama. Before I knew what was happening, I found myself being steered by the elbow out of the garden room by the man with the cufflinks. I was aware of intrigued guests watching us leave. The handsome stranger spotted a quieter part of the hall, over by the grand staircase and guided me over there. 'What the hell do you think you're doing?' I gasped, wriggling my elbow free. My face was sizzling with consternation.

Now that I was out of the garden room and not the spectator sport, I seized another chance to look again at the man who'd taken the glass from me and removed me from the situation.

He towered over me. I reckoned he was in his mid to late thirties. The pinstriped three-piece suit he was wearing was beautifully cut. Lord knows how much it cost.

'In answer to your question, Miss, I was trying to stop you from being sacked. Tipping drinks over guests – even if they are behaving like an utter knob – isn't a good look.'

I glowered up at him. 'I didn't need your help, thank you very much. The twat deserved that champagne all over that posh suit of his.'

He raised his two slashes of dark brows at me. 'Would he really have been worth losing your pay over? I think not.'

His enviable black lashes thrust down at me. I cleared my throat. 'I'd better go. The boss is looking for me.'

My dark-haired rescuer appraised me. 'Aren't you going to thank me?'

'For what?' I bristled. 'For stopping me from teaching him a lesson for once?'

Underneath, buried deep inside my common sense, I knew that he'd done the right thing by stopping me from doing something so rash. I would've been dismissed on the spot and not paid a penny. Probably been in the papers as well. Octavia would've loved that. I just didn't want to lose face and admit it.

Cold, hard reality started to bite. I folded my arms. 'Come to think of it, I could still lose my job. No doubt that idiot will complain about my attitude anyway, if he hasn't already.' Shit! I should've taken a breather. Counted to ten. A sliver of panic shot through me. I really needed the money from this event today. Oh bugger!

The man pushed both hands into the pockets of his suit trousers. 'No, he won't. I'll talk some sense into him. Make sure he doesn't say anything to your boss.'

I blinked in surprise. I stood there, feeling self-conscious and laced and unlaced my fingers together. 'Oh. Er. Thank you.'

'Hey Daisy, sorry to interrupt.' Iris had materialised at my elbow. She was grasping a tray of assorted, sharply cut sandwiches. She blushed up at my rescuer. 'Sue is looking for you.'

I gave my dashing rescuer a brief nod of gratitude and

hastened away, tapping furiously across the black and white tiled hall and back towards the kitchen.

For the last hour of the event, the cold, hard realisation that Fox might and very well could still lodge a complaint about me, throbbed away in my head. I could feel my chest prickling with worry.

But he didn't complain. In fact, not long after our showdown, he vanished with his two friends, and I didn't see him again for the rest of the lunch.

The more I thought about it, the more convinced I was that the knight in shining armour had kept his word and persuaded Fox not to speak to Sue about me.

As I helped clear up in the kitchen, I thought again about what had almost happened. I'd let my emotions almost spiral out of control. And although it would've been satisfying seeing that expensive champagne trickling down that bulbous face of his, I was taken aback at how glad I was that Cufflink Man had stepped in when he had. So was my bank balance.

Fox wasn't worth losing today's generous pay over. And if I was to succeed in the acting profession, I'd have to learn to suck up negative reviews. Although, there were negative reviews, and then there were the infamous ones penned by the likes of Fox. They weren't constructive reviews, they were annihilations.

Monty and Minnie Lockwood, who it turned out were

the owners of Carston Manor, told us to avail ourselves of the downstairs shower room if we wanted to get changed at the end of the event.

We dashed in there once we'd cleared up. I enjoyed the hot needles of water, and once I dried off, I threw my jeans, glittery trainers and one of my pretty, sparkly cotton T-shirts back on. I stuffed my sweaty uniform back in my bag.

Relief swamped me as we prepared to leave. At least I hadn't ruined my reputation in the hospitality industry.

We'd already been thanked profusely by Monty and Minnie, who said she'd had the most wonderful birthday. Monty also owned a very exclusive eatery in London's West End, at which the rich and famous dined regularly, and so his list of celebrity friends over the years had become the stuff of legend.

Most of the guests had vanished by now, as had countless bottles of the champagne.

Sue and the rest of us made our weary way out of the side kitchen door, towards the staff parking. 'What are you up to for the rest of your Saturday, folks?' she asked us all.

'A soak in the bath,' sighed Iris, followed by Jasmine, who informed us she was going to take her dog for a walk and then collapse in front of the TV.

Jason revealed that he and his boyfriend were going to catch the latest Brad Pitt movie at the cinema, while Kieran was planning on going to a new nightclub with his mates. He let out a huge yawn. 'That's if I can muster up some energy.'

Now it was my turn to reveal my Saturday plans.

'I'm about to drive up to Scotland. I'm going to visit my grandfather.'

Sue squinted in the mid-afternoon sunshine spilling through the trees. She jangled her car keys in her hand. 'Goodness! That's a long drive, but I bet he'll be looking forward to seeing you.'

'He is. I can't wait to see him either. We FaceTime and call each other a lot, but I haven't seen him properly for a good few months.'

'Oh, that sounds wonderful,' enthused Sue. 'Whereabouts in Scotland are you headed?'

'Highland area. Strath Ross.'

Sue's mascara-lashed eyes danced. 'I've never been as far as that. I've visited Edinburgh and Perth, though.'

'Good job you're not flying back,' piped up Kieran, as he prepared to clamber into the driver's seat of his black Ford Escort. 'Nationwide IT failure at all UK airports. All flights cancelled.'

'What?'

Our heads snapped round to see where the other voice had come from. It was my rescuer from earlier.

Kieran nodded. 'It's true, sir. Just saw it on my phone. Came up on the news.'

The man scrambled about in his suit pocket and pulled out his mobile. He jabbed at the screen. 'Shit!' He pushed a furious hand through his dark waves. 'I don't believe this.'

'Have a safe drive to Strath Ross,' smiled Sue at me, unlocking her car and dumping her bag on the back seat.

I made to walk across to where Marlene was parked.

'You're driving to Strath Ross? As in Scotland?'

Morganite Man's questioning voice made me start. I frowned over at him. 'Yes.'

'When?'

'I'm setting off now.'

He strode closer. A slow expression of hope spread across his face. 'So, you can drive me there?'

My shocked mouth sprang open. 'Sorry?'

'To Scotland. You can take me there. You just said that's where you're headed.'

I floundered. 'Yes, that's right, but…'

He stuffed his mobile into the inside of his suit jacket. I caught a flash of electric blue satin lining. 'I was supposed to be flying up there this evening, but that's not happening now.' He oozed confidence. 'Under the circumstances, I think it's the least you can do.' He flexed a brow, which made my breath catch. 'I think you owe me one, don't you?'

Chapter Three

My indignation spiked. Who the hell did he think he was?

I didn't even know his name. I didn't know anything about him. Yet he was asking to tag along with me on the drive to Scotland?

Ok, I thought with a stab of irritation. He *was* a treat for the eyes.

But to just invite himself along on my journey back to Strath Ross? The damned cheek!

Part of me did appreciate his intervention earlier, but the other part – the petty part – wished he'd let me chuck that drink over Fox.

I stared up, struggling to comprehend the boldness of this man. 'You're not backwards in coming forwards, are you?'

'If you don't ask, you don't get.'

From the front of the manor, I could hear gaiety and the slamming of taxi cab doors.

Strobes of sunlight sifted through his dark hair, illuminating shoots of blue.

'But I don't know you,' I blustered. 'You could be anyone.'

'Evan Lord,' he replied, extending a hand.

I shook hands with him. 'I'm Daisy Madden.' He had elegant long fingers. I withdrew my hand as fast as I could under his intense gaze.

He fished his wallet out of the lining of his fancy suit jacket, produced a business card and handed it to me. His name, email address and other contact details were on it. It also said he was a freelance journalist.

I gave it a flap. Today wasn't working out as I'd planned. All I wanted was to jump into Marlene and head back to Scotland, enjoying my own company and brooding over where my acting career was going or not going.

I realised I was studying him a little too long. I snapped my attention back to his business card and mentally scurried around, latching onto any excuse I could so as not to agree to him becoming my passenger. 'You could've stolen this,' I insisted. 'There's no proof this is yours. I've only got your word for it.'

Evan Lord's mouth twitched. 'Have you actually seen who was at this shindig? If I was a thief, you really think I'd be ignoring the bling being flashed around in favour of a business card?'

I scowled up at him. Was he laughing at me?

He sighed. 'You're still not convinced, are you?' His eyes widened. 'Wait! I've got my passport with me. It's in my case in the cloak room. Come with me.'

I opened my mouth to protest, but I found myself being steered around, back through the kitchen door and along the great hall, to the mobile cloak room.

There was an attractive young woman with a long, dark plait handing stragglers their jackets. When she saw Evan smiling at her, her face lit up. It looked like he had that effect on a lot of women. Probably one of those shallow charmers. Another Leon, I concluded.

'Excuse me. Could I have my case, please?' he asked.

'Of course, sir. Do you have your cloakroom ticket handy?'

Evan retrieved his wallet and pulled from it a pink ticket with the number fifty-eight printed on it.

The cloakroom attendant moved to the left, bent over and fetched Evan's case. It was a plush, leather effort.

Evan thanked her and moved it over the desk. Around us, the final partygoers were saying long goodbyes to friends and associates.

Evan deposited his case on the grand hall tiled floor, unzipped the front pocket and slid out his passport. 'There you go.'

He handed it to me. I stared down at the shiny navy-blue leather document in my hand. Who did he think I was? Passport Control?!

Feeling self-conscious under his burning gaze, I

concentrated my attention on his passport and flipped through the pages.

I located his photograph and personal details.

Evan's chiselled features stared up at me.

I noticed that his full name was Evan Nathaniel Lord, he was thirty-seven and that he'd been born in Forrest Bank…

I drew up in surprise. 'Forrest Bank?!' I blurted.

'Yes.'

'As in Forrest Bank in the Scottish Highlands?'

'No. Forrest Bank in the Amazon.'

I pulled in my lips at his sarcasm. He didn't sound like he came from that part of the world. His accent was all privately educated sounding vowels.

'I was supposed to be flying to Inverness Airport this evening and then picking up a hire car for the short drive home to visit my family who still live there.' He scrutinised me. 'And then I overheard you say you're from Strath Ross. We're practically neighbours.'

True enough, Forrest Bank wasn't far from Strath Ross; around half an hour. It was a pretty little place too, bursting with forestry and gorgeous woodland walks, with Loch Crawe sandwiched in between us.

Bugger! Typical, that he was heading in the same direction as me.

I thrust his passport back at him.

The grand hall was almost empty now, except for the cloakroom attendant and an older man in overalls, who'd appeared and was helping her dismantle everything and pack it away.

I gripped the strap of my bag tighter and started to head back down towards the kitchen. Evan trundled his designer case behind him as he followed me. I could hear the squeaking of the wheels on the tiles. This wasn't looking good. It was appearing more and more likely that I'd have to drive him to Scotland. 'Don't you drive?' I scrambled, hoping I could still come up with an alternative travel suggestion for him. 'Didn't you bring your car?'

'No, I caught a taxi here.'

We both exited the kitchen again, which was back to its pristine, sparkling glory. Another couple of cabs scrunched away over the gravel. 'And even if I had been foolish enough to bring my car, I wouldn't have been able to drive the thing. I've been drinking.'

Bloody hell, seethed my inner voice. He's got an answer for everything! Forget about being a journalist, he'd make a wonderful politician.

I drew up beside Marlene and slid my car keys from my bag. I didn't want this man beside me for the five-hundred-mile journey. *Why?* whispered a voice. I ignored it. 'Look, Mr Lord, I don't mean to sound rude, but I had planned to have a quiet, relaxed journey back to Scotland—'

His deep voice interrupted. 'It's Evan. And I'll pay you.'

'Pardon?'

He adjusted the handle of his case and made it stand to attention beside him. The warm breeze made his silky, ice blue tie flutter. 'I said I'll pay you for the cost of your petrol and also for the inconvenience. Is five hundred pounds acceptable?'

My eyeballs popped in my head. 'Excuse me?'

'I'll pay you five hundred pounds for taking me.'

I wrapped my arms around myself for something to do. This was ridiculous! But boy would that amount of money come in handy. My cheeks stung. 'But that's too much.'

He shrugged. 'I need to get home and you're holding all the cards.'

Oh God. I didn't want to be cocooned in a car until tomorrow beside this man. He made me feel all fingers and thumbs. But the amount of money he said he'd pay me would more than cover the petrol costs and meant I could be a bit choosier about where I stopped overnight tonight.

Evan flexed a brow at me. 'Do we have a deal?'

He stuck out his hand.

I eyed it. From under his suit jacket sleeves, I got another glimpse of his glittering cuff links.

I sighed inwardly. What could I do? He had stopped me from getting sacked, I supposed, and it wasn't his fault that the UK airports had grounded all the flights. Then there was the generous amount of money he'd offered me to get him there.

God, I hated being beholden to people. If I could just get over this acting slump!

Glossing over the reluctance flickering in my chest, I took his hand and gave it another shake. His skin was warm as his fingers brushed mine. I pulled my hand away first, as though I'd received an electric shock.

I cleared my throat. 'Alright. Deal.'

Relief flooded his features. 'Thank you, Miss Madden.'

'Daisy.'

He seemed to relax a little under his pinstriped suit jacket. 'Excellent. Thank you, Daisy.'

He nodded down at my bright, daffodil-yellow car, looking bemused. 'And this is yours?'

'Yep. Why?'

'You won't misplace her in the car park.'

I halted at my driver side door, the afternoon sun glancing off the window. 'If you don't like my car…'

Evan let go of the handle of his case and raised both his hands in a mock act of surrender. 'Not at all. She's … she's funky.' His mouth flickered.

I momentarily closed my eyes. Could I do this for the next twenty-four hours?

I glanced over the car roof at him. Evan was preparing to open the passenger side. 'Well, are you driving then, Miss Daisy?' His face was deadpan, but there was a glimmer of teasing.

I prickled. *Very funny, Captain Smirk.*

This was going to be one *long* journey back to Scotland.

Chapter Four

The Hertfordshire countryside slid past in a haze of thatched cottage roofs, willowy trees and billowing fields in the late afternoon glow.

Evan tried to rearrange his long legs on the passenger side.

I made sure I kept my eyes fixed on the road ahead.

I gripped the steering wheel tighter. 'M1 and then M6,' I commented. 'Then I thought we could break up the journey and stay the night in the Lake District. Ambleside.' I wondered if I sounded like a tour guide, but I didn't care. A mixture of disbelief and annoyance were still firing through me over me agreeing to take Evan back to Scotland in the first place. Still, I did feel like I owed him.

I glanced over at the digital clock on my dashboard. 'If we stop for an hour, I reckon we should hit Ambleside around nine o'clock tonight.' My voice sounded odd to my own ears. All I wanted to do right now was blast out some Lady Gaga at top volume in an attempt to lift my spirits.

Evan glanced down at his solid silver wristwatch. 'That late?'

'Ok, I'll turn on my turbo thrusters. How's that?'

Evan raised a brow.

He was making me put up my barriers and get all defensive, which was making me feel even worse. Then more pictures reared up in front of me of that smug sod Fox at the party: the way he'd smirked at me; his mocking gaze.

I followed the signs for the M1 motorway. 'Pity that Monty and Minnie weren't more selective about the company they keep.'

'You're not still festering over what happened earlier, are you?'

I glided Marlene off the slip road and onto the motorway. Other traffic whipped past, but it wasn't quite as busy as I'd expected. 'Excuse me? Festering? That man savaged the TV series I was in. My first big break. And all the cast, the crew, everyone; they all worked so hard on *Sinister* and put so much time and energy into it.'

Evan studied me. 'So that's what that was all about. You're an actor?'

'Struggling.'

'And that mouthy guy? Who was he?'

I flicked the indicator. 'Fox. You've heard of him, right? The ignoramus who calls himself a TV and film critic?'

Evan's brows jumped in surprise. 'Of course I've heard

of him. Wow. Well, I guess his reply would be he's only doing his job.'

'Well, I'd rather be unemployed than do what he does. Do you have any idea how hard this industry is to break into? How tough it can be? It's all I've ever wanted to do, and in just a few cruel words, that cretin has slighted so many promising careers.' I bit back furious tears. 'I've got no more acting work lined up right now, and I'm sure it's the fallout from Fox's review.'

Sunlight was glancing down the planes and angles of Evan's face. 'I'm sorry about that, but I'm sure things will turn around for you.'

'Oh, gazing into your crystal ball, are you?'

The atmosphere in the car was becoming icy and tense.

'Like I said, some people should rethink their circle of friends.' I shot him a loaded glance. 'I'm afraid I have a rather dim view of journalists.'

Evan twisted round in his seat. 'I didn't realise being driven by you meant that I'd be subjected to a verbal tongue lashing about my career choices.' His eyes blazed. 'I should've got a coach back home instead.'

'Yes, perhaps you should. There's still time.'

The silence hung there.

I couldn't help how I was feeling. I was dreading telling Grandpa about my current situation, as he could and often did worry about me being down in London, despite him denying it. And having Evan stationed beside me for hundreds of miles was making my nerves jangle.

'In that case, drop me off at the next services and I'll sort myself out from here.' His peppered jaw jutted out. 'But don't worry, I'll still give you the money I promised.'

The traffic was slowing into a chain of cars.

I shook my head. I was struggling to keep my voice calm. 'I don't want anything from you, thank you.'

The cars ahead of us began to creep along again. I was able to pick up a little more speed. I didn't want Evan in my car anymore. Damn this bloody airport tech outage!

'I'm not in the habit of breaking promises, Daisy.'

'And I'm not in the habit of begging for cash. I can manage fine, thanks.'

Evan's back stiffened. 'Jesus! Has anyone ever told you how stubborn you are?'

I didn't answer. I just raised my chin and kept driving.

There was another awkward silence for a few moments before Evan let out a pained sigh. 'Look. You're right. I think that Fox individual could've been a bit more careful with his choice of words.'

'A bit more careful?' I repeated, incredulous. More fields flew past the car. 'There must've been poison dripping from his keyboard when he wrote that. In fact, whenever he writes most of his reviews!'

I shook my ponytail and eyed the white Lexus in front of us. 'Why does he have to be so cruel? I'm all for constructive criticism, but what he said was well out of order.' More dark thoughts about Fox crept back in. 'I bet he's a talentless, sour individual without a creative bone in his body.'

Evan eyed me from the passenger side. 'That's often said

about critics. They can be a bit harsh, and yes, he was acting like an arse just now.'

'A bit?' I clutched the steering wheel more firmly again. Around us, other frustrated drivers and passengers edged forward in their vehicles along the M1. 'I got the distinct impression from the way he acted towards me that he would be an arse most of the time.'

Evan forced a hand through his floppy, thick hair. 'Look, I'm getting the vibe you'd rather me not be here and you'd much prefer to do the rest of the journey on your own.'

I didn't say anything and stared ahead through the windscreen.

Evan spoke again. 'Not all journalists are like him, I can assure you. To be honest, I wouldn't describe him as a proper journalist anyway. But if you still want to drop me off…'

Oh bugger. My conscience nibbled at me. It would take him forever to get from here by coach back up to Forrest Bank, and that's if he could even get a seat on one. Because of the mess at the airports, the coaches would no doubt be swamped with additional bookings, as well as the trains. I wasn't that heartless, even if he was irritating me.

'I'm not dropping you off by a major motorway. I like to think I've got a moral code, unlike some people I can mention.'

I puffed out my cheeks. 'Just stay put. You might as well, now we're on our way.'

It was a relief to get out of the car prior to hitting the M6 to catch some fresh air and indulge in a cup of tea and an Emmental toastie.

Evan bought himself a coffee and a club sandwich.

We sat opposite one another at the motorway services, which seemed to be occupied by frazzled families heading home after a day out in the May sunshine.

Evan persisted in offering me brief, indecipherable glances whenever he looked up from his phone.

If anyone was looking at us, they'd probably assume we were a couple who'd just had an exchange of words.

I drained my tea, stood up and popped the recyclable cup in the nearby bin. 'I think we should head off again.'

Evan's lashes jutted up at me. 'So, you're not intending on abandoning me here?'

'Not if you behave yourself.'

'That sounds boring.' His eyes locked with mine.

I gripped the strap of my bag tighter. He was doing it again. Somehow, he was managing to make me feel discomfited. I spun away him. 'Come on then. Let's hit the road.'

―――――――

Coventry, Birmingham, Walsall, Stafford, Stoke-on-Trent, Preston, Lancaster; we pushed on past them all, Marlene like a bright yellow daffodil negotiating the roads.

The evening sky was bleeding into a delicious raspberry

ripple shade. I'd checked Google Maps on my phone, and Ambleside was now only about half an hour's drive away.

My eyes were beginning to feel gritty with tiredness.

I guided Marlene off at Junction 36 and flashed a brief look across at my passenger.

Evan had nodded off.

The kaleidoscope of colours drifting across the sky, lit up his features. He had such a confident, capable air about him. Everything about his appearance gave off the air of being broad and strong. I took a closer look at him as we flowed into another slowing line of traffic, from the cut of his stubbled jaw and the sharp sweep of his nose, which tilted slightly upwards at the end, to his bold, black brows and the way his mouth pursed in an almost petulant way as he slept.

Someone parped their car horn behind us. It gave me a start, and Evan's lids flickered.

I pushed my attention back to the road. The last thing I wanted was him thinking I was checking him out.

The A591 opened out with dry stone walls racing here and there, lush grass and hedgerows basking in a bronze edged sunset.

Weariness pressed down harder on me. I was longing for a long soak in a bath and then to sink into fresh, crisp bed linen.

Evan had drifted back off to sleep again.

He was all legs, and his dark hair was flopping onto his brow.

His suit was beginning to rumple, but it didn't detract from his elegance, I concluded with a jab of irritation.

I was still mulling over the prospect of losing myself in a bubbly bathtub at the bed and breakfast which I'd booked for us when we'd stopped for a break, when a blur of movement caught my attention on the right-hand side of the road. We were about to pass a heavily wooded area.

I slowed down and peered out of my driver side window. It appeared to be a little white blob of something moving this way and that in front of some dense trees.

Evan was still dozing beside me, his head slumped backwards, with one lock of hair falling forwards.

I eased off the accelerator and squeezed the brake. There were no other vehicles behind me, so I eased into the kerb for a closer look and hit the hazard lights.

I squinted out of my driver side window again. The evening light was shining into my eyes.

The white blur moved again.

I unclipped my seatbelt and angled myself against the window so I could see better.

It was a lamb.

It looked like the poor little thing was all alone.

Evan shuffled in his seat, but his eyes remained closed.

I flicked a look into my rear-view mirror. There was a car making its way over the brow of the hill behind us.

I turned my attention back to the lamb.

The cute little ball of fluff had edged away from the trees and was getting closer to the road. Oh no! If it shot out, it wouldn't stand a chance against the traffic, and it would soon be dark.

I yanked open my driver side door.

The noise of it must have disturbed Evan. He shot up straighter. 'What 's going on?'

I whipped round in my seat.

He rubbed his eyes. 'Where are we?'

'We're almost at Ambleside.'

I turned back to check that the lamb hadn't got closer to the road.

Evan let out a big yawn and stretched his arms above his head. His shirt lifted, exposing a smattering of dark hair and taut stomach. I pretended not to notice.

When he yawned again, this time making a louder noise, I shoved my finger to my lips. 'Sssh! You'll frighten it!'

Evan looked at me, confused. 'What?'

But I knew I didn't have time to explain as another car was glinting over the hill on its way towards us.

I scrambled out of Marlene and left my driver side door open. I straightened my T-shirt and started to edge my way towards the lamb, who was eyeing me with a mixture of fear and suspicion.

Evan was staring across from the passenger side, as though I'd lost all leave of my senses.

'Here, cutie. It's ok,' I soothed.

'I bet you're not talking to me.'

I snapped my head round and rammed my finger to my lips again. The baby sheep was like a blob of cotton wool with a black patch over one eye and a curly-wurley tail. The furball took a couple of faltering steps backwards.

Behind me, more cars zipped past on the country road. Darkness was beginning to close down now, giving the trees an eerie, long-shadowed silhouette.

I crouched down a few feet away, the grass brushing against the knees of my jeans. 'Come on, sweetheart. I won't hurt you.'

The lamb made a couple of nervous bleats.

'Daisy!' hissed Evan from the car. 'What the hell are you doing?'

I looked back. 'Shush! You'll see in a minute,' I whispered. If the poor thing got spooked, it could take off into the road.

Very gently, I outstretched one hand.

The lamb eyed me and my extended hand with an element of caution. I noticed as he moved that he had what looked like either the letter S or a figure eight on his right flank in light blue spray.

After a few moments of inspecting my hand, he moved closer and closer, until I was able to reach out and stroke him.

I glided my hand down his small, white, downy back. 'It's ok. I won't hurt you.' Giving him another few strokes, I managed to then pick him up, cradled him in my arms and carried him back to my car.

The warm, marmalade glow of the day seemed like a distant memory now. The Lake District darkness was inky black, and the stars were peppered across the sky like scattered seeds.

Evan's mouth dropped open as I juggled the lamb and me into the driver's side. I handed the lamb over to him and closed the door.

Evan stared in horror down at the lamb, who was peering back up at him. He gawped across at me. 'What the hell?!'

I let out a bark of laughter at the sight of Evan holding the little animal, as though it were some alien life force. 'Well, I can't take care of him while I'm driving, can I?'

I negotiated our way back out onto the road, and we set off again.

I nodded over. 'There's a smudged blue marking not far from his tail on his right side. That must be which farm he belongs to, so we should be able to find out which one.'

Evan's gaze was incredulous. His eyes glinted with disbelief out of the darkness. Only the lights from my dashboard were lighting up the angles of his features. 'Are you serious? It's after nine o'clock on a Saturday night, and you want to play detective and locate Farmer Barley mow?' The lamb wobbled as he sat on Evan's lap and seemed fascinated by him, giving him prolonged gazes. 'We're in the middle of the bloody lakes, Daisy! There must be dozens upon dozens of farms around here.'

I focused on the taillights of the car in front. 'Yes, but they all won't be using that colour of paint on their flock, will they?'

Evan shook his head. 'I don't believe this.'

The surrounding hills were rising and falling like dark, slumbering giants.

'Oh, look! A pub!' I erupted, pointing over to the right-hand side, to where a lit-up, cosy-looking public house with lattice-style windows was crouched further back from the road.

Frothing spring flowers were bursting out of hanging baskets either side of the glowing entrance. A couple of cars in the parking area shone under the spray of stars.

'Don't tell me you want to take Shaun the Sheep for a drink?' ground out Evan. He waited for me to kill the engine and, as soon as I did so, bundled the lamb back over to me.

I gave him a sarcastic look.

'Because if he doesn't want one, I do.' He adjusted his suit jacket. 'I feel like I'm in a Monty Python sketch.'

I tutted at his sarcasm. 'What did you expect me to do? Just ignore Pirate and let him be mowed down?'

'Pirate?' echoed Evan. 'Who the hell is Pirate?'

'Well, it's not a nickname I've conjured up for you.' *I could think of a few, but they aren't polite ones*, I concluded darkly to myself.

I gave the lamb a gentle squeeze as he nestled in my arms. 'I think he looks like a sweet little pirate, with that black patch over his eye.'

Evan groaned. 'Oh my God… I really am in a Monty Python sketch.'

I ignored him. 'I thought if we took him into the pub,

someone might recognise that blue mark on him and know which farm he comes from.'

'I need that drink more than ever now,' murmured Evan, although I thought I detected a faint smile teasing his mouth for a second. But it was gone as quickly as it appeared, so I wasn't sure.

He clambered out of the passenger side while I retrieved my bag from the back seat and slung it on, all while juggling Pirate in my arms. He seemed to have become used to being carted around.

I locked up Marlene and hurried to catch up with Evan who was stalking ahead across the pub car park in his designer suit. Pirate bumped gently in my arms.

The gold wooden sign creaked over our heads, proclaiming the pub's name to be The Lake and Lantern.

Evan frowned down at Pirate in my arms. 'Are we really doing this?'

I scowled up at him while rubbing Pirate's head. 'Of course. Unless you want me to drop you back at that dark woodland, and I'll take this little bundle onwards to Scotland with me.'

Evan rolled his eyes. 'I don't doubt you're serious.'

I could feel Pirate's little piston of a heart bumping against my chest. 'Believe me, the more I see of some people, the more I like animals. They love you unconditionally, and they don't lie to you or let you down.'

Evan gave me a long look. 'Not everyone's like that, Daisy.'

I arched one cynical brow. 'I've yet to be convinced.'

He straightened his shirt collar. 'A journalist, an actor and a sheep go into a pub. That's the start of a joke.' The amber glimmer from inside the pub slid down his compelling features. I turned my attention back to Pirate and gave him a reassuring squeeze.

'I just hope I don't bump into anyone I know,' grumbled Evan, pushing one of the double doors.

'I think that's unlikely.'

The three of us stepped inside to be greeted by a handful of customers propping up the polished, semi-circular bar. It was all velvet green, cushioned chairs and booths, brass ornaments and dramatic black and white framed photographs of Lake Windermere, Coniston and Derwent Water adorning the walls.

It wasn't packed out for a Saturday night, but a couple of the cosy booths were occupied by patrons.

I gave Pirate another stroke.

A few of the drinkers, who were casually arranged around the bar, turned to see who'd just stepped inside. Evan dropped his voice. 'I've seen horror films that start like this.'

'Oh, for pity's sake,' I complained out of the corner of my mouth. 'Do you ever say anything positive?'

Not waiting for his pithy reply, I gathered my confidence and strode up to the bar with Pirate cradled in both my arms, as though this was no unusual occurrence on a Saturday night in these parts.

'What would you both like?' beamed the man behind the bar. He had a shiny, red face and a thin, fair combover.

Evan stepped up beside me and moved to speak.

'I was talking to the lady and the lamb,' he joked.

I guessed that was his punchline, so I laughed. I ruffled Pirate behind one ear.

Evan jumped in and asked for a pint of Guinness. He turned to me. 'What can I get you?'

'Just a fresh orange juice, please. I'm driving, remember?'

'And your friend?' persisted the barman, gesturing to Pirate. 'Would he like a baaa supper?'

The barman chuckled at his own joke. I pushed out a smile. Pirate was providing this middle-aged man with an endless supply of chronic one-liners that I'd expect to find in a Christmas cracker.

While the barman fetched our drinks, I ignored the quizzical looks from a few other punters. I nudged Evan. 'My purse is in the front pocket of my bag. Can you fetch it for me, please?'

Evan shook his head. 'This is on me, even though you've made us late getting to our accommodation because of Shaun here.'

'Thank you. I think. Oh, and it's not Shaun. It's Pirate.'

Evan offered the lamb a withering look. 'Stupid me. Yes, of course it is.'

The barman set down Evan's pint of rich brown Guinness and my orange juice, complete with a paper straw. He accepted Evan's credit card and put it through the machine.

'I wondered if you might be able to help?' I asked him, adjusting the dozy Pirate in my arms.

The barman handed Evan's credit card back to him. 'Yes, I'll try to help if I can.'

I took a gulp of the fresh orange out of the straw. It was cold and zingy as it hit the back of my throat. Pirate wriggled in my arms for a closer look at my liquid refreshment before blinking wearily again.

'I found this little fella alone by the side of the road, not far from here.' I pointed at his wriggly tail. 'He's got a blue daub of paint, which looks like either the letter S or the number eight.' I turned Pirate around in my arms, so the barman could see. 'I don't suppose you might know which farm he belongs to?'

Evan took a long, satisfying pull of his pint. 'Please, sir. Tell Daisy you do know, otherwise I think we could end up as a threesome on the way to Scotland.'

I scowled up at Evan, whose face was deadpan. Then he winked down at me. 'I'm not interested in threesomes,' he whispered across at me. 'I'm too selfish.'

My face flooded with colour. My mouth pursed. 'I can assure you, I've got absolutely no interest whatsoever in what might or might not float your boat.'

I hugged Pirate tighter but managed to throw Evan what I hoped was a disdainful expression.

That made Evan's eyes glitter with amusement, which made me even more bad-tempered.

The barman leant across and took a closer look at the blue smudge on Pirate's curly white coat. 'Sorry, Miss.

I've no idea. There are a fair few farms around here, so he could belong to any of them.'

'I don't want to say I told you so,' murmured Evan from behind his pint glass.

'But no doubt you will.'

Oh bugger. What if we couldn't locate the farmer who Pirate belonged to? I wasn't prepared to just leave him here to fend for himself.

Observing me with a growing look of concern, Evan set down his Guinness on the bar. The pub lights shone behind him. 'Don't tell me you're thinking of bringing him along with us to the bed and breakfast?'

I jutted out my chin. Pirate snuggled against my chest. 'I haven't decided yet.'

Evan raised his beer to his lips again. 'I'm staggered you'd prefer the company of a walking woolly jumper than a tall, dark and rugged journalist.'

I cradled Pirate and took another sip of my orange juice through the paper straw. 'I think that speaks volumes, don't you?'

Evan's eyes sparkled at me.

'Excuse me?'

A middle-aged woman who'd been nursing a white wine a little further down the bar approached us. A man about the same age, who I presumed was her partner, sidled up behind her.

She hooked a chunk of highlighted blonde hair back behind one ear. 'Oh, isn't he adorable?' She set her wine glass down on top of the bar and fussed over Pirate in my arms. She turned her attention to me, her light grey eyes creasing with friendliness. 'We couldn't help but overhear what you were saying just now. He's lucky someone like you spotted him.'

I slid Evan a loaded look. 'Oh, I'm just glad we were passing by at the time.'

Pirate twisted as I held him. The woman angled her head when she saw the blue marking on his coat. 'Henry. Come and take a look. Isn't that the marking Murdo uses on his flock?'

Her partner peered at the faded blue image through his Harry Potter style spectacles. 'Yes. It is. A blue S for Sylvester. Murdo Sylvester.'

I gave Pirate a happy hug. 'You're sure?'

'One hundred percent,' answered the man with a decisive nod. 'I've done some work on Murdo's farm over the years, just to help him out. We've been friends ever since we were at secondary school together.'

Evan finished his pint and offered Pirate a triumphant, smug smile.

'So, Mr Sylvester's farm is near here?' I asked, feeling a pang of happiness and relief that we'd found the lamb's owner, combined with a silly stab of sadness.

The blonde woman waggled her wine glass. 'Just ten minutes up the road. You can't miss it. Take the second right when you see the sign for Brock Wood Farm.'

I finished the last of my orange juice and adjusted the position of Pirate in my arms. 'Ready to go then?' I asked Evan.

He gave me a frustrated look. 'So, I take it we're now off to take Shaun the Sheep back to his owners?'

'Yes. Then we can head on to our accommodation.'

Evan frowned down at Pirate. 'I'd have been quicker walking from Hertfordshire to Scotland.'

'Don't let me stop you.'

We thanked the barman and the helpful couple and departed from the pub. The stars reminded me of spilt glitter above the hills.

We clambered back inside Marlene, and again I plopped Pirate into Evan's resistant lap.

Evan tutted down at his suit.

I turned over the car engine. 'Don't worry about your designer clobber. We can get it dry-cleaned. Pirate will soon be back home safe and sound.'

'Not soon enough,' mumbled Evan under his breath. He eyed Pirate, who'd flopped down in his lap. But then the lamb nuzzled his sooty black nose into Evan's stomach, and when Evan thought I wasn't looking, he gave the little furball a quick stroke.

I smiled to myself.

The journey to Brock Wood Farm took us past an old crumbling castle ruin, its turrets bursting upwards in the dark, and by a sweet little humpbacked bridge with silvery water dancing underneath it.

'Here it is,' I announced, clicking the car indicator to the right.

As though recognising the farm road, Pirate shifted in Evan's muscular arms and peered out of the passenger side window.

We trundled up the tree-lined lane. Up ahead of us, a farmhouse beckoned, warm tangerine lights shining out of the sash windows.

'We'll deposit Pirate and then head on to the B&B.'

'Finally,' sighed Evan. 'When I joined you on this road trip, I never envisaged I'd be babysitting a sheep.'

'He's not a sheep, he's a lamb,' I corrected, easing us into a space at the front of the farmhouse and switching off the engine. 'And when I woke up this morning, I didn't think I'd be giving a lift all the way to Scotland to a friend of the biggest critic dickhead in the UK.'

Evan puffed out his cheeks. 'I'm not a friend of that boorish idiot. I'd never set eyes on him until today.'

We got out of the car. Evan scooped up Pirate and brought him round to me. As soon as the lamb saw me, he launched himself into my waiting arms.

Evan tutted. 'What it is to be popular.'

'Stop feeling so sorry for yourself and come on.'

The entrance to Brock Wood Farm was illuminated by a gorgeous, old-fashioned oil lamp either side of the farmhouse door.

Evan raised one hand and was about to knock when a voluptuous woman in her sixties with fiery, red hair swept out of the door.

She looked at me, then at Evan, and then her inquisitive, hazel eyes fell on Pirate. He wriggled in my grasp. 'Oh, my goodness, Murdo!' she called. 'Come here! Come and see!' She grinned at both of us. 'Thank you so much. Where did you find him? His poor mum has been going spare.'

'I spotted him just a few minutes up the road, near the woodland. Not too far from that pub,' I explained.

A man with an impressive ZZ Top grey beard came barrelling out next. 'We didn't realise the little bugger was missing until late. Looks like he squeezed under my fencing. That's getting repaired first thing tomorrow morning.'

The lady beckoned for me to hand over Pirate. I gave him another hug and offered him to her with a strange, dull throb of reluctance. I'd got attached to the little toot.

The farmer shook both our hands and offered his grateful thanks again. 'Sorry, I'm Murdo by the way, and this is my wife, Carla. How did you know to bring him here?'

'A lady in the pub told us. She and her husband recognised the blue marking on his coat,' said Evan, pointing at Pirate in Carla's arms.

Carla laughed as Pirate shimmied against her ample bosom. 'Would you both like to come in for a cup of tea? Or something stronger?'

I shook my ponytail. 'That's very kind of you, but we just want to reach our bed and breakfast and crash out for the night. And I'm driving anyway.'

Murdo gave Pirate a rub on his flank as he peered out of his wife's arms. 'Ah. Young love, eh? I remember it well.'

It took a moment for me to register what the farmer

meant. 'What? Us? You mean…? Oh God, no! As if! It's nothing like that.'

Evan's eyes danced down at me. 'Daisy here is giving me a lift back to Scotland to visit my family. As a favour. That's all.'

Carla nodded her understanding. 'Oh, I see. Right. Well, thank you so much again for rescuing this little devil.'

Evan moved to leave. I darted up to Carla and gave Pirate a stroke on the nose, and was rewarded with a hot, wet lick on the face, which made me laugh.

We waved our goodbyes and jumped back inside the car.

I fired up the engine and clicked my seatbelt back into position.

'They thought we were a couple,' glittered Evan across from me, in the dark.

I adjusted the rear-view mirror for a little longer than was necessary. 'I know. They must have a terrific sense of humour in these parts.'

Chapter Five

E van's expression was carrying almost as much weariness from the journey as mine was.

He fetched his case from my car boot and then manoeuvred out my pink wheelie one. He tugged up the handle for me. 'There you go.'

'Thanks.'

'You're welcome.'

Under the Lake District stars and the soupy glow from the streetlamps, he towered over me. But our Entente Cordiale was short-lived. When he saw me let out a big yawn, Evan gave me a wry, 'I told you so' expression. 'If we hadn't got involved in rescuing that furball, we'd have got here earlier.'

I locked my driver side door.

Even though I knew deep down that Evan had done the right thing by stopping my impulsive streak, he could protest all he wanted. He was more like the arrogant critic than he thought. 'And if you hadn't interfered this morning, your critic friend Fox would've been wearing champagne, and I'd feel satisfied.'

Evan shook his head in exasperation. 'Yes, satisfied but out of work. And like I told you, that ignorant idiot is no friend of mine.'

My mouth flatlined. Yeah, right. He would say that.

Just across the street was our snug little bed and breakfast, with blossoming planters stationed at the windows. From outside, I could see twinkling gold lights strung around a couple of paintings by the reception area.

All I wanted to do after such a long drive was sink into a deep sleep.

Evan studied me. I shuffled from trainer to trainer on the lit-up pavement.

I tried to cover up my appraisal of Evan with a dry laugh. 'People like Fox only think of themselves. They're narcissists.' More pictures of Leon went through my head. 'Believe me, I've come across guys like him before.'

Evan gave me a prolonged look. 'That guy certainly didn't do himself any favours earlier today.'

Behind Evan were the smoked glass windows of an Italian restaurant. A loved-up couple inside were clinking glasses, lost in each other's eyes.

There was a slight bite to the evening breeze now.

I huddled deeper into my pink denim jacket. 'He's a judgemental, unfeeling piece of work.'

I snatched hold of the handle of my case and brushed past Evan, the wheels rumbling. Tiredness was pulling at me. 'I wonder how that man can sleep at night, which is what I intend to do right now.'

I headed onwards, tugging open the door and stepping ahead of Evan into the softly lit, welcoming interior.

The reception desk was to the left, and stationed behind it was a lady with shiny, copper hair and a pair of spectacles draped around her neck on a chain. I gave my name, and she replied, 'Double room, is it?'

I blinked at her. 'Sorry?'

'A double room for you both.'

In my post-driving fog, it took a few seconds for me to realise that she thought Evan and I were a couple. Not again. This was getting embarrassing. 'Oh no! Good grief, no!' I blabbed, before letting out an odd laugh. 'We're travel companions. We've travelled together. I mean, I'm giving him a lift…'

Evan bent down by my ear. I got a shot of his woody cologne. 'You don't have to tell her your life story, Daisy.'

I threw him a look and gave the lady at reception a pleading smile. 'No, separate rooms please. I did say that when I rang earlier to make the booking.'

As she got us to sign in and took our details, Evan lowered his voice. 'Let me know if you change your mind about the room situation. I could ask for a connecting door.'

I tutted and turned away from him. 'No, you're fine, thank you.' I should never have agreed to giving this man a lift back to Scotland.

For many reasons.

It was a relief to sink into the bed, which smelled of

sunshine and lavender, and to try to put behind me my disastrous day, my troubling travel companion and the reasons why he was making me feel on edge.

After a deep sleep, I fumbled out of bed, showered, dressed myself in clean jeans and my American baseball T-shirt and fired my hair up into a messy topknot.

The dining room had a few guests enjoying their breakfast when I entered.

I took a table up by the window and gazed out past the tie-back cream curtains. I could see the Sunday morning sunshine lighting up the stippled roofs opposite.

It was like a paintbrush over the hills beyond, sweeping across to highlight the different mountainous palettes of jade and burgundy.

The breakfast room consisted of circular tables draped in long, white tablecloths. Dinky little vases of shocking pink roses sat on each, giving the room an extra pop of colour.

The crockery was like something out of a Victorian dollhouse: delicate china, sprigged with poppies.

The efficient-looking bed and breakfast owner, a lady with a blue rinse, took my order of scrambled egg, potato scones, fried tomato, button mushrooms and a pot of tea. I vowed to walk it off when I got back to Strath Ross.

I looked down at my watch. It was approaching half past eight. My attention drifted to the dining room entrance.

I wondered when Evan might appear. I wanted to set off straight after breakfast. I couldn't wait to see my grandpa.

Not only that, but I was keen to deposit Evan and put yesterday behind me. He made me feel self-conscious and defensive, like I suddenly consisted of awkward limbs and angles. He rubbed me up the wrong way with his sarcastic remarks.

It would be wonderful to step back into the fresh, clear scenery of Strath Ross and try to reset. I couldn't give up on being an actor. The very thought of it made my heart sink. It was what I was. It was all I wanted.

But after Fox's savage review of *Sinister* and the drought of acting roles my agent felt she could put me forward for as a result… My mind drifted back to Fox's self-satisfied red face and twisted mouth. The way he'd been holding court with his two friends, braying and bellowing.

For something to do while I waited for my breakfast and for Evan to arrive, I delved one hand into my bag, which was swinging from the back of my chair, and pulled out my mobile.

I clicked into my emails in the desperate hope Octavia had sent me a message telling me that the most fantastic theatre/TV/film role had come up; that it was perfect for me, and she was putting me forward for it. But there was nothing apart from Amazon recommendations and an African President asking me to send him fifteen thousand pounds for an emergency operation.

Jade had sent me a text though, confirming that she'd arrived at her writing retreat safely and that she would be taking part in a free verse writing session today with her crush poetry lecturer. I dashed off a reply saying to keep me posted, and that in a matter of hours I'd be back home in Scotland. I decided not to mention Evan. She'd want a full briefing. I'd tell her later on in the week about him, and about rescuing Pirate. I smiled to myself, and a little glow of satisfaction lit up in my chest. At least I'd done a good deed there.

I was busy scrolling through an online copy of *The Stage*, hoping that a suitable audition might leap out at me, when a flicker of movement to my right made me look up.

Evan was approaching the table. He was dressed in a dark pair of jeans and a black, tight-fitting, V-neck T-shirt that clung to his muscles. It was a far cry from the well-cut three-piece suit and slick tie.

I found myself fumbling around with my phone. Frustration gripped me. For goodness' sake!

'Morning Daisy. Sleep well?'

'Yes, thanks. Did you?'

At that moment, the bed and breakfast owner materialised at the table with my breakfast and teapot on a tray.

Evan eyed the plate with appreciation as he sat down opposite me. 'That looks wonderful. Same again for me, please, but with coffee instead of tea. Thank you.'

As soon as the blue-rinsed lady had scribbled on her notepad and vanished, Evan pinned me to the spot with his melting, chocolate eyes. I shifted in my chair and tried to appear nonplussed. I bet he did this to every woman he met, laying on the sexy smiles and the flirtatious looks. Little did he know that I'd been privy to Leon. I'd been treated like his consolation prize. It was all a show. An act. And acting was something I was good at.

At that moment, my mobile pinged at my elbow.

I snatched it up. Maybe it was an email from my agent after all, or a text telling me about an audition?

My eyes greedily read the screen.

As if.

It was a reminder from my opticians, telling me that my next eye test was due.

Dumping the phone, I reached for the pot of tea and glugged it into my cup.

'Another acting job?' asked Evan with interest.

I set the teapot down. 'No. It wasn't. It was a reminder from my opticians to get my eyes tested.' I folded my arms. 'I'll contact the hospitality agency when I get back to London and ask for whatever shifts they can give me.'

'Oh, come on, Daisy. Don't you think you're jumping the gun a bit?'

My jaw clamped shut. 'Are you kidding?' I shook my head, exasperated. 'In the acting profession, you're only as good as your next role, and you can go months and months without any money.' I shook my topknot, exasperated. 'I wonder what it feels like to wield the sort of power that critics like Fox have? To be able to make or break people's careers with just a few sentences?'

I picked up my knife and fork again and proceeded to cut into the tomato with relish. A part of me was imagining it to be Fox's head. 'I bet he really gets off on it, the tosser.'

Evan eyed me across the table as the sound of clinking cutlery echoed around us. 'I read the review of *Sinister* online. He was complimentary about your performance.'

I made a snorting sound, which drew a few curious looks from other guests. 'Complimentary? Did you read the same review of *Sinister* that I did? He said my acting was competent; satisfactory but unable to rescue a car crash of a show. That's hardly glowing.'

Our tense conversations screeched to a halt, as Evan's breakfast and coffee arrived at the table. As soon as the woman disappeared, Evan picked up his knife and fork. 'Look, if it's any consolation, I watched *Sinister,* and I thought you were great. In fact, I thought you were the best thing about it.'

My fork stilled half way to my mouth.

'I wouldn't have recognised you, though, if you hadn't explained who you were. I think it was the platinum blonde bobbed wig you wore for the role.'

'Thank you,' I managed, surprised.

Evan sliced into his bacon. 'And I just want to apologise on behalf of those journalists who don't take their jobs seriously enough. It shouldn't be about hurting people or making them feel less than they are.'

I took a sip of my tea, studying him across the rim. 'I think you're right. It's just, you have no idea what it's like to put all your energy into something and then find it's been trashed.' I lowered my cup and held it in my hands. 'When

I heard I'd got that role in *Sinister*, I couldn't take it in. I was beyond thrilled. All the hard work and trailing around auditions, to finally secure a spot in a new TV drama like that.' I set my cup down on its saucer with a decisive rattle. 'And now, the names of the cast are being treated like a bad smell.'

We spent the next few minutes eating in comparative silence. All around us, there was the clink of teacups. Some gentle violin music wafted from the speakers.

'What sort of journalist are you? I mean, what do you write?' I asked, finishing off my scrambled egg.

'I'm a freelancer. I tend to write topical news features. Anything from pieces about dating apps and romance scammers to the increasing popularity of women's football and how politicians use social media.' Evan took a mouthful of coffee. 'I'm lucky. I know a lot of editors, so I tend to have a good in when it comes to having my pitches accepted.'

I drained the remainder of my tea and pushed my almost-finished breakfast plate away. 'And would you ever be tempted to follow in the likes of Fox's footsteps? Become a critic, in the loosest sense of the word?'

'Never say never…' Evan began.

Of course. Why did I ever think otherwise? Any glimmer that this man was different to the bombastic idiot at the lunch yesterday withered inside me. I might have guessed as much. I shot up from my chair. Birds of a feather flock together, echoed the voice of my late grandmother. She always used to say that. Looked like she was right. 'I'll see you outside in half an hour. I want to leave here no later than quarter past nine. Please don't be late.'

And with that, I stalked off to check out and ring Grandpa to give him my estimated time of arrival.

Marlene was packed up. Evan and I had both checked out of the bed and breakfast, and he was now back in the passenger side.

Sunday morning sunshine, like patches of soft, golden marmalade, pooled on the tree tops. It bathed the stirring Ambleside and brought out the keen ramblers and water sports enthusiasts.

A nearby stream slid over the rocks in a twinkly silver ribbon as we prepared to drive off.

I'd rung my grandpa and told him that he could expect me in around five hours. He was delighted, saying he'd have the kettle on and couldn't wait to hear about London and my next acting roles. My stomach had dropped when he'd said that, and I'd changed the subject.

I'd also told him that I was dropping someone off in Forrest Bank on the way back to Strath Ross. As soon as I'd said it was a male passenger, my grandpa had asked, 'Och, handsome, is he?'

I'd gripped my mobile tighter to my ear back in the guest room. 'No. Ok, yes, well, I suppose he is, but he's not my type.'

My grandfather had then proceeded to ask me his name

and occupation and what his prospects were. I think he was trying to suss out if he was good breeding stock. 'Nothing like that, Gramps. Just a favour, that's all. He couldn't fly up to Scotland because of all the technical problems.'

My grandpa's voice brightened even further. 'Scottish, is he?'

'Yes, he's actually from Forrest Bank, but he's spent a lot of time in London.'

'Och, never mind. You can't have everything.'

I'd laughed, but my heart had shrivelled in my chest when he'd repeated that he was desperate to get an update on my acting career. I was dreading telling him.

I resolved to reassure him though. I'd just talk around it; say there were a few possibilities in the pipeline. Hopefully, if I sounded convincing enough, he wouldn't fret.

As I drove along, I allowed myself a brief glance over at Evan. Then I wished I hadn't.

He was looking across at me at the same time.

I almost gave myself whiplash and drilled my attention back on the road.

'Daisy?' His voice washed over me. I could feel the sun kissing the tops of my shoulders through my T-shirt. 'You ok?'

'Yes. Fine, thanks.'

Evan brandished his mobile phone in his hand. 'Just saw the headlines. Seems the airports are back in business, but it's going to take a good few days to get everything sorted out.'

We drew up to a set of traffic lights.

'Thank you again for giving me a lift. Really.' His voice softened. 'I do appreciate it.'

I turned to look at him. He pulled a pair of aviator sunglasses from his T-shirt pocket and slipped them on. They suited him.

I snapped my face away and waited for the lights to turn to green. 'You're welcome.' *Oh, please don't start being nice to me.* I felt all tangled up and despondent inside, and the last thing I needed was empathy.

Now it was my turn to hesitate. There was the sense of a truce unfurling between us. Less of an awkward tension and more of an acceptance. It caught me off guard. I cleared my throat. 'And I should thank you again, too. For stopping me from throwing that champagne over Fox.' The light shifted to green, and I moved off. 'I know you did the right thing. I would've looked like such an idiot in front of all of those people, not to mention losing my job when I really needed it. It's just…'

Evan stretched his legs. 'I get it. I do.' A small smile tugged at his mouth. 'I agree with you, if that helps. That guy deserved a headful of champers and then some.' He rubbed at his chin, his eyes concealed behind his smoky sunglasses. 'He was asking for it.' Now it was his turn to pause. 'But you're the better person. Know that, Daisy. Please.'

My cheekbones glowed. 'Thank you. I appreciate that.'

A flicker of a smile crossed my mouth. Wow. What was happening here? Had we reached some sort of understanding after all?

'Just try not to pick up any more stray passengers on the way please, will you?' he joked. His mouth hinted at a smile, as he shook his head at me in mock disbelief.

'Well, I picked you up,' I replied back.

'I'm glad you did.'

There it was again; something zinging between us.

I concentrated on the traffic up ahead. 'Scotland, here we come.'

Chapter Six

The M6 soon became the A74 at Gretna.

Its sentimental, romantic aura gave way to the Borders, with its quaint little bridges, farmland, cute towns and ragged skyline.

As we grew closer to Glasgow, the stately buildings, reaching spires and imposing, heavy stone architecture gave way to the M80 past Cumbernauld.

We appreciated the fairytale beauty of Stirling Castle, perched on top of a rocky outface. The green trees reminded me of clumps of broccoli, enhancing the rise and fall of the castle above it.

Then there was the imposing Wallace Monument, gold edged in the sunlight, as it soared like a solid, frilly needle into the sky.

The M80 soon vanished in Marlene's rear-view mirror, leading us through Perth, with its shining River Tay, clusters of shops and sprinkling of woodland walks and museums.

We glided past the town of Dunkeld, with its pretty string of pastel houses built in the 1700s and now restored by the National Trust for Scotland. No wonder it was known as the best-preserved historic town in the country.

Pitlochry came next; it was one of my favourite Scottish towns to visit. I loved meandering around its scenic little town, strolling past the River Tummel and drinking in its rich history.

If I'd been alone, I'd have parked up and taken myself for a wander, indulged in a coconut and cherry scone in one of its sweet little cafes and watched the tourists exclaim in delight at the allure of the all-year-round Christmas shop on the high street.

But with Evan accompanying me, I thought it best just to get him to his family home and then head to Strath Ross as soon as I could.

The prospect of being back in Strath Ross, surrounded by its rich, Celtic echoes of the past, and traipsing over its humpbacked bridge to the shops, made my heart lift.

Evan and I exchanged small talk on the last leg of the journey, in between him dozing off in fits and starts.

I found myself snatching more and more opportunities whenever I could to study his strong profile when he was asleep. It was the way his nose glided down to meet his full lips, and that lock of stubborn, dark hair that would tumble forwards onto his forehead.

I gave myself a mental check and turned back to the

road. No! I was walking a tightrope here, and it would be so easy to fall off. *Remember Leon, Daisy. Remember Leon. Evan is nice to look at, but he's cut from the same cloth,* I assured myself. *Don't even think about opening up your heart to more hurt.*

Tourists and day trippers were clogging up Aviemore. People were making the most of the gorgeous spring weather, walking, biking and climbing.

Evan had stirred and was arching his back in the passenger seat.

'How come you were at the birthday lunch yesterday?' I asked him.

The scenery slipping past us was lush forests tickled by snow-powdered Cairngorms as its backdrop. Aviemore was known as an ideal location for sailing, windsurfing, stand up paddleboarding, kayaking, canoeing and mountain biking.

'I know Monty through his local rugby club.'

'You play?' I asked, glancing away from his sinewy arms.

'I used to. I'm more of a gym bunny nowadays.'

I can see that, teased a flirty voice in my head. I got frustrated with myself and straightened my back as I gripped the wheel.

We left its sparkling shores and pushed onwards. Evan slipped into another light sleep.

Tourist signs for Strath Ross and Forrest Bank loomed ahead. As I slowed to a stop at a set of lights, Evan woke up. He propped himself up in the passenger seat. 'Sorry.

Was up late finishing a piece I was commissioned to write for *The Recorder*.'

'Anything juicy?'

I angled the steering wheel and pulled away from the lights.

'A feature about the minimum wage and how it impacts people who are trying to break into the creative industries.'

'Well, that's great. At least you're writing about something that helps people. It's positive, you know?'

More trees slid past my driver side window.

Evan turned his attention to the country lane. 'You can just drop me off on the next right.'

I clicked the indicator and eased Marlene around the corner.

The hedgerows were bursting with white and lemon buds.

I was so busy appreciating the delicate prettiness of them and the heady waft of the scented air that I almost didn't see a couple of police officers in the middle of the lane a short distance away. I slammed on the brake and instinctively threw my left arm out to protect Evan.

I apologised. 'Sorry about that. Blimey. What's going on here?'

There was a police van parked on the verge and several officers stationed further along.

One of the policemen, who had a short, clipped, blond beard, came striding up towards the car.

I wound down my driver side window. 'Where are you

supposed to be heading to, Miss?' His accent was lilting and sing-song Scottish, like mine.

'I'm just about to drop off this gent at his family's house just up the lane there and then head on to Strath Ross.'

The officer gave his head a slow shake. 'You're fine to drop off your friend if it's just up that side road. But as for heading onto Strath Ross, I'm afraid that's not possible right now.'

I blinked up at him in confusion. 'Sorry?'

The officer threw out one arm and indicated further up the sun-spilt lane. The fields shone like waggling, gold fingers. 'There's been a serious incident, Miss. You can't reach Strath Ross at the moment.'

I stared up at the police officer, who was squinting down at me from under his cap. 'But why? What's happened? My elderly grandfather's expecting me.'

The policeman sighed. 'I'm sorry. But this is a serious situation, and we've had to close the road from Loch Crawe to Strath Ross.'

I twisted round to look across at Evan. This was crazy! What the hell was going on? Nothing ever happened in these parts, and we were all grateful for it. The worst situation would be some flooding or a wild forest fire, which would be under control in no time. The sight of these police officers and the police van made me think it was more than some bonfire.

Evan stooped lower in his seat to speak to the police officer. His face broke into a smile of recognition. 'Hey! Karl. How are you?'

The police officer took a moment to study Evan's face. His eyes widened. 'Evan Lord! Bloody hell! What are you doing back in the sticks? Had enough of the city types?'

'I'm up visiting my folks. How's Roxy and the kids?'

'Great, thanks. Starting to get a bit more sleep now that Elliott is sleeping through the night.'

Evan pointed through the windscreen. 'What's going on, Karl? Any clues?'

Karl rolled his eyes. 'You can take Forrest Bank out of the journalist but you can't take the journalist out of Forrest Bank.'

Evan craned his neck. 'Hold on. Isn't that Sacha?'

I followed Evan's attention. A woman had appeared out of nowhere and was brandishing her mobile and a notebook. She had tousled, strawberry blonde hair skimming her shoulders and was dressed in black cropped trousers, a red strappy top and trainers. She was flitting from police officer to police officer, talking to them and scribbling notes down.

I noticed a change in Evan. His expression was guarded.

'Do you know her?' I asked him.

'Yes. Her name's Sacha Nicholson,' he answered. 'She's a journalist with Highland News Radio.'

'And?' pushed Karl in a teasing voice.

My attention swept from Karl to Evan and back again.

'And nothing,' replied Evan, sinking back against the passenger seat.

Karl raised his brows at me.

Hmmm. I wonder what that meant.

'Anyway, you were asking what was going on.' Karl looked towards his colleagues. 'We're waiting on the arrival of a military expert from Inverness.'

'Military expert?' I repeated.

Karl nodded.

'A chap out with his little grandson walking his dog in the fields up by Loch Crawe stumbled across what looks like two unexploded World War Two bombs.'

'Bloody hell!' breathed Evan. 'Are you joking?'

'Nope. Wish I was, mate.'

Bombs? Loch Crawe? That was the only way I could get home to Strath Ross. Panic flooded me. 'But I have to get back.'

Karl shook his head. 'Nobody is going anywhere near that road for the time being. We need this expert to take a look.'

'And then what?' I asked, my optimism and excitement at the prospect of seeing my grandfather today withering fast.

'And then he'll advise us on what should be done next. Bomb disposal will be called in.'

Oh shit. This was not going to be solved in a matter of hours. I recalled a similar incident in Wales a while back. The bomb had to be exploded, and the nearby locals ended up being evacuated from their homes for several days.

Karl spoke again. His expression was sympathetic, as the sun glided down one side of his face. 'Is there somewhere else you can stay for the time being, Miss...?'

'Daisy Madden,' I faltered.

'Miss Madden, I can let you head on down to Evan's folks', but you can't go any further.'

I watched the blonde reporter still buzzing around the police car and the officers chatting amongst themselves. This was just what I needed!

I'd have to ring Grandpa and tell him. He'd be every bit as disappointed as I was. My shoulders sank under my T-shirt. I'd just have to deposit Evan at his parents' home, turn around and then head back down the road and find a bed and breakfast somewhere.

I'd planned to put the money Evan had given me towards the cost of petrol for my journey back to London, not on accommodation. So much for the best laid plans.

The hotels round this area were sumptuous but on the pricey side. If I couldn't find a reasonably priced bed and breakfast, I'd have no option but to fork out more money. It would either be that or sleeping in Marlene.

Karl stepped back from my driver side window. 'Apologies again.'

I pressed the accelerator and pulled away. I was churning with disbelief and annoyance. I had to shrug off the enveloping feeling of self-pity. These bombs could've killed someone. In the scheme of things, my predicament wasn't that serious. It was just so infuriating and disappointing.

'My parents' place is just up here, if you take the sharp right.'

My mind stuttered back to focus on what I was doing.

The lane, sandwiched between two thick bands of

hedgerows, had a huge corn field on the left protected by a long fence. Beyond the field, I caught a glimpse of hills weighted down by heather.

I steered Marlene on as the trees ahead parted.

Wow.

Facing me was an imposing Edwardian mansion. It possessed a glossy, oak double door at the grand entrance and half a dozen glinting windows. Furling crenelations of unicorns and eagles twisted like elegant cake decorations in the afternoon sun.

Surrounding the property was an endless throng of swaying Scots pines and ferns. All it needed was a dusting of snow, and it'd make the most stunning Christmas card.

'This is beautiful,' I breathed, resting both my arms on top of Marlene's steering wheel.

Evan didn't say anything for a moment. I could feel his eyes on me.

'I suppose it's not bad. It's called The Ramblings.' He gave me an eye roll. 'Oh, please don't look like that, Daisy.'

'Like what?'

'Like you've just had a spell cast on you.' He gestured out of the windscreen. 'I know it's impressive, but it eats up money. The place belonged to my late paternal grandparents, and they left the property to my dad in their will. He grew up here and adores it, so my parents moved in and took it over.' Evan gazed out. 'Louise, the housekeeper, is a lovely woman, and she's stayed on.' He rolled his eyes. 'But like I said, places like this cost a fortune to heat and maintain.'

I set off again, the car wheels scrunching over gravel.

'You're welcome to stay here until this bomb situation is dealt with.'

Evan's words took me by so much surprise that I screeched to a halt. Had I heard him correctly? Marlene's engine burred away. 'Sorry?'

Evan fixed me with his dark stare. 'I said you're welcome to stay here for the time being, until the bomb situation is over.'

I opened and closed my mouth like a goldfish. The windows of The Ramblings were like diamonds, shining down on the car.

'We've got plenty of space here, as you might have guessed, and my mum loves having guests.'

I fidgeted behind the steering wheel. Ahead of us, The Ramblings glowed like butter in the Sunday afternoon sunshine. The trees around it appeared to be alight. Evan's lips flickered. 'We're not The Munsters. Well, some might disagree about that.'

I wondered what on earth to say. I barely knew him. We'd only been sandwiched in the car together for twenty-four hours. And I'd never met his family. It was kind of him. But being here with Evan, in his parents' home…

I found myself appreciating the way his mouth tilted up at one corner when he was thinking. *No. Remember what you promised yourself, Daisy. Keep your distance and you'll keep your dignity.*

I pushed my thoughts back to The Ramblings. 'Thank you. Really. That's very kind of you, but…'

'But what?'

Oh bugger.

My head was struggling to find a reasonable excuse to say thank you, but no.

'Come on, Daisy. Don't be stubborn. This is my way of saying thank you for putting up with me on the journey here.'

Evan was still training all his attention on me.

I felt vulnerable under those dark pools of his. It was annoying. 'But you've already paid for the petrol, and you gave me too much money anyway.'

Evan cut me off. 'Yes, I know I've paid you for the petrol, but we weren't to know about two unexploded bombs.' He pushed his hand through his flop of black hair. 'It's a no-brainer as far as I can see. Just means you'll have to put up with me and my eccentric family for a day or so, and then you can be on your merry way to Strath Ross.'

I still wasn't sure. I'd envisaged dropping Evan off and then heading on home. To my grandfather. To safety, in a way; to where I could lick my wounds in private about my life and seek solace in familiarity.

Maybe the authorities would be able to handle those bombs faster than they anticipated. Perhaps several days was the worst-case scenario, like it had been with the incident in Wales. Perhaps I'd only end up having to stay the night here.

One of Evan's brows arched at me for a reply. The sunshine was spooling through the windscreen, rifling its golden fingers through his hair. 'Well?'

My emotions bounced against one another.

I didn't want to appear rude, but … those bloody bombs! It looked like I had no other option, and considering that I was having to be so careful about my finances at the moment, it didn't make sense to fork out for accommodation if I didn't have to.

I'd have to ring Grandpa and tell him what was happening. What with the technical issues at the airports and now undiscovered explosive devices, this whole trip seemed doomed!

Evan leant forward in the passenger seat. With his unshaven jaw and long legs, he seemed to take up most of the space in my car. 'Could I have an answer today please, Daisy?'

I pulled myself backwards in my seat, putting a decent amount of space between us, both physically and mentally. 'Thank you,' I managed, pushing out a smile. 'That would be good.'

Chapter Seven

E van instructed me to park Marlene round the back of the property.

Once I'd driven into a space and killed the engine, Evan jumped out and fetched our bags from the boot of the car.

While he was doing that, I pulled my phone from next to the handbrake and called my grandpa to tell him about the bomb discovery in case he didn't know about it already or hadn't heard it on the news, and also to reassure him I was ok and to tell him where I was staying. 'Hopefully they'll have it all sorted in a day or two, Gramps. But as soon as it is, I'll be on my way to you, ok?'

'Och. Don't you fret, sweetheart. As long as you're safe and sound, that's all that I'm bothered about. Hold on a second and I'll switch on the news. I had no idea all this was going on.' I heard him rattling the TV remote control and the volume rising. There was the sound of a live broadcast from the area. Grandpa fell silent while he listened to what the TV reporter was saying. Then he jumped back on the phone. 'But I think you're being a wee bit optimistic about it all being sorted in a day or two, if this reporter is right. This isn't a stray firework they're dealing with.'

I groaned. So much for escaping quickly from Evan.

'So, a fancy place you're staying, is it?'

I gazed up at the swirling detail of The Ramblings, its pointed roof and beams shooting upwards. 'It's lovely. I'll take a photo of it and send it to you.'

'And it's this Evan's house?'

'It's his parents'.'

'Oh, I see. Right. Well, no disgracing the family name and creeping over to his bedroom in the wee small hours.'

My spine stiffened. 'Grandpa! No. No! It's not like that. I mean, I'm staying as a guest. Evan wanted to thank me for driving him all the way up here after the airplane issues.' I took a quick breath before I rambled on again. 'It's nothing like that whatsoever.' I could hear my voice picking up speed. I sounded like I was inhaling helium.

'You're a grown woman, darling. You don't have to explain yourself to me. As long as he treats you proper, otherwise he'll have me to answer to.'

Around me, the abundance of trees sashayed in the sunshine. I gripped my mobile. Evan was lingering with our two bags several feet away, looking at his phone. 'I appreciate that Grandpa, but there really is nothing to explain.'

There came a deep chuckle down the line. 'Alright sweetheart. If you say so.'

My eyes locked on Evan again, who glanced up from his phone screen. I spun away from him. I hoped he hadn't heard any of that. 'I'll call you tomorrow, ok Grandpa? I'm so sorry about this.'

'It's not your fault, chicken. You just behave yourself, send me a photo of this posh house when you get a moment and we'll speak tomorrow.' His crumbly voice softened even more. 'Love you.'

'Love you, too.'

I slipped my phone into the back pocket of my jeans and walked over to Evan.

He pushed his mobile into his jeans pocket, and I reached for the handle of my case.

'Your grandfather ok?'

'Yes, thanks. Disappointed at not seeing me today, but he's good.' I pulled a disgruntled face. 'I was so looking forward to seeing him, too.'

Evan squinted down at me against the sun. His sunglasses were dangling from the top of his T-shirt. 'You're close, aren't you?'

'Like two coats of paint.'

He grinned at me. It was the first time since I'd met him that he'd smiled like that; a big, genuine one that made his eyes crease. It lit up his entire face. 'Is he retired?'

I found myself appreciating that smile for longer than was necessary. I gave myself a mental check. 'Yes, he used to work for the local council, maintaining their parks and gardens. Very green-fingered.'

Evan pulled a wry expression. 'I wish I was. I've just got to look at a rose and it withers.'

I buried a smile. 'That doesn't come as any great surprise.'

Oh no. There was that killer grin again. 'Come on then, Miss Daisy. Let's introduce you to The Addams Family.'

'I thought they were The Munsters?'

'Yeah. On a good day.'

Evan gave me a wink that made my stomach do a weird flip-flop thing.

I gritted my teeth. Was he doing this deliberately? Probably his usual charm offensive, I reminded myself.

'Something tells me you're easy to tease.'

I could feel my neck turning blotchy, but I stuck my chin out. 'That's where you're wrong.'

I began to follow Evan through a side door that looked like it would lead into the hall, when I remembered something. 'Oh. Sorry. Hold on a second. I've left my handbag on the backseat. I'll just go and get it.'

I darted out of the back door and headed towards Marlene. I fished my car key from my jeans pocket and aimed the fob at my car. I tugged open one of the rear passenger doors, bent forwards and reached along the back seat to collect my bag.

I was still bent forwards, my bottom up in the air as I dragged my bag towards me, when a male voice startled me. 'Need any help over there?'

I closed the car door, locked it with the fob and turned around. 'No. I'm fine, thanks.'

A tall man with long, flowing, dark blond hair like a Viking warrior was standing there. He was sporting a tight, olive green, sleeveless vest top, dark jeans and heavy walking boots. He had a smattering of blond stubble.

'You ok there, Daisy? Oh.'

Evan had reappeared and was frowning from me to the Viking warrior and back again.

'Yes, thanks Evan. I'm fine. This kind gentleman was just asking if I needed any help.'

Evan's expression twisted. 'I bet he did.'

Was it my imagination, or was there some tension swirling around all of a sudden? Nope, not my imagination.

I noticed that a green garden trowel was dangling from the Viking's grasp. I also picked up on his light, sky blue eyes appraising me. Who was this man with the rock star looks and the swagger to match? Whoever he was, Evan was in no rush to introduce him.

The silence continued.

Well, this wasn't awkward – much.

I clapped both my hands together for something to do, to fill the void and then wished I hadn't. I must've looked like a performing seal. Around us, there was the fizzing of blackbirds singing in the trees.

'So,' I said brightly to the Viking, pointing at the trowel in his hands, 'are you the only gardener who tends to the grounds here? You must be kept busy if you are.'

Viking threw his head back, making his hair stream out behind him and laughed.

Had I said something funny?

'Gardener? Seriously?' He looked over at Evan. 'Didn't this one tell you he has a handsome baby brother?'

Evan pushed both his hands into the pockets of his jeans. His body tensed. 'Haven't had time yet. We only just arrived.' He slid a sarcastic smile over at his younger brother. 'Still, I don't have to introduce you to Daisy now. You've just done it.' There was an odd, alien inflection in his voice.

Something was telling me I'd really put my foot in it, whatever 'it' was.

I felt like a prize idiot. 'Oh, I'm so sorry. Evan didn't tell me he had a brother.'

Viking's mouth carried the ghost of a smirk. 'I gathered that.'

'And I just saw you holding the trowel, and I put two and two together and made five.' I extended a hand. 'I'm Daisy. Daisy Madden.'

Viking reached for my hand and shook it. His ornate dress rings sparkled on his fingers. 'I'm Dane. Dane Lord.' He held my eyes for a few moments. 'Very nice to meet you, Daisy.' His attention lingered on me for a few more seconds.

'What with all the hoo-ha at the airports and flights cancelled, I gave your brother a lift back up to Scotland.'

Dane's fair brows lifted. 'That was very generous of you.'

'I was coming back up to Scotland myself anyway.'

'Ah.' Dane bathed me in a toothy grin. 'Where are you from?'

'Strath Ross.'

His blond hair lifted in the light breeze. 'Really? We're practically neighbours.'

'Hardly,' remarked Evan. 'You're living in Glasgow now.'

Dane gave his older brother a mischievous look. 'I'm not at the moment though, am I?' He refocused on me. 'Me and my rock band have got some gigs here in the local area, which is why I'm back home at the moment.'

Evan stepped in, taking me by surprise and cutting the conversation short. 'Now that the formal introductions are over, Daisy, let's take you inside and you can meet Mum and Dad.'

'You're a fast mover,' said Dane with a twinkle. 'You've only just met the girl.'

Evan's soft, brown eyes grew hard. 'Daisy's staying here for the time being. Don't know if you've heard yet, but two unexploded bombs have been found up by Loch Crawe, so she can't make it home.'

Evan started to accompany me back towards the rear door of the house, our cases trundling behind us, when Dane's gravelly voice rang out. 'Welcome to The Ramblings, Daisy. Maybe I can show you around while you're here?' There was another charming smile.

But I didn't have time to answer, as Evan was already steering me inside.

He guided me through the side entrance and into the

hall, which was huge, with a butterscotch and white tiled floor. On the opposite wall was stationed a gold, oval mirror which looked like something out of *Game of Thrones*.

Greek-style vases sat in all four corners sprouting dry reeds and rushes.

A white, marble, Cinderella-style staircase on the left spiralled to the upper floor. To the right was what looked like a massive sitting room, which consisted of polished maple furniture and a thick, pillar box-red carpet. It looked out onto the gardens through a set of double doors.

Trees lined up like soldiers on the far side, and the lawns sloped and glided downwards.

From out of nowhere, an older, smartly dressed couple appeared, making me start. 'Evan! Darling!'

The woman's cream heels clicked on the tiled hall floor. She bundled Evan into her arms.

'Hey, Mum.'

She planted a big kiss on his cheek and took a step back to admire her eldest son.

Behind her, a dapper man with a greying beard emerged. He gave Evan a brief hug. 'Hi, Dad.'

Then his father's attention fell on me, loitering in the background. 'Are you going to introduce us, son?'

Evan beckoned me over. 'Mum. Dad. This is Daisy. Daisy, these are my parents, Alison and Bennett.'

Alison Lord's ice blue eyes, which reminded me of Dane's, creased as she smiled at me. We shook hands. 'Lovely to meet you, Daisy.'

'And you.'

Bennett shook my hand next. 'Is this the young lady you told us about on the phone? The one who kindly drove you up here?'

'Yes, Daisy got me out of a tight spot.' Evan smiled at me, and I found my skin prickling.

'It was fine. No big deal,' I insisted.

Alison tutted. 'You never told us we were going to have company, Evan.'

Evan sighed. 'It's not an issue, Mum. Not as big an issue as those unexploded bombs. That's why Daisy is staying with us, until that's sorted out.' He gestured to me. 'Daisy comes from Strath Ross.'

'I don't want to put you to any unnecessary trouble,' I bleated.

Alison wafted her manicured hand. 'Of course it isn't any trouble.' She wrapped her arms around herself. 'Just heard about those bombs on the radio news. Hope they can sort it out soon.' She turned her attention back on me again. 'The main guest room is already all made up, and I'll make sure there's clean towels.' She twinkled. 'Unless I've got the sleeping arrangements wrong.'

Not again! Maybe I should wear a sign around my neck in capital letters saying, 'EVAN AND I ARE NOT A COUPLE!' I shook my head and refused to think about her inference about Evan and me sharing a bed. 'Oh no. It isn't like that.'

I flapped my hands around like a windmill. 'I was providing hospitality at a birthday lunch yesterday; Evan was there as a guest and after he found out the planes were grounded and heard me saying I was driving to Scotland, and, well, I gave him a lift.'

I slipped Evan a look out of the corner of my eye. His mouth had flipped into an amused hint of a smile.

'Oh, I see,' said Bennett. 'Well, thank you very much again for helping him out.'

'Anyway,' exclaimed Alison, 'you get yourself settled, and then we can have dinner. Evan, please show Daisy to the main guest room.'

And with that, she flounced off in a haze of caramel outfit and blonde hair, and Bennett followed up the rear.

My trainers slapped on the ornate staircase as Evan assisted me with taking my trolley case to my room. I'd assured him I could manage, but he'd insisted, taking the handle with one firm grip, his muscles bunching under his T-shirt as he manoeuvred it.

We reached a large, closed, panelled door.

Evan cranked the handle and opened it.

I was greeted by a sumptuous four-poster bed, decked out in lemon and white bedding. There was an ensuite bathroom with white fittings and peach and cream accessories. The whole pastel effect reminded me of a cornucopia of delicious summer ice creams.

Pale, gold, satin curtains framed the bedroom window and pooled down to the biscuit-coloured carpet. Sunshine was splashing over the bed covers.

'This is stunning,' I breathed.

Evan set my case down by the foot of the bed. 'I hope you'll be comfortable in here.'

'Are you joking? It's beautiful!'

'Good. You relax for a bit before dinner.'

'What are you going to do?'

'No rest for the wicked.' He flashed me a loaded grin.

I ignored a squiggle in my stomach and faffed around with a corner of the duvet.

'I'm going to start a piece about men and romance in the twenty-first century that I've been asked to write for a woman's magazine.'

He clicked the door handle and stepped out into the hall. He hesitated and turned to look at me. 'Did it seem so outlandish?'

'Sorry?'

'The idea of us being romantically involved?'

My heart zipped in my chest. Bloody hell. What was going on with me? Why was I reacting like this? 'No. Of course not,' I floundered. 'I mean, you're very good-looking.'

I froze. Shit! What did I just go and say that for? Was I losing my mind?

Evan smiled. 'Thank you. Ditto.'

I found myself fascinated by my bedroom window and the glimpses of the lawns. 'It's just… Well, we're not; I mean, we're not involved. We're not a couple. Obviously. So, it's ridiculous.' I felt like I was scrambling for a lifebelt as a wave tried to pull me under. 'You did me a favour, making sure I didn't get sacked, and I did you a favour, driving you to Scotland, so we're even.' I was saying the words, but they sounded hollow, even to my ears. I'll soon be out of your hair anyway.'

Evan gave me a thoughtful look that I was struggling to read. 'See you for dinner.'

I was sure I wouldn't be able to walk ever again after Alison and Bennett Lord's hospitality.

Their housekeeper, a cheery, effervescent and widowed middle-aged lady called Louise Compston, was tasked with coming up with something special for Sunday evening dinner.

Boy, did she achieve that!

She served Scottish sea bass in a lemon and chive sauce, accompanied by boiled potatoes and assorted vegetables. For pudding, there was homemade sticky toffee pudding with a dollop of clotted cream ice cream.

Dane didn't join us for dinner.

'He's got a gig in Aviemore tonight,' remarked Alison across the table to me.

'So, Dane's a musician?' I asked, recalling his earlier comment.

'He's lead singer with his own rock band,' interjected Bennett. 'Disciple.' He rolled his smoky grey eyes. 'Dane's got a great voice, and the lads in the band are talented musicians, but whether they'll have any huge commercial success, I don't know. He tends to treat this place like some sort of hotel when he's visiting.'

'Dane's a bit of a free spirit,' remarked Alison dryly, taking a gulp of her white wine. 'Does his own thing.'

'That's putting it mildly,' ground out Evan beside me.

I frowned. The two brothers didn't seem especially close. I thought about my own situation, being an only child, and my parents' selfish approach to parenting. Maybe I wouldn't have felt as though I always had to prove something growing up if I'd had a sibling.

The drive from England to Scotland was catching up on me with a vengeance, so I thanked Alison and Bennett for their kind hospitality and said I was heading for an early night.

I just wanted to crawl into that regal four-poster bed and lose myself in the cosy fuzziness of sleep.

It was as I was approaching my bedroom door that I heard tapping from across the hallway.

The door was ajar, and I could see Evan seated at a writing desk in his room, concentrating on his laptop. The screen was highlighting his serious features, the light sparkling off the Clark Kent spectacles he was wearing. A lock of thick, dark hair kept tumbling forward onto his brow as he focused. Every so often, he'd push it back with one, pensive hand.

I found myself appreciating him and gave myself a mental shake. *Come on, Daisy. Remember what you said to yourself before.* What I'd been saying to myself on a loop, in fact, ever since Evan and his classy cufflinks had appeared at the posh cream tea.

I was about to turn around and head back to my room when he spotted me.

He slid off his spectacles and dumped them on top of his desk. 'Hey.'

Oh no. I hoped he hadn't seen me lurking about watching him. 'Hi.'

He beckoned me in through the partially open door and stood up.

His room had a queen-sized bed, topped with navy blue and silver bedding to complement the blue-toned carpet. There was an ensuite bathroom off to the right and long, deep, sapphire-coloured curtains at the far window.

'I was just going to say goodnight,' I said, fidgeting on the spot and not understanding why. I'd intended to slip away to my room without Evan seeing me. 'Thank you again for your hospitality.'

Evan's gaze flickered. 'You're welcome. I'm the one who should be thanking you. You got me here when British aviation didn't.'

'Like I said before, you stopped me from getting sacked yesterday after my moment of seeing red.'

Evan's mouth morphed into a smile. 'Believe me, we've all been there.'

I remained standing close to his bedroom door.

'Well, goodnight then, Evan,' I said, knotting my hands together.

I began to turn away, when what was on his laptop screen caught my attention. It was branded 'News Update.'

Evan's gaze followed mine. Underneath the words 'News Update', flashed, 'Bomb find.'

I moved towards his desk for a better look.

It has been confirmed in the last few minutes that two unexploded bombs discovered on the outskirts of Loch Crawe in the Scottish Highlands are both SC-500 devices, weighing 500kg each, used during the Second World War.

Renowned Inverness-based war historian Professor Morris Sneddon confirmed the findings only a short while ago. 'These bombs are around eighty-five years old and could potentially cause a great deal of damage.'

An expert bomb disposal team are now in the Loch Crawe area assessing next steps. The leader of the team, Captain Susan Muir, said, 'This is a highly complex operation, with a disposal team comprised of army and search squadron.' She added, 'We will be assisted by other emergency services and partners, who can all provide expert knowledge in their field.'

Captain Muir confirmed that the two unexploded bombs would be dealt with on site, and that one option would be to construct a sand-filled pit around the two bombs to mitigate any surrounding damage to the area when they are neutralised.

An army disposal spokesperson explained that the operation to neutralise both bombs would take several days to complete.

I let out a loud groan. Oh, you had to be kidding!

Several days? A week in other words? I'd been trying to convince myself it would be just a couple of days at most, and then I'd be gone.

Evan straightened up beside me. 'That bad, huh?'

'It's just … well … several days? I was so looking forward to seeing my grandfather and Strath Ross again.' *And putting distance between me and you.*

Then another voice chipped in with, *Why would that be?*

'And you still will get to Strath Ross and see him,' assured Evan, his lips curling in a sympathetic smile that made his eyes shine.

My breathing did a funny, raggedy thing. I had to leave here as soon as I could. My acting had to come first, especially now when I was struggling to secure auditions and roles. Allowing myself to fall for a pair of sexy, chocolate eyes wouldn't help me.

Evan continued to look at me.

My breathing picked up a sterner pace.

It was then that his mobile trilled to life by his laptop.

I glanced down at Evan's phone.

I recognised her photo on his phone screen. It was that blonde reporter from earlier. Sacha whatsit.

My fast breathing vanished. A dull, odd feeling took over.

Evan's gaze followed mine to his ringing phone screen.

I could feel my wobbling emotional walls growing stronger again, shooting high up into the sky, impenetrable and solid. Her picture had reminded me of why I had to stay strong, forge my own path and not allow myself to become emotionally attached to another man.

I flicked a dismissive look at Evan's phone, lying there ringing on his desk. 'Aren't you going to answer that?'

Then I strode out of his room and headed across to mine.

I banged my bedroom door shut behind me. Maybe Sacha calling when she did had been a godsend. It had brought clarity where there had been initial thoughts starting to creep in about Evan, a stirring attraction threatening to shake my resolve.

I suspected there had been something between them when Evan had caught sight of her on the country lane earlier today. That police officer friend of Evan's had hinted as much.

As soon as the bomb situation was over, I'd leave.

I couldn't wait.

Chapter Eight

I was about to get ready for bed when my mobile trilled in my jeans pocket.

It was Jade.

'I've just seen the news,' she gabbled into my ear. 'Christ, unexploded bombs?! Are you alright? Where are you?'

'I'm fine,' I reassured her, sinking down onto the corner of the four-poster bed. It was almost nine o'clock, and the May night outside my bedroom window was slipping into darkness.

I got up and closed the long, silky curtains, clicked on the ornate bedside lamp and flopped back down again on the bed. 'I'm staying at someone's until all this blows over. Oops, wrong choice of word.'

Jade immediately jumped on this. 'Someone?'

'A guy,' I faltered. 'Someone I met at the cream tea. I drove us back to Scotland.'

Jade let out a shocked gasp. 'You gave this guy a lift all the way back up to Scotland?' She didn't give me time to answer. 'I hope he's ok. He's not a creep, is he? What's going on? Where are you?'

I sighed. 'Jade, if you'll just give me a chance, I'll explain.'

'Ok. Sorry.'

'Right. So, because of the bomb situation, and it all taking place by Loch Crawe, I couldn't get back to Strath Ross, so Evan insisted I stay with him at his parents' place in Forrest Bank until it's sorted. That's only about half an hour away from Strath Ross.'

'Oh, yes?' Her voice was loaded, teasing.

'What's that supposed to mean?'

'It doesn't mean anything.'

'Lady Jacintha, you're a terrible liar.'

'Oh, please don't call me that.'

There was a pause. 'So come on then, Madden, what's he like?'

'Who?'

'Sir Keir Starmer. Who do you think I'm talking about?! This Evan.'

My mind drifted through my closed door and across the hallway, with its heavy-framed paintings and vases of flowers, to Evan's room.

'He's ok.'

There was a triumphant snort. 'You like him.'

'How old are you? Eight?'

She pushed on and ignored me. 'You think he's attractive.'

The image of Sacha, with her swishy blonde hair, grinning up from Evan's mobile phone screen lodged itself in my head. 'Like I said, he's ok,' I dismissed. 'Anyway, how's things with you?'

'There she is. The Daisy Madden I know and love. Avoiding the personal questions and changing the subject. Too scared to open up.'

I prickled on the bed. 'I'm not scared. I just don't want to talk about Evan, that's all.'

'Why not?'

I knew why I didn't want to talk about him with Jade. I refused to answer the questions that were prodding at the corners of my mind. It had been as though we were on the verge of another connection just now, and then Sacha had called, and that brought back all the tumbling thoughts about Leon's deceit; the hurt, the betrayal, the way he'd seen me as a temporary distraction before he could trade me in for a better model and elevate his chances of a successful acting career at the same time.

I'd grown used to forging my own path while I was growing up, relying on myself, apart from my grandparents. My parents were both selfish, thoughtless individuals who put themselves front and centre, and that had taught me that investing all your trust and emotion into another person just wasn't worth the hassle.

But then, of course, Leon had come along, and I'd ignored my own advice.

That would teach me.

Nevertheless, it didn't matter, I reassured myself. I wouldn't get stuck in another situation where I felt out of control. Again.

'So,' I carried on. 'Your brooding poetry lecturer? What's happening there?'

Jade's voice morphed into a more honeyed version of her usual self. 'I've got a poetry workshop tomorrow. I intend to impress him with my villanelles.'

'Sounds painful,' I joked. 'But if anyone can, you will.'

Jade laughed, 'You can bet on it. So … any news on more acting jobs?'

I frowned down at the bedroom carpet. 'Not so far.' I hoped I sounded more optimistic than I felt. 'But something will come up. I'll just have to take on more hospitality gigs when I get back to London.'

'I'm not worried about the money,' she insisted into my ear. 'You don't have to concern yourself with that. Just pay me your next rent when you can.'

'I know, and that's so kind of you, but I'm not a freeloader.'

'I know you're not.'

When I let out a loud, noisy yawn, Jade wrapped up the call and blew me a kiss, and we said goodnight.

———————

Monday morning dawned with me spread-eagled in bed, gazing up at the four-poster canopy.

I couldn't believe that it had only been a couple of days since the Fox incident.

So much had happened.

Driving Evan up to Scotland, rescuing a lost lamb in the Lake District and then finding I couldn't get home thanks to two unexploded German bombs from World War Two.

Not to mention the cringeworthy review from Fox, and then finding myself struggling to secure any new auditions.

Now I was sat in Evan's parents' sprawling mansion, having breakfast with him and his Mum and Dad and mentally willing my agent to call me with some good news.

Desperation started to take chunks out of me again. It was like my life was going backwards, not forwards.

Evan glanced over his cup at me. He took a bite of toast. He looked like he might be on the verge of saying something but was interrupted by the sudden, blond whirlwind that was Dane striding into the dining room.

He'd secured his hair back in a long, low ponytail and was dressed in a Metallica T-shirt and dark green combats. 'Good morning, Daisy,' he dazzled, reaching for a slice of the golden toast in the toast rack. He turned to Evan. 'And good morning to you too, tall, dark and arms.'

Evan smirked. 'What Christmas cracker did you find that in?'

Dane ignored him. 'Just heard on the local news that the bomb guys are building a huge sandpit around those two tin cans.'

'They're hardly tin cans,' muttered Evan.

Dane scraped out a chair and sat down next to Bennett. 'The good news though is that it looks like our very attractive house guest won't be leaving just yet.' He awarded me a big, flawless grin.

I found myself grinning back. I couldn't help it. Dane didn't take himself too seriously, and it was nice to meet another soul from the creative industry.

Evan shot his brother a dark look but didn't say anything.

'How did your gig go last night?' I asked Dane, trying to push some conversational lightness into my voice.

Dane sat back in his chair, all louche, rocker charm. 'Great, thanks. Appreciative crowd.' He left the inference hanging in the air. 'Very appreciative.'

Alison rolled her eyes at her younger son.

Dane just laughed at his mother's expression and savoured his toast. He started to butter another slice. 'So, what are you up to today, Daisy?'

'Studying *The Stage* and social media, looking for acting work.'

Dane twinkled across the table at me. 'You won't have to look long. You'll get snapped up.'

The spring sunshine was competing with his hair for golden brilliance. I laughed, forgetting that I had a lump of toast in my mouth. I coughed. Coughed again. One panicked hand flew to my throat. I was struggling to breathe.

I let out a raspy gasp. Evan leapt out of his seat, as did

Dane, who managed to reach me first and jerked me out of my chair. He snaked both his golden, solid arms around my waist and jerked me upwards like a rag doll three times before the offending piece of toast flew out of my mouth and across the breakfast table. 'Are you ok?' he asked, staring down into my face.

'Thanks to you, I am,' I croaked, taking ragged breaths.

Evan was standing across the table, his expression etched with concern. When he noticed his brother still holding me, his jaw throbbed.

Alison and Bennett ordered me to sit back down and take it easy.

After a few moments of everyone asking if I was ok and me gratefully getting my breath back and sipping some water and tea, Dane glittered across the table at me. 'Fancy joining me on a woodland walk this morning?'

Evan's glass of fresh orange juice stilled at his mouth.

'It's just a short drive from here.'

I could feel Evan studying me for my reaction. I pretended not to notice. I should get out of The Ramblings. Put space between Evan and me. It was for the best. He had willowy, blonde journalists ringing him anyway. And Dane had just stopped me from choking. I returned Dane's attention with a bright grin of my own. 'Yes, that sounds great. Thanks.'

Evan's stubbly, dark jaw tightened, but his gaze remained impassive.

'Great. Ok.' Dane drained his coffee. 'Let's finish up here, and then we can get going.'

We zipped back down through the high street in Dane's white four-by-four truck, past the Highland countryside with its ribbons of pines and inviting, mossy, woodland paths.

Hillsides criss-crossed over each other beyond the trees, emerging phantom-like in rich palettes of chocolate brown, jade and emerald.

I stretched my legs in the passenger seat beside Dane. I'd fished out my walking boots and tied my hair back in a high ponytail.

I sneaked a look across at him as he focused on the road. He was attractive in a full-of-himself kind of way. At least with someone as openly flirty like him, I knew where I stood.

'Got any siblings?' Dane asked, as he indicated right onto a bark strewn public car park and picnic area.

'No, I'm an only. I often think it would've been nice to have a brother or sister.'

Dane let out a low, dry laugh. 'Yeah. Well...'

I thought about Dane and Evan together; their prickly barbs at one another and the simmering atmosphere. I wondered whether I should pose the question, but it was out before I could do anything about it. 'Are you and Evan close?'

Dane sneered as he switched off his car engine. 'Are you joking?!'

When he saw my surprised expression, he tapped the

steering wheel. 'We're just very different.' There was that smile again. 'I don't know if you've noticed.'

'Yes, I have.'

We both jumped out. I reached into the back seat to collect my bag, and Dane fetched his rucksack.

Dane locked up the truck. Around us, the birds danced and flitted between the trees, and a couple of lazy clouds scudded overhead in the soft, blue sky. 'Evan's a bit of a stuffed shirt,' announced Dane. 'You've just got to take a look at some of his mates. They're all designer running shoes and TAG watches.' He snorted. 'He needs to lighten up.'

I realised with an odd stab that I suddenly didn't want to participate in this verbal critique of Evan. It didn't feel right. Ok, so Evan had received a call from Sacha last night, which had thrown me, but talking about him this way and seeing his own brother mock him? It felt wrong. Deceitful.

I switched the conversation to Dane's music. 'So, you write all your own material?'

'Oh yeah.' Dane gazed across at me. His gravelly, Scottish accent carried. 'I'm very creative, especially when I see something beautiful.'

I smiled. 'Talk about having the gift of the gab.'

'It's true,' he laughed. 'We all need to get our inspiration from somewhere.'

I stifled an amused smile.

Yes, he was a little over the top, but he was fun and creative; not like some men I'd met recently.

We moved off, crunching our way over the strewn twigs and bark. The air was heavy with the sweet, tangy scent of damp moss.

'So, you're an actor?' asked Dane, his light, icy eyes scanning my face and coming to rest on my lips. He was a born flirt. He did it as easily as breathing.

'That's right. I trained in Glasgow, got my degree and have worked in a lot of theatre productions. Then I got the part of Tammy in that ITV drama *Sinister*...'

'I saw that! I thought it was great, actually.'

'Really?' I was oddly touched; with so much on TV these days, I wasn't sure whether many people had actually seen my show.

'Absolutely.' He smiled. 'Me and the guys are performing at a local pub tonight. Fancy seeing me in action?'

I considered his question. 'Is Evan going?' I asked as airily as I could.

Dane laughed. 'No. He never comes to see the band play. Our sort of music isn't his thing.'

A night out of The Ramblings, not having to see Evan. That sounded like a plan. 'Ok. Thanks.'

'Great. It's a date then.' He grinned down at me as the sun shimmied through the trees. 'Come on. I'll show you this special place – I think you'll love it.'

Dane suddenly took his cue and moved off in big, long strides, leaving me staring in his wake. I watched him hurry on ahead. 'Hey. Hold on a sec. Let me catch up.'

I picked up speed, feeling the sun tickling my back through my T-shirt.

Dane, however, was focused on his destination and was walking even faster now. All I could see was the back of his black T-shirt and glimpses of his swinging ponytail. 'Dane. Can you wait for me, please?' I called.

His faint voice echoed back. 'Come on, Daisy. Let's get there before the light changes. I want you to see it.'

In my hurry to catch up with him, I'd not been looking where I was going and planted my foot down on something hard. 'Argh! Shit!' A burning pain shot up my leg. I'd twisted my right ankle on a jutting rock.

I hopped about on my left foot on the path, still swearing. 'Dane!'

From the ether, I heard an irritated voice. 'Yeah. What is it?'

'I've just twisted my ankle.'

'Och, you'll be fine. Come on. You need to see this view.'

What?! I waited to see if he might dash back, just to check that I was alright, but he didn't. Instead, I caught a glimpse of him taking his phone out of his combat trouser pocket and recording the view.

Frustrated, I set my right foot back down on the path, but a few indignant throbs from my ankle soon made me lift it back up again. 'Ow!' I glowered into the distance. 'Dane? Dane!'

But he didn't reply. He'd gone off without me.

I hopped on my left foot, incredulous. The sun was

warming my skin even more through my cotton T-shirt, and I had no clue where I was.

Now what?

I put my right foot gingerly back down on the path, but it was still hurting. I winced and tried to move myself so that I wasn't putting any pressure on it. I really was having a great day! First I almost choked on some toast, and now I'd injured my foot?!

I had to make it back down to Dane's car. I didn't want to try to find him. I could end up getting lost or falling over. But if I did reach his car, I didn't have the car keys anyway. He had them. Bugger! What now?! What should I do?

Fury ate into me. This was my fault. I should never have said yes to Dane asking me along. Why the hell had I? I'd just wanted to show Dane I was grateful to him for what he did at breakfast. But was there something more to it than that? Something I didn't want to acknowledge? Was it because I wanted to annoy Evan? Make him jealous? Get back at him because Sacha rang him last night? Let him think I wasn't interested in him? I wasn't anyway, of course. Had I come on this walk with Dane to get away from Evan's simmering presence for a while? A combination of all of them? No, of course not. That was ridiculous.

Wait. I had my phone with me. I could ring for help. I dumped my bag at my feet and swiped one brow across my sweaty forehead as I pulled out my phone. I tapped the screen.

My shoulders sank. There was no signal.

Panic was rising in me faster.

'Need a hand?'

I almost stumbled over in fright as I twisted round.

It was Evan.

It took me a few stunned moments to process that he was standing there, talking to me. I gasped in surprise, almost forgetting my throbbing ankle. 'What are you doing here?'

He shrugged. 'Thought I'd take a morning stroll.'

'At exactly the same place as Dane and me?'

'A happy coincidence.'

I narrowed my eyes. 'How did you know we'd be here? Did Dane tell you where we were going?'

Evan shook his head. 'He always brings his lady friends up here. He's a creature of habit.'

I stiffened under his enquiring eyes. 'I'm not one of his lady friends.' In my indignation, I forgot about my delicate ankle and set my foot hard down on the path. 'Aaargh!'

'What is it? You ok?'

With two strides on those long legs of his, Evan was right in front of me. I could make out the curve of his upper lip under his stubble and the prick of his ebony lashes. 'You're not having a great day so far, are you?' he asked, with a hint of amusement.

I fought to look calm and collected. 'I've twisted my ankle, but it's fine.'

'It doesn't seem like it.' Evan peered around. 'And where's Thor got to? Breaking up tree trunks with his bare hands?'

Despite my tender toe, I laughed. 'He was taking photos on his phone, and I seem to have got left behind.'

Evan's lip curled up with evident disapproval. 'Very gallant of him to leave a lady in distress.'

'Well, he did perform the Heimlich manoeuvre on me earlier.'

'Only because I didn't get to you first.'

'Oh, sorry about that. Next time I'm choking, I'll make sure I give you a head start.'

With one swift movement, he took my left arm and draped it around his neck. I could feel the warm glow of his skin against my arm. 'Just stop being mardy for two seconds, Daisy, and let me help you.'

I swallowed. 'What are you doing?'

'Well, we're not about to do the Argentine Tango.'

I tutted at him.

'We're going to head back to my dad's car, and then I'm taking you home to The Ramblings. You need to rest your ankle.' He nodded down at it. 'Is it broken?'

'I don't think so. I can waggle it.' I gave it another wiggle and winced. It was still tender but not raging with pain like it had been ten minutes ago.

'Right. Let's go. Just keep holding onto me, and don't let go.'

Our eyes sought out each other.

I jerked my head away and trained my attention on the trees ahead. How come he could be so charming and attentive towards me one minute and almost stand-offish the next?

I took gentle steps, the solidity of Evan a reassuring and intoxicating presence, as he guided me along. 'What about Dane?'

Evan assisted me back along the path. 'What about him?'

'Don't you think we should tell him what's happened? I couldn't get a signal on my phone just now, though.'

Evan clicked his tongue at the mention of his brother as we carried on walking; well, me hobbling and Evan supporting me. Evan's muscles glanced against the side of my body every so often. I took a deep breath and tried to focus. Think about Sacha. She called him. There's history there, and what looks like unfinished business if she's ringing him as soon as he gets back to Forrest Bank.

Evan's voice made me concentrate again. 'He should've thought about you instead of taking off like some long-haired Bear Grylls.' He sighed. 'Ok. Let's get back to the car and I'll see if I can call him or text him from there and tell him I've got you.'

There was that lingering, dark look again. A wisp of breath caught at the base of my throat. 'Thank you,' I managed.

After another five minutes or so of dogged determination on both our parts, the picnic area appeared. I'd never thought a car park could look so beautiful.

We stopped while Evan fished one hand in his jeans for his car keys. He assisted me round to the passenger side and unlocked the door.

Evan braced himself. 'The door's open. Here.'

Ever so gently, he stooped over and helped me into the passenger seat. I got a cloud of his tangy, citrus shampoo.

I tugged at the neck of my T-shirt for something to do. My car door was still open, and I was glad. My cheeks were on fire. Maybe the woodland air would take the sting out of them. 'I'll try to call Dane now,' said Evan, gazing down at me as I arranged myself in the passenger seat. His expression was soft; thoughtful.

Then he seemed to check himself and reached for his phone from his back pocket.

'Thank you,' I blurted. 'For coming to my rescue.'

Evan halted his fingers on his phone screen and nodded. He returned his attention to his phone. 'He's not picking up, so I'll send him a text.' I watched Evan's fingers flash over his phone screen. 'There. Done.'

He stalked round to the driver's side, and I closed my door. 'Now, let's get you back. You need to rest that ankle for a bit. Something cold on it, and maybe some arnica cream.'

I nodded. 'That sounds like a good idea, seeing as I'm going out tonight.'

Evan switched on his car's ignition. 'Oh?'

'Dane invited me to go and see him and his band play at a local pub.'

His expression tightened. 'Did he?'

I nodded.

Evan steered the car out of the picnic area and indicated to turn right and back out onto the main road. 'I'll see you there then.'

An odd, flickering feeling like an escaped bird took off in my chest. 'You're going?'

Evan shrugged. 'I might as well. Even though Dane does act like a prick a lot of the time, he's still my brother.'

There was a loaded silence in the car.

'Right, peg leg,' he teased, negotiating us back down the country lanes. 'We need to get you sorted, otherwise Cinderella won't be going to the ball.'

Chapter Nine

T he Ramblings was lit up inside with the sun spilling in through its mullioned windows.

Its golden kaleidoscope rays criss-crossed the tiled floor and staircase.

I shuffled inside with Evan at my back.

'Mum? Dad?' he called, his deep voice echoing around the space.

'Your parents have gone out,' replied Louise from somewhere around the corner. 'Helping with a charity auction at the residential home.'

I could hear her shoes tapping on the tiles as she approached. 'How are things? Oh!' She saw me waggle my booted foot and wince. 'What happened?'

'I went for a woodland walk with Dane and ended up twisting my ankle on a rock.'

Louise clicked her tongue and crossed her arms over her aproned chest. 'Och no! Was it up by that pine forest? With the picnic area? I overheard Dane asking you to go out for a walk earlier.'

At Louise's words, I felt Evan stiffen beside me.

I nodded. 'Yes. That's the place.'

Louise indicated to my foot. 'How is it now? Can I get you anything?'

'No, thanks. It's a lot better than it was.'

'Well, just shout if you do need anything.' She bustled off.

'I still think you should pop a frozen bag of peas on it,' insisted Evan. 'It won't do any harm.'

We'd reached the bottom of the staircase.

I put my right foot on the first step and slowly edged onto the next.

Evan folded his big arms behind me. 'It's going to take you about three hours to get up there at this rate.'

'Well, what do you want me to do? Jump on a hovercraft?'

'Very droll.'

Before I could say anything else, I felt the ground move away from me. Evan had swept me off my feet and into his arms. 'What on earth…?!' I gasped, finding myself staring up into his serious face. Part of me wanted to insist that he put me down right away. I could bloody well make it up those stairs by myself, thank you very much!

But the other half of me was savouring every moment of being held by this sexy, strong man. I wanted him to hold me like this. I wanted to breathe him in; feel his muscles around me; be protected by him; feel the thud of his heart against me. I wasn't used to being protected or sheltered. I was used to being the independent one; self-reliant. Embarrassment flooded me as I found I liked it very much, especially as Evan was the one doing the looking after.

He held me as though I weighed nothing, gazing down at me for the longest time. His flickering, black lashes; the arch of his brows. Slowly, he proceeded to thud up each step of the ornate staircase in his walking boots, holding me in his arms.

Neither of us said anything. It was as though the only noise reverberating around the great hall was our breathing and the crashing of my heart.

My fingers located Evan's neck, and I laced them around him as he continued to transport me upstairs. Common sense was screaming at me, but I refused to listen.

Evan's black hair bounced against his forehead. I wanted to raise my hand and brush that irresistible flop of hair back from his face.

'I'll take you to your room,' he murmured. His attention travelled to my mouth.

My insides turned to water. I couldn't think properly. My head was lost.

This was wrong. I should've stumbled up the stairs by myself. I shouldn't have allowed myself to be in this position. I was making myself vulnerable. But despite the protests racing through me, my fingers tightened around Evan's neck.

We reached my bedroom door, and Evan raised one booted foot and pushed against it. It swung open.

The sight of my bed and the two of us alone, me still wrapped in Evan's arms and him carrying me … I was struggling to concentrate on anything except him. My tumultuous emotions clashed with the charged silence. The feel of his arms encircling me was a sensation I'd never experienced before.

With so much care, Evan laid me on top of the bed and proceeded to remove my socks and boots. Thank goodness I'd given myself a pedicure at the weekend.

Evan took a step backwards, still studying me as I lay there on top of the bed. 'How are you feeling now?'

I wanted to say, 'Hot and bothered,' but I bit it back.

Lying here, feeling so vulnerable under the watchful hot gaze of Evan, was making bubbles explode in my stomach. This wasn't me. It shouldn't be me. I never allowed men to get this close after Leon. Much less risk being left heartbroken and used that way.

How I wished I was wearing something sexier than a sparkly T-shirt and jeans. Then I remembered I wasn't speaking. I hadn't answered his question. I hurried to gather my thoughts. 'It's feeling a lot better, thanks.'

I pushed myself upwards onto my elbows. 'Thank you again, Evan, for taking such good care of me. I mean it.'

Evan sank down on the edge of the bed. 'Don't mention it.' He pointed at my right ankle. 'You've got an impressive bruise there. Give me a second, and I'll fetch that bag of peas and some arnica cream from the kitchen cupboard.'

'Evan. There's really no need.'

But he just rewarded my protests with a withering look.

I heard him bound back down the stairs, and he returned moments later with a bag of frozen peas wrapped in a tea towel of Edinburgh Castle and a tube of arnica cream. 'Can you manage?' he asked, waggling the bag of peas.

'I think I can.'

I accepted the peas from him and set them on my ankle. I made a satisfied, groaning noise.

He grinned. 'That good?'

'Oh yes.'

I'd keep it on for a few more minutes before removing it.

'Are you ok for me to apply the arnica, or do you want to do it?'

I sat up a little straighter. 'I can manage,' I insisted. I didn't think I could take the idea of Evan's hands touching me.

But I couldn't apply the cream myself. I tried reaching down to my ankle a couple of times, but it was an awkward angle, and every time I did, it niggled as if to remind me to be careful.

'Here,' ordered Evan. 'Give it to me.'

He squeezed some of the soft, white cream onto his finger and proceeded to rub it gently into my ankle. His fingers glided up and down my skin. His lashes were thick and black as he continued to look down. 'You don't like accepting help, do you?'

I flinched at his question.

'Keep your foot still while I apply this.'

There was a beat. 'Well?' He pushed. 'You don't, do you?'

'I like to be independent.' I was in danger of gasping, but I managed to turn it into a weird cough.

A couple of blackbirds chirruped their song right outside the bedroom window.

I had to remind myself to keep breathing as Evan finished applying the cream. The ache had subsided now, replaced by the zinging sensation of Evan's fingertips playing against my skin.

We continued to study each other.

My mind slotted Evan and Dane side by side. Dane was attitude, charm and confidence. But Evan was … he was caring and intense, with that dry sense of humour. What with the way his muscles bunched, too… *Stop, Daisy! Just stop!*

'You rest for a bit.' Evan's voice broke through my meandering thoughts. 'Just shout if you need anything, ok?'

The kindness and concern in his voice took me by surprise. I wasn't used to it; being fussed over by others. My grandparents and Jade, but that was about it.

Emotion rose in me, and I bit it back. 'I will. And thank you again.'

He moved towards the bedroom door and turned around. 'And no heroics on the stairs, otherwise I'll have to insist on carrying you again.' The lingering look he gave me made my insides quiver.

As soon as Evan closed the door behind him, I let out a frustrated sob, grabbed a pillow and sank my teeth into it.

Chapter Ten

I spent the rest of the day trawling through social media in desperate search of acting work.

Louise made Evan and me Scottish salmon and cream cheese bagels for lunch, accompanied by salad and ruby red, juicy tomatoes.

I made sure I was ok to negotiate the stairs myself. I'd been tempted to ask again for Evan's help but concluded that was a road I shouldn't be going down. Common sense prevailed. Evan had to be kept at arm's length, I decided inwardly. I knew my emotions were threatening to tip over where he was concerned. It was ridiculous. I'd only known him for a few days, and yet whenever he was around or looked at me, I'd come over all gawky and struggle to look at him.

I also had to keep Sacha at the forefront of my mind. It appeared she was back on the scene.

I struggled to ignore the wriggle of jealousy.

Maybe this was gratitude I was feeling rather than anything else. Evan had stopped me from throwing the champagne over Fox, and he'd come to my aid earlier that day with my bruised ankle. He'd been like a superhero, flying in to show me that I wasn't all alone and that I could rely on someone else apart from my grandfather.

Yes, stated a strong, insistent voice inside my head. That was all it was. Gratitude and appreciation.

After a delicious early dinner of beef stroganoff and rice, I made my way up to my room to get ready for Dane's concert.

I had thought about not going. After all, he'd abandoned me and my ankle on that walk. Maybe it had just been Dane's keenness to show me the area? Maybe that was why he'd strode on ahead. But something else persuaded me that I should go. Dane did come to my rescue at breakfast, and Evan was going, too. Would it look churlish if I didn't?

Evan's voice made me spin round outside my room. 'Managed ok then?'

A shiver of excitement shot up my spine.

I pushed a loose hunk of hair back behind my ear which had escaped from my ponytail. 'Yes, I did, thanks.'

Evan leant on the wall, looking like a Greek God. 'That's a pity.'

'Why's that?'

'I was hoping my maiden-carrying services might be required again.'

'You need to concentrate on exposing the bad guys.'

'Not as much fun, though.'

I reached for the door handle, struggling to steady the clattering of my heart.

Was Evan flirting with me?

Then images of Sacha danced in my head.

I closed the door behind me and slumped my back against it.

As I showered, washed my hair and got dressed, I resisted all thoughts of Evan, and instead I concentrated on what I should wear for Dane's gig.

The man in question had appeared briefly at dinner, showing concern over what happened and enquiring after my ankle before helping himself to some stroganoff. Then he'd headed off again ten minutes later, saying he had to go and get ready to meet his band mates.

Alison and Bennett had exchanged exasperated looks.

He and his older brother were polar opposites.

Dane had the sass and cockiness, while Evan … oh, for pity's sake! I was doing it again.

This was going nowhere, me thinking about Evan. It was fruitless. No doubt if anything had happened it would have ended up a disaster anyway, and with Sacha in the mix, it was a no-brainer.

After I'd finished applying my makeup, I rifled through the contents of my case.

I pulled an agonised face. What should I wear? I hadn't expected to be invited to a rock gig.

My ankle was much better, but I decided to avoid the couple of pairs of strappy heels I'd thrown into my case and opted instead for my more sensible, sparkly trainers. I'd team that with my rose pink, strappy, summer top, my slim-fitting, black jeans and my rhinestone belt. I'd throw my denim jacket on over it all in case it got cooler when the gig ended.

I pinned my hair up at each side and dashed on some of my favourite Dior perfume. I grabbed my bag and phone and was just rounding the corner after heading downstairs when I collided with a chest. 'Oh!'

Evan.

He was wearing a white T-shirt under a loose, black, linen shirt and dark combats. He smelled of cedarwood and his hair was tumbling back from his face in dark layers.

His serious expression shifted as he drank me in. 'You look gorgeous.'

The air around us bristled. 'Thank you. You don't look too shabby either.'

There was a poignant crackle again between us. It was as if The Ramblings was holding its breath, eavesdropping in on our conversation.

'I thought we could take my dad's car.'

'Don't you want to walk there if it's not too far? You won't be able to have a drink.'

'We can get a cab back, and I'll collect the car in the morning.' He nodded down at my right foot. 'And yes, I know you said it's much better, but let's not risk it.'

His words wrapped themselves around me. Something told me I could get used to this, being watched over and protected rather than having to do the watching over and the tending. But that warning klaxon about staying self-reliant and not getting hurt exploded in my head again.

The spectre of Leon reappeared. God, I hated him for the emotional debris and distrust he'd left in his wake.

Evan smiled down at me. 'Come on, then. We don't want to keep Bryan Adams waiting.'

I cocked a brow at Evan and laughed. 'Something tells me Dane and his band would like to be compared to someone grittier than Bryan Adams.'

'I know,' he grinned. 'That's why I said it.'

Louise called out to us to have a great evening and returned to singing along to Michael Ball and Alfie Boe in the kitchen. Alison and Bennett had gone to visit friends in Aviemore.

We made our way out of The Ramblings and down to where Bennett's car was parked up: the silver Mercedes which Evan had used to rescue me and my twisted ankle.

We jumped into it and set off.

As Evan edged us out of the grounds and onto the main road, in the far distance we could just about see the faint, grey shimmer of Loch Crawe and what looked like drones hovering like black dots. 'Hopefully it won't be much longer, and then you'll be able to leave and see your grandfather,' pointed out Evan.

He steered us towards a small line of traffic lights and then along the high street.

'What's he like?' asked Evan. 'Your grandfather?'

'He's wonderful, although I am biased. He's funny, insightful and very caring.' *Just like you*, whispered a voice in my head. I reset my head and concentrated on my grandfather again. 'He used to work for the local council in their parks and gardens department, as I said. He loved it.'

'And what about your grandmother?'

'She was a hairdresser. She passed away fifteen years ago now.'

'I'm sorry.'

I appreciated the winding shops beyond the passenger side window. 'My grandma meant so much to him. He misses her like crazy, as do I. We just make sure we're always there for one another. We always have.'

Evan clicked his indicator to the right and took us down a narrow street, sandwiched with quiet little gift shops and restaurants and cafes decked out with awnings. 'And what about your parents?'

My protective shield experienced a sudden wobble under Evan's questioning. 'What about them?'

When he gave me a quizzical look, I blanched. 'I'm sorry. I didn't mean to sound rude.'

'No. It's ok. That's the journalist in me rearing his head. You don't have to tell me anything.'

Evan guided us into a car park situated at the side of a pub called The Whiskey Jar. I remembered that was where Dane said Disciple were staging their gig.

Evan turned off the engine and rested both his arms on top of the steering wheel. His sleeves were rolled up a little, and I could see a smattering of dark hair. My stomach flip-flapped around. Dear God, woman!

Something was pulling at me, encouraging me to talk to Evan; to open up and reveal a part of me I liked to keep hidden. Vulnerability. This was a sudden, scary sensation. Part of me wanted to jump out of the car and not say anything to him, but the patient, soft expression in his eyes was hypnotising.

I sighed. 'It's fine. Really.' I picked up my bag by my feet and cradled it in my arms for something to do.

Snapshots of my mum and dad drifted like gossamer in front of my eyes. They didn't register with any sort of emotion. Maybe a touch of sadness at what they felt they hadn't been able to do for me – what they thought they couldn't do and give to each other – but nothing else. 'You can tell you're a reporter.'

'Like I said, please don't feel you have to tell me anything you don't want to.'

I lifted my right hand from the top of my bag where it was resting and flapped it. 'No. It's ok.' I gathered myself. 'I'm not close to my parents.' I hesitated, gathering my resolve to delve deeper into my past life. Outside the car, the pub lights shone like torch beams into the descending darkness. 'My mum got pregnant at eighteen and decided she wasn't cut out for motherhood, so my maternal grandparents brought me up from the age of three months old.'

The chatter of pub goers outside disturbed our conversation for a brief moment. We heard the pub doors clanging open and shut.

'I'm sorry, Daisy.'

'Oh, don't be. I had the most wonderful childhood thanks to them.' I shrugged my shoulders. 'You don't miss what you've never had.'

'What about your dad?' he asked.

'Oh, he disappeared down to London as soon as my Mum told him she was expecting and never came back.' I glanced out of the windscreen at the glowing pub. 'He was a struggling actor, and my mum wanted to become a singer.' I let out an ironic laugh. 'They were both so frustrated with their lot and never achieved what they wanted to in life.' I delivered a small smile. 'I think that's why I'm so hell-bent on being successful. I want to make something of my life and not live like my mum does. She wallows in regret all the time, and it's eaten her up.'

'Do you see your parents?'

I shook my head. 'My mum very occasionally, if she's got nothing better to do, but my dad never kept in touch. He got married and has four kids of his own now. Lives in the south of England somewhere. Ironic really. Dad of the year when it suited him.'

'Well, they're missing out on so much, not having you in their life.'

I drank him in. I couldn't believe I'd just sat in a strange pub car park and revealed so much of myself to a guy I'd only known for three days. If someone had said to me I'd do just that, I would've thought they were nuts. No way would Daisy Madden, struggling actor, very independent, have even considered that. I could feel a shaky smile tugging at my face. 'That's a lovely thing to say.'

'It's true.'

I noticed the way Evan's mouth arranged itself when he was thinking; how it tilted up at one corner, almost like he was bemused. What would his lips taste like? How would his mouth feel on mine?

I fidgeted in my car seat. 'So, enough about me. How about you, Evan Lord?'

'What about me?'

'What's your story? You seem to get on so well with your parents. Still, I'm not surprised; they're amazing.'

Evan toyed with his dad's car keys. 'Yes, they're great. Very kind and supportive.'

'And Dane?'

A strange flash of something passed across Evan's expression. 'He's self-obsessed.' His lips curled. 'Life's a game to him a lot of the time.'

I waited for Evan to elaborate but he didn't. He cranked open his driver side door and clambered out. 'Time to go and have our eardrums assaulted for the next ninety minutes.'

We entered the pub doors to be greeted by a sea of bodies, with varying degrees of length of hair and ages. Rock T-shirts were being sported by the vast majority of the crowd.

The interior of The Whiskey Jar consisted of sea green and grey walls, with a semi-circular bar with mirrored panels behind it.

Booths ran all the way towards the back, and tables and chairs were clustered close together.

There was a makeshift stage several feet in front of us, on which Dane was testing the microphone and the other band members were getting themselves arranged with their instruments. The clinking of glasses could just be heard over the sound of chatter and laughter.

Dane's fellow band members of Disciple all had the same look, with their snake hips and longer hair.

Dane adjusted the microphone stand, spotted me, grinned and winked. I found myself blushing, grinning and waving back.

Evan's expression darkened, but he didn't say anything.

Then Dane noticed his brother beside me, and his brows shot up in surprise.

'I'll get the drinks,' said Evan, setting off towards the bar.

'No you won't,' I protested. 'You and your parents are putting me up in that gorgeous house. The drinks are on me.'

Evan gave me a long look. 'You're very determined.'

'Pig-headed, some say.'

'I thought that as well, but I didn't want to be rude.'

'Hasn't stopped you before.'

'I'll go and get them then,' said Evan.

I thrust a twenty-pound note into Evan's reluctant palm and requested a white wine. He ventured into the pub crowd and made his way towards the bar.

'Hey, Daisy. Wow. You look stunning.'

Dane had bounded off the stage, his loose, blond hair flying behind him. I felt myself glow under his compliment. He was like a firework that you couldn't help but admire. He jerked his head in his brother's general direction. 'Am I hallucinating, or did I just see Evan with you?'

'No, you're not hallucinating. Evan wanted to come along.'

'Evan?' he repeated. 'Wanted to come to one of our gigs?' Dane folded his arms. He was wearing several leather bracelets. 'He doesn't usually come along. He never has before.' His lips twitched at a smile through his fair stubble. 'Snow Patrol and Bastille are about his limit.'

'Dane. You ready?'

One of the other band members, a tattooed guy in a red Alice Cooper T-shirt signalled from behind where we were standing.

'Yep. Just coming, Jay.' Dane bathed me in another of his flashing smiles. 'If you're lucky, I might dedicate one of our songs to you.'

I grinned back at him. 'I bet you say that to all the girls.'

'No, I don't. Well, only the most stunning ones.'

Then he was off, striding back towards the stage as though he owned the whole pub and everyone in it.

'What did Barbie want?' Evan handed me my glass of white wine.

I arched one brow at him. 'That's your kid brother you're talking about.'

'I know. Don't remind me.'

I took a savouring mouthful of the crisp, white wine. What was going on between Evan and Dane? They were forever sniping, trying to get one up on each other, scrambling to come up with snarky comments to fire in each other's direction. Any more thought about their fraught relationship was brought to an abrupt end by Dane's gravelly voice booming into the mic. 'Good evening, folks. We are Disciple.' He craned his neck across the top of the heads of the applauding and cheering crowd. 'And this first song is for the beautiful girl over there in the pink top. This is just for you, Daisy.'

It took me a moment to realise that Dane was referring to me. The blood rushed to my face as a number of curious heads turned to look in my direction. A couple of girls in leather jackets scowled over at me.

Evan muttered something under his breath which sounded like 'Prick.'

Dane had a powerful singing voice as he belted out lyrics about love and losing your mind over it. The other guys in the band played their guitars and drums respectively with so much passion and concentration. I found myself captivated by Dane's performance. He was a true showman, prowling about the stage and engaging with the crowd.

At the end of the song, Dane soaked up the whoops and thunderous applause.

It was as Dane was about to launch into his next track, which he said was called 'Losing your Levity', that my mobile rang in my bag. It was Octavia. My heart gave a little skip of optimism. Did she have good news on the acting job front?

I set my half-empty wine glass down on the corner of the table nearest us and caught Evan's attention. He was supping his pint and looked the epitome of boredom. If he didn't enjoy Dane's music, why had he come along tonight? Was it because I said I was going? Or was I flattering myself? I blinked away my wandering thoughts. 'Evan, I've just got to take this. It's my agent on the phone. Won't be long.'

'Ok. I'm not going anywhere. Unfortunately.'

I couldn't help but smile at Evan's tortured expression.

I weaved my way through the pub crowd, then stepped out of the languid atmosphere and into the fresh, zinging spring evening. Darkness was pushing out the tangerine sky over the shop rooftops.

'Oh! I can hear loud music. Having a great time, sweetheart?' asked Octavia.

'Yes, not bad, apart from not being able to make it the rest of the way home, due to those two bombs they discovered.'

'I saw that on the news,' she breathed into my ear with drama. 'Crikey. It's all going on there, isn't it?'

I thought about Evan and The Ramblings.

'Anyway,' she carried on, with an air of importance. 'I just wanted to let you know that there's a couple of auditions in a few weeks' time that I'd like to put you forward for.'

I clutched my phone harder to my ear. 'Really? Oh, that's great, Octavia. Thank you!'

Excitement dared to flare in my chest. 'So, what are they for? Who are they with?' I started to pace up and down the pub entrance, with bouts of clapping, stomping and music filtering out. A kernel of optimism bloomed in my chest. 'Do you think the fallout from that review is starting to wane then?'

Octavia started to speak, but I was so delighted to hear that there might be some new roles on the horizon that I didn't give her an opportunity to explain. 'Is this for a new project? A TV series? Do I know anyone involved?'

'Daisy, for heaven's sake!' Octavia's bark made me stand to attention. 'If you'll just let me get a word in, I'll explain!'

'Sorry. I'm just relieved, that's all.'

'I got that impression.' Octavia cleared her throat. 'Now, please don't get carried away. We're not talking about the London Palladium. One is for a new, bespoke furniture company in South Kensington for their TV advert, and the other is the part of a nurse in a new BBC daytime soap opera.'

I digested this information. 'A nurse? How big is the part?'

'Oh, it's not a regular gig. It's a brief walk-on. You get four lines.'

My stomach felt like the bottom had fallen out of it. I didn't want to sound ungrateful. I really didn't. But a furniture ad and four measly lines? 'And that's it?' I managed.

'I'm afraid so. At least for the time being.'

I let out a long, low breath of resignation.

'But you never know. They could lead to something else,' said Octavia, trying to jolly me along.

I wasn't sure what a furniture ad and four lines about someone's medical condition could do to boost my dying acting career. I shook my head, even though Octavia couldn't see me. Disappointment hollowed me out. 'Thanks, Octavia. I really appreciate it, but there's no point.' I swallowed. 'I'm taking a break.'

More drums and wailing guitars seeped through the closed pub doors.

Octavia's voice became crisp. 'Suit yourself, Daisy, but lots of other people will be chasing those roles. Beggars can't be choosers, and all that.'

There was a brittle silence before she spoke again. 'I'll let you get back to your partying.'

I slung my mobile back in my bag.

I banged through the pub doors, leaving behind the sweet May night and stepping back into flying, long hair, leather and denim jackets and clanking beer glasses.

Evan had his back to me.

I started to approach and was about to tap him on the shoulder. I was thinking about telling him about the call with Octavia just now so I could get it off my chest. I'd confided in him about my parents just now, so why not this? He was a good listener.

But as I drummed up my nerve to talk to him, I noticed he was engaged in an animated conversation with someone.

It was only as I drew closer, that I recognised who he was talking to. It was Sacha.

I screeched to an embarrassed halt. They were both laughing.

My breath trapped itself in my throat as she stretched out one hand and rested it on Evan's arm. She was gazing up at him, her lips slightly parted, and every so often, she threw her head back in an exaggerated laugh. She was dolled up in black, strappy kitten heels and a glittery dark jacket, and she was wearing charcoal leather trousers that looked like they'd been sprayed on.

My stomach twisted.

She must've noticed the staring woman with the long, mink-coloured hair, because she dragged her attention away from Evan and gave me a look.

But I remained rooted to the spot in morbid fascination as she leant up and pushed that stubborn lock of dark hair back from Evan's forehead.

And I'd been blaming Dane for being a compulsive flirt. At least he was open about what he was. You knew what you were getting into. But Evan, with his straight moral compass demeanour ... had he been playing me for an idiot these last few days? Letting me think he was genuine, when in fact he was a deceiver like Leon?

There was more laughter burbling between Sacha and Evan. I felt such an idiot. But it was my own fault. The pain I was feeling was self-inflicted. I'd suspected there was something still lurking between them, and it looked like I'd been proven right.

Dane finished singing the band's latest song on their setlist about a lost love, and the riotous applause took off again.

I managed to clap and pin a smile on my face as Dane caught my eye from the stage. 'Daisy, Daisy, give me your answer, do.' He crooned into the mike. His light eyes were glittering. I suspected he'd downed a few pints.

On hearing Dane mention my name, Evan spun round.

His expression was unreadable.

Sacha followed his gaze, and her mouth flatlined when she saw Evan looking back at me.

I stared ahead towards the stage and waved at Dane. I knew I was being petty, but I gave him what I hoped was my most dazzling smile. What was the matter with me? What did I think I was doing? Was I trying to make Evan jealous?

Evan's jaw clenched.

I folded my arms and wrapped them around myself for comfort as Evan was then barrelled by Sacha right past me and out of the pub.

Chapter Eleven

O h please, please let these bloody bombs get dealt
with as soon as possible!

I gazed down into my cup of tea, stirring it with the
spoon around and around. I was doing it so much I was at
risk of making myself dizzy.

My thoughts kept creeping back to Evan and the way
Sacha had corralled him out of the pub last night.

I was annoyed at being annoyed in the first place. My
teaspoon stilled in my hand.

All the compliments Evan had been paying me, the
teasing and the flirting, the charged looks, and then he
disappears off with her? But then, what should I have
expected? She'd rung him the other night, and then there'd
been the loaded comments from the police officer friend of
Evan's about her.

I resumed stirring my tea. It was my own fault. It was
self-inflicted. I'd sleepwalked into this where Evan was

concerned. I'd assured myself after the mess with Leon that I could keep a lid on my feelings.

But here I was, teetering on the brink again.

I should never have allowed Evan to carry me upstairs. His eyes raking my face, drifting down to my mouth, resting there with that burning, dark intensity; feeling his muscles shifting against me. If I'd known what I knew now, I would've limped up them myself, even with a dodgy ankle.

A dull ache inside me wondered where Evan was. There was no sign of him. Same with Dane.

I was still the only one at the breakfast table, with Louise zipping back and forth with conserves and cereal. Her thick, bouncy, blue-toned curls jumped around her face.

Even Alison and Bennett hadn't appeared yet.

I forced myself to stop clattering the spoon. My tea resembled a beige whirlpool. I had to stop thinking about where Evan might be and who he was with.

I got frustrated with myself again. I tapped idly on my phone screen, which was lying on the tablecloth at my elbow.

'Good morning, Daisy. Sleep well?'

Bennett came striding into the dining room. looking suave in a coffee coloured, short-sleeved shirt and light trousers.

I pushed myself straighter up in my chair and forced a smile. 'Yes, I did. Thank you, Bennett. How about you?' This was a lie. My mind had kept racing in the dark, torturing myself about whether I'd imagined any connection between Evan and me and what he and Sacha might be up to.

'Yes, slept well, thanks,' carried on Bennett, oblivious to me dwelling on his oldest son. 'Did you have a good night at Dane's gig?'

I was about to reply when Evan's voice interrupted. 'Morning.'

I reached for my teacup and all but pushed my face into it. I wished he hadn't stopped me from drenching Fox on Saturday. I wished I'd never given him a ride to Scotland. I wished that there had never been a sodding tech outage at the airports. I wished there hadn't been two unexploded bombs. I wished he'd never invited me to stay here. I wished I'd never accepted. I wished he hadn't been so gallant and insisted on taking me in his arms and carrying me upstairs. I was knotted up inside, and my head was going into a tailspin.

'Morning,' I sing-songed, hoping I sounded so laid-back I'd look horizontal.

Don't sit opposite me, Evan, hissed an inner voice. *Don't sit opposite me… oh shit!*

He dragged out the chair opposite me at the table and sunk into it.

Why couldn't he have taken that irresistible mouth and eyes of his off down to the far end of the table?!

Evan reached for the coffee pot and glugged the steaming, hot, dark liquid into his cup. 'Did you enjoy the gig then?' His voice was strained.

'Yes, it was wonderful, thanks,' I said with forced

joviality. 'After it finished, I stayed behind with Dane and the rest of the guys. We had a great laugh.'

Actually, it had been anything but.

I'd been bored rigid.

Dane had to be centre stage, even in conversations. He'd sat there with the other band members and a few hangers-on from the pub crowd, preening and managing to turn every topic around so that in the end, whatever the subject was, the chat invariably came back around to be about him. It was admirable in a way. It really was a talent.

But there was no need for Evan to know that.

Dane had flirted with me, of course, introducing me to his friends and band members, stationing me beside him; but in the end, I'd made my excuses, saying I was tired, and I left the pub and booked a taxi back to The Ramblings.

I tried to look nonchalant about the whole night, pushing images of Sacha in her skin-tight trousers to the back of my mind. 'And how about you?' I asked, not wanting to know. 'Did you have a good time?'

'Yes, great, thanks.' Evan savoured a mouthful of his black coffee. 'I caught up with Sacha.'

'Yes, I could see that. Well, she wasn't hard to spot, was she?' My smile was rigid. What the hell was the matter with me? Anybody would think I was jealous. 'It was a great night.'

Evan's brows stiffened. 'Yes, I could see what a good time you were having by the way you kept winking at my brother. Unless you have a medical condition?'

I let out an exaggerated laugh. If I didn't know any better, I might think he was jealous!

I wasn't jealous of him and Sacha, though. Nope. Not at all. I was irritated by him. And that was a different thing entirely. Completely unrelated.

At that moment, Alison entered the dining room in a pair of light-coloured jeans and a sleeveless, copper T-shirt with, ironically, daisies printed on it. 'Everyone have a good night at Dane's gig, then? Was he on top form?'

Evan rolled his eyes. 'What do you think, Mum?'

'Yes, it was great, thanks,' I chipped in, slipping Evan a covert look out of the corner of my eye. 'The pub was packed.'

Alison helped herself to some tea from the pot. 'That's good. Bennett and I have been before to see him and the band, but it's a bit on the raucous side for our liking.' She slid me a smile. 'I'm more of an André Rieu kind of girl.'

'I'd love to see him in concert,' I replied. 'It looks like such a spectacle.'

'It is. We saw him live in Venice a couple of years ago, and it was like stepping back in time, with all the gorgeous ballgowns and the atmosphere.' Alison seated herself and sipped her tea. 'Daisy, I was wondering if you were up to anything this morning? I have to drop some old fabrics at the local high school's art department.'

I'd just finished my cereal and clanked the spoon against the side of the bowl. I could feel Evan's eyes landing on me. 'That's a blast from the past. That's my old secondary school.'

Alison beamed across at me. 'Happy memories?'

'Mostly,' I replied, thinking of my gangly self racing to drama class. Some of the other kids had taken the mickey out of me for wanting to act, and because I'd loved it when we studied Shakespeare in English class.

I returned my thoughts to Alison's offer. It would be a relief to get some fresh air and escape from that dark gaze of Evan's. He could do whatever he wanted with Sacha, I thought, an odd twisting sensation in my chest. None of it was my business. I wasn't going to get played again.

'I'm not doing anything.' I nodded over at her. 'More than happy to help you. Thank you.'

The drive to Forrest Bank High School wasn't a long one.

I recalled my daily school bus trips from Strath Ross to school and home again, with some of the other kids blasting out Maroon 5 and One Direction, and the bus drivers tutting at Freya McMaster and Leo Anderson snogging on the back seat.

Alison slid on her sunglasses and guided us in her nippy little gold Punto through the high street. 'Is everything alright between you and Evan?'

I stiffened in the passenger seat. 'What do you mean?'

I could see her choosing her words carefully. The sun glanced off her blonde highlights. 'It's just I thought there was a bit of an atmosphere between you two at breakfast. Sorry if I've put my foot in it.'

I twitched my nose. Crikey. What was I supposed to say? I couldn't tell her that I found myself attracted to her eldest son, despite my best efforts, but I was pissed off at him because he'd left Dane's gig with his reporter girlfriend. 'No, I don't think so,' I struggled, forcing my attention back to the shops swishing by the window.

There was no way I was admitting any of this to Alison. Prising that information out of me couldn't be done by tugging off my fingernails. My insides were in a confused knot. Every time I thought about Evan, my breath would catch at the base of my throat as I conjured up more pictures of him gazing down at me from under his lashes. Had I been deluding myself? Had I read it all wrong?

Maybe I'd imagined that he was showing signs of finding me attractive? Perhaps it was wishful thinking? It wasn't reciprocated?

If I'd created the whole situation in my head, it was my own fault. I'd let myself down by allowing myself to find Evan attractive in the first place. I should've fought it more. Ignored it.

Angela turned off the main street and down past a sign which read, 'Welcome to Forrest Bank High School. Twinned with Lamarr College, Nice, France.'

As we drew closer, I could see my old school emerging. It was a two-storey brown brick and glass building with smaller annexes stationed at the back. It was fringed by thrusting trees and had a generous-sized football pitch and a wild garden, which was tended by the students. Apart from more greenery, it hadn't changed, I thought with a pang of sentiment.

I waited until Alison manoeuvred her car into a space located in the visitor's car park. She swiped off her sunglasses and popped them on top of her head. 'I was very surprised Evan went to Dane's gig last night.'

I didn't want to keep talking about Evan. If I didn't think about him, it would help, wouldn't it? I would've thought the pain I went through with Leon would've taught me something, but obviously it hadn't.

Alison switched off her car engine. 'To be honest, I was stunned when he told me he was going. He's never shown much interest in Dane's band before.' She lowered her voice a little, even though we were the only ones in the vehicle. 'That sort of music isn't usually to Evan's taste.'

I fetched my bag from the footwell, dumped it on my lap and proceeded to fiddle with the strap. 'He was chatting to a blonde woman in the pub. Very pretty. Sacha.'

Alison's expression tightened. 'Sacha? Are you sure that was her name?'

'Yes. Why?'

She rested both her ringed hands-on top of the steering wheel. The way the golden May light was slipping down her profile, highlighting the strong sweep of her nose and the pout of her bottom lip, reminded me of Evan. 'She's bad news, that one. She'd sell her own grandmother to get a byline.' Alison adjusted her sunglasses perched on top of her head. 'And you're sure that it was her?'

I nodded. 'He wasn't with her at the start of the evening,

but they left together at the end of the night.' I contorted my mouth into what I hoped was a casual smile.

Alison looked like someone had stood on her foot. 'Maybe I should speak to Evan. Ask him about her.'

'No. Please don't,' I blurted. 'He might work out that it was me who told you.'

Alison gazed ahead through the windscreen at the rise and fall of the high school roof. 'I don't want him getting involved with that bloody woman again. She hurt him so much the first time.'

Her words jabbed at me. I kept replaying the image of Sacha pawing at him last night. I wondered what had happened. It must've been a messy affair if Evan ended up getting hurt by her. Maybe Sacha was still an itch that Evan wanted to scratch?

The very idea made hurt and resentment well up inside me. Well, I wasn't prepared to be somebody else's reserve.

I wanted to push the conversation on further, though. What had Sacha done? What had she done to Evan to make Alison say that? Had she broken things off? Had he ended it and regretted it?

I shook my head. No. I'd be gone soon. Hopefully only another two or three days at the most. It wouldn't be right to pressure and probe Alison about Evan's previous relationship, even though a part of me was desperate to.

I shifted my position in the passenger seat. 'Please, Alison. Don't say anything to Evan. At least not yet.'

Alison cranked open her driver side door. 'Ok, Daisy. I promise I won't mention Sacha to Evan, at least for the time being. But if that woman thinks she can just swan back into his life and hurt him all over again, she's got another think coming!'

I clambered out of my side of the car and slung on my shoulder bag. We both headed round to the boot, and Alison unlocked it. The material we'd packed in there, glossy, patterned rolls of fabric, was stashed in huge holdalls. There was everything from chintz to paisley and from silk, satin and velvet to cotton.

We retrieved them and set them down by our feet. 'Can you tell I used to be in the drapery trade?' She grinned at me.

'Now you come to mention it.'

Alison locked the boot, and we set off towards the school building. 'When did you work in drapery?' I asked her.

'I had my own little business when Evan and Dane were younger. It was a place in the local high street. It's now the little tearoom on the corner.'

'What made you decide to stop, if you don't mind me asking?' I squinted in the light.

Alison's sunglasses bobbed on top of her head as we got closer to the school entrance. 'People stopped spending as much money on that sort of thing. Then my in-laws passed away, and Bennett found out his parents had left him The Ramblings in their will.' Alison adjusted the strap of the holdall in her hand. 'Don't get me wrong, it's a beautiful house and I love living there, but it costs so much to maintain it. It swallows up money.' She sighed. 'We've even had to let our full-time gardener Freddie go recently. He'd been with us for years. Lovely man.'

We slowed as we drew nearer to the entrance of the high school. 'At least Dane is good with plants. He's been trying to keep on top of the grounds as much as he can whenever he happens to be here.'

I recalled meeting Dane when I first arrived, clothes dirty and trowel in hand, and assuming he was the gardener.

'Bennett loves the place and is so sentimental about it. He grew up there, and it's been such a huge part of his life.' She frowned. 'Evan is very fond of The Ramblings as well, whereas Dane doesn't have the same emotional connection to the place. He just sees it as bricks and mortar. I think it's because he's on the road so much with his band.' Alison stared up at the sky for a moment, appreciating the duck egg blue shade and the waltzing puffs of cloud. 'Do you know Evan insists on giving us a monthly contribution towards the upkeep of The Ramblings?'

I stared at her, surprised. 'Does he?'

'Oh yes. We didn't want to take it, but Evan got really annoyed. He said it's part of his childhood, too, and that he would be really offended and hurt if his father and I didn't let him try to help out.'

My heart shifted. Why did Alison have to tell me that? I was trying to dredge up any reason I could to try and switch off my attraction to him. I hoped I'd got him wrong, and it would turn out he was vacuous and self-centred.

Instead, I learned he was giving his parents a monthly amount of money to maintain their stately home.

Alison dropped her voice. 'Please don't say anything to Evan, but even that amount of money he gives us is being swallowed up. If it's not the roof, it's the heating, or we stumble across dry rot. It's never-ending.'

Alison pressed the intercom, and we were put through to the school office. 'Alison Lord here, with Daisy Madden. I called earlier. I've got some materials to drop off for the art department.'

'Oh yes,' croaked a lilting Highland female voice. 'Hold on a second please, Mrs Lord, and I'll buzz you in.'

The double doors whooshed back, and Alison and I entered, negotiating entry with the holdalls of rolled up fabrics.

I gazed around. It was just how I remembered it, except for more large, white, ceramic, square tubs housing greenery dotted around the place.

'Changed much?' asked Alison, as though reading my mind.

I shook my head. 'The mosaics are new over by the stairwell, and there's fancier photography on the walls, but apart from that, no.'

One of the school secretaries gazed up from her computer screen and approached the glass partition. Her trendy spectacles glinted at us.

There was the odd student drifting up and down between classes, resplendent in their black and gold piped uniforms and silvery, striped ties. It reminded me of being a teenager, charging about the school corridors here the same way.

The school secretary took our names and tapped at her computer screen. 'I'll just let Ms Carnegie know that you're here. Please take a seat over there.'

Alison and I took up seats on a couple of black and chrome leather chairs in reception, still armed with the spare materials, while the secretary contacted the art department.

A few moments later, a young woman in a waistcoat and flared trousers came striding towards us from along the left-hand corridor and pumped Alison's hand up and down. Then she shook mine. 'Thank you so much for all of this! I promise it will go to very good use.'

'No problem, Nadia. Glad to be of help.' Alison smiled at me. 'I won't be a second.'

The teacher assisted her with the canvas bags of material, and they vanished back up to the left, chatting together.

I'd just taken up my seat again to wait for Alison to return when I had the feeling I was being watched. I shifted in my chair and admired the mosaic artwork of Loch Crawe up on the wall and the black and white photographs of the high street in years gone by.

Still, the feeling remained that someone was watching me.

I glanced around before realising that I was right. Someone in the school office was indeed peering through the partition at me.

It was a woman who I estimated to be in her mid-forties with rich, burnished, short hair and soft lines around her wide-set, pastel green eyes. Maybe she thought I was someone else.

I trained my attention again on the impressive mosaic for a few moments and then glanced back at the school office. She was still there, staring through the glass at me.

I delivered a brief, nervous smile.

I got a big, dazzling grin in return. Then she beckoned me over.

I peered around, looking for anyone else, but no, it was me she was indicating to.

I stood up and tentatively approached. 'Hello,' I said, not sure what else to say and wondering what was going on.

'Hi.' Her eyes popped at me. 'I hope you don't mind me saying, but aren't you Tammy from that ITV drama series?'

My cheeks flared with delight. Someone recognised me? 'Yes,' I faltered, my smile getting wider. 'I am. I mean, yes, I'm the actor who played her.' I wanted to shake her hand, but she was stationed behind the school office glass. 'I'm Daisy Madden.'

'I knew it!' she gasped, one excited hand fluttering up to rest on her chest. She was wearing a white blouse with a black, velvet pussy bow. 'Och, I'm brilliant at spotting celebrities. Wherever me and my husband go, if there's someone famous around, I can see them a mile off.'

I laughed, flattered. 'I'm not a celebrity or famous, believe me, but thank you very much for saying so.'

The woman kept grinning at me. 'You were wonderful in that series! I loved it!'

Ha! Up yours, Fox, I thought to myself in triumph, still beaming at the school secretary. 'Thank you. I appreciate that.' This was just what my confidence needed. After Fox's appalling review of *Sinister*, my current acting work drought and then Evan making me feel at all sixes and sevens, it was lovely to be recognised.

It was at that moment that the woman flapped her hand to get someone's attention behind me. 'Mrs Hazelwood? Excuse me? There's a phone message that's been left for you.'

It took a moment to process. Mrs Hazelwood? My old drama teacher?

I whirled round.

She had hardly changed at all in thirteen years. Her auburn hair was shorter, now skimming the top of her shoulders, and her face had filled out a little, but she was still pretty in an effervescent sort of way. 'Thanks, Gillian.'

Mrs Hazelwood leaned closer to the other side of the partition to collect the note. Behind it, a few of the school secretaries were tapping on their keyboards.

I took in her smart, fitted trousers and shimmery top, memories flooding back. How she would stride into drama class, bubbling with enthusiasm and telling her students to throw off the shackles of feeling self-conscious. She'd always greet us with a cheery 'Howdy!' and proceed to ask what dramas or films we'd been watching that week on TV; what actors stood out for us and why.

'Mrs Hazelwood?' I blurted.

She was about to walk away. 'Yes?'

Her ice blue eyes grazed my face. A slow smile grew as she examined me. 'Wait a minute. Daisy? Is that you?'

'It's me.' I laughed, delighted she'd recognised me after all these years.

She bundled me into a hug, much to the bemusement of a couple of passing teenage boys. 'My goodness! How are you? What are you doing back here?'

'I was supposed to be heading home to visit my grandfather, but this bomb situation has put paid to that, at least for another day or two.'

She nodded vigorously. 'Oh, of course. Hopefully they'll have it resolved by the end of this week.' She clapped her ringed hands together. 'Last I heard, you were treading the theatre boards, and then you were in that wonderful TV drama!' She turned to grin at the school secretary, who was watching us both with keen interest. 'One of my former drama students. A stand-out pupil was Daisy. I always knew you had talent.' She folded her arms, waggling the note she'd just been given. 'So, you're staying locally at the moment?'

'For the time being, yes,' I answered. 'And how are you, Mrs Hazelwood?'

Her dangly ruby earrings shimmered as she moved. 'Oh, still married, three teenage kids now though, and a springer spaniel. And please stop with the "Mrs Hazelwood", Daisy. Call me Josie.' She shot me a long, smiley look. She appeared to be debating something. 'I don't suppose I could grab a very quick word with you?'

'Yes, of course.' I wondered what she might want to talk about.

Mrs Hazelwood led me over to the staircase, and we huddled under the stairwell. She shuffled from foot to foot in her loafers, and said 'Daisy, I don't suppose I could ask a favour of you?'

'Ask away.'

'Would you consider coming to give a short talk to my senior drama class? I know they'd love to hear about your career and how you got your break in the business, especially after your appearance in *Sinister*.'

Behind us, the school office buzzed with chatter and the odd ringing phone.

I looked at Josie. Her eyes were pleading.

'Some of the kids sadly don't have the support and encouragement you had. I mean, I do my best, but they aren't getting that additional support at home to follow their acting dream.'

I'd been lucky that I'd had my grandparents as my constant cheerleaders. Everybody needed encouragement and help, no matter how strong they insisted they were. I offered a flattered smile. 'I'm delighted you've asked me. If I can help in any way, I'd be glad to.'

Josie looked like she'd been on the receiving end of a huge lottery win. 'Are you sure, Daisy? I mean, please don't feel any obligation.'

'It's fine. I'd be honoured, and it's the least I can do after all the encouragement and support you gave me when I was one of your students.'

Josie took my hand and gave it a grateful squeeze. 'I know it's rather short notice, but I don't suppose you're free at half past two this afternoon to come back and speak to the students? See a few of them perform? That's when I have my next class with them.'

'That's fine by me. I've got nothing else planned.'

This seemed like a win-win all right. The more I could avoid Evan until I departed The Ramblings and headed off to Strath Ross, the better.

The way he'd left Dane's gig with Sacha last night.

My heart contorted at the memory.

I wouldn't let him make me feel like that again.

Chapter Twelve

The gym hall consisted of a polished, pale, wooden floor and a dozen students sat around cross-legged, dressed in an assortment of jeans, T-shirts and leggings.

Memories of me struggling to leap over the pommel horse and getting whacked in the ankle by a hockey stick still haunted me.

'Howdy, guys!' chimed Josie.

She turned to me and indicated with one hand. 'Now, we have a special guest with us this afternoon. This is Daisy Madden, a former pupil at this school and one of my former drama students. She's trodden many theatre stages, and no doubt you will recognise her from her role as Tammy in the recent, excellent and gritty ITV series *Sinister*.'

There were excited nods and murmurs and a burst of applause.

'Daisy has kindly agreed to come and chat to you all today, so Daisy, over to you!'

I dumped my bag on a nearby chair and thanked Mrs Hazelwood for her introduction before giving a potted version of how I got started: the endless auditions, the chilly theatres I'd acted in and then my biggest role to date in *Sinister*. 'How about some of you give me a performance of one of your favourite pieces, and then I'm more than happy to take any questions?'

There was a sea of enthusiastic nods.

'Right. Who'd like to go first?' I asked.

There followed a procession of very good performances from the students; they each stood up and acted out a scene from one of their favourite movies or novels.

There were scenes performed from *Of Mice and Men*, *To Kill a Mockingbird*, *West Side Story* and *Wuthering Heights*. Their range and maturity blew me away, and I clapped and encouraged them, advising a couple of them to throw themselves even more into the person they were pretending to be. 'Don't think about your audience,' I suggested. 'In fact, don't think. Just be.'

I was revelling in the drama student's enthusiasm and passion, but at the same time, bouts of melancholy hit, making me wonder when or even if I would ever act again myself.

My attention fell on a pretty, strawberry blonde-haired girl sitting close to the gym hall windows. She was appraising me with sea green eyes. She dropped her attention to her trainers when I smiled and nodded over at her. She was the only one who hadn't got to her feet to perform.

Josie sidled up beside me. 'That's Cayla Sweeney,' she whispered. 'All my students are great, but she's something else. So, so talented. Just a pity she doesn't believe it herself.' She nodded her head in the direction of the school's entrance. 'Cayla is Gillian's daughter. The school receptionist you were chatting to this morning.'

'Ah. Right.'

'Gillian's one of my closest friends,' added Josie, giving Cayla a smile.

The girl returned a nervous one back, before peering down steadfastly at her trainers again.

The other students noticed us looking over at her.

There was a hush.

'Cayla, isn't it?' I asked.

She nodded her long, straight hair, making it tumble further over her face.

'Would you like to perform something?'

She bit her bottom lip.

'Do what you like; poem, scene from a book, an excerpt from a play.'

'I don't know,' she murmured, avoiding eye contact.

'You can do a scene from *Pride and Prejudice*,' suggested Josie.

Cayla shook her head. 'No, Miss.'

I searched around my mind for something to suggest next. 'What about some Shakespeare?'

Cayla glanced up at me from under her straight fringe.

'I love *Twelfth Night*,' I said. 'It's my all-time favourite of his. I think it's the first rom-com.'

Cayla's eyes widened. 'Seriously, Miss? I love it too.'

'Well then,' announced Josie, looking delighted.

Cayla stared around before slowly rising to her feet. Her glittery trainers squeaked on the shiny gym hall floor.

She knotted and unknotted her fingers in front of her. The pale blue hoodie she was wearing looked like it was ready to swallow her up at any moment.

'Take your time,' I told her. 'When you feel ready.'

The afternoon May sunshine was tumbling through the gym windows making Cayla's hair light up. She stole a deep breath, took another furtive glance around at her fellow drama students and then began to recite part of Olivia's monologue from act one, scene five.

'What is your parentage?'
Above my fortunes, yet my state is well.
I am a gentleman.' I'll be sworn thou art.
Thy tongue, thy face, thy limbs, actions, and spirit,
Do give thee five-fold blazon. Not too fast! Soft, soft!

I watched her possess each famous word, delivering it with clarity and conviction, as her contemporaries observed her with open admiration.

It was as if she'd morphed into Olivia herself, self-assured and regal, with an element of steel coursing through her.

When she finished, there was a stunned hush before we all broke into rapturous applause.

Cayla sank down again, cross-legged, on the floor. Her face was zinging pink under her curtain of hair.

'That was incredible,' I assured her. 'Mesmerising.'

We then held a question-and-answer session, where I was asked everything from who my favourite playwright was and which actor I envied, to what role I dreamt of and which theatre had the best atmosphere. It was so heart-warming to be able to share everything I loved about my craft.

The class soon came to a close, and the students thanked me as they filed past to go home, clutching their bags and folders.

Cayla was the last one to leave.

'You were wonderful,' I assured her. 'You're very talented.'

She hooked some hair behind one ear. 'Thank you, Ms Madden.'

She scurried out of the gym with her straw bag clutched to her side and her head down.

'School bullies,' said Josie, breaking through my thoughts.

'Sorry?'

'Cayla had a hard time recently with being bullied. It's knocked her confidence. Made her think she isn't good enough. That's why she's so reluctant to perform.'

My own experience of bullying at this very same school echoed in my head. 'I've been there. I know what that's like and what effect it can have on you.'

Josie examined me as she zipped up her bag. 'You were bullied? I never knew that.'

'It didn't go on indefinitely, thanks to my grandpa getting a couple of the local farm hands to have a quiet word with the ring leader.'

Josie grinned. 'Now that I can believe.'

'But I can appreciate what it must be like for Cayla. What's happening with the situation now?'

'The girl in question got excluded, and quite right too, but Cayla is still carrying the after-effects.' Josie slipped on her denim jacket. 'Gillian keeps asking me to try and have another word with Cayla; talk her round and make her realise how amazing she is and what potential she has, but I think she thinks I'm only telling her what her mother wants her to hear.'

Josie studied me. 'Hold on. What about you?'

'Me?'

'She probably thinks I'm some old luvvie fart, whereas you seemed to hit it off with her, especially with the *Twelfth Night* love-in.'

I blinked at her. 'You think I might have more luck?'

Josie shrugged as we strolled together out of the empty gym hall. 'Worth a try. Would you at least give it a go? See if Cayla might listen to you?'

I conjured up images of her performances of Olivia. I remembered getting sneered at myself by that nasty piece of work Gideon Turner and his cohort who didn't understand my love of drama. They used to say I thought I was better than everyone else just because I wanted to pursue acting.

The truth of it was that I knew what I wanted to do from an early age, and nothing would dissuade me.

I thought again about Cayla. 'Ok. I can't promise I'll succeed, but yes, I'll chat with her.'

Josie gave my arm a squeeze. 'Let's go and tell Gillian. She'll be delighted! And thank you!'

I pulled up outside number 12, The Grove in Forrest Bank just before five o'clock that afternoon.

Gillian had said Cayla would be home by then, but she wouldn't tell her I was coming. I didn't know in hindsight whether that might be a good idea or not.

Maybe it was. If she thought I was coming to deliver a pep talk, she might decide to go straight back out again before I arrived.

The house was a spotless, white, pebble-dashed, detached affair with a cheery, bright red front door and a small but well-tended front lawn, fringed with flower beds bursting with pops of spring blooms.

I parked Marlene in the street and clambered out.

The late afternoon air was languid and peaceful, tinged with lazy sunshine.

No sooner had I locked my car and started to make my way up the brick path than Gillian yanked the front door open and hauled me inside. The air smelled of apple air freshener. 'Thank you so much again, Daisy. I can't tell you what it means to me and Morris, my husband.' She gestured around. 'He's at work at the moment. He works in IT.' She stopped and let out a nervous giggle. 'Sorry. I'm babbling. It's not every day I have a famous actor in my house.'

I let out a snort. 'That's really sweet of you to say that, Gillian, but like I said before, I'm not famous.' And I never would be, if the likes of bloody Fox had their way and the lack of acting roles continued.

I refocused on Gillian and her daughter.

The hallway consisted of a polished, pale, wooden floor, with an ornate, heavy, cherrywood sideboard and a couple of vases of fresh flowers. Family photographs lined the walls.

'Cayla's up in her room,' said Gillian in a hush. 'Come on. This way.'

Gillian swept up the carpeted staircase, and I followed. I wasn't quite sure what Gillian wanted me to say to Cayla, but I'd already decided to just wing it and hope that I could reignite some of her acting spark.

Gillian had changed out of her businesslike blouse and skirt from the morning. She was now dressed in a loose, denim shirt and Capri pants.

We reached the top of the stairs, and Gillian lowered her voice again. She pointed at a closed, white, panelled door ahead of us. Cayla's name was painted in pink italics on a lilac, ceramic plaque.

'Just please try to convince her not to give up on her dream,' said Gillian in a hush of desperation.

'I'll do my best,' I assured her. 'Her performance this afternoon was breathtaking.'

Gillian's eyes misted over. 'I just wish she'd believe in herself again.' She tugged at the hem of her shirt before she knocked on her daughter's bedroom door. 'Sweetheart, can I come in?'

There was a monosyllabic grunt.

Gillian waggled her plucked brows at me and opened the door.

Cayla was perched on the edge of her bed. She was frowning down at a book in her hands.

'Cayla?'

When she snapped the book shut, I noticed it was *Twelfth Night*.

She set it down on the bed covers beside her and looked up through her long fringe. Spotting me, she did a double-take.

'Look who's come to see you,' said Gillian.

Cayla appraised me for a few seconds with wide eyes.

On her bedroom walls were glossy posters of Austin Butler and Millie Bobby Brown. Her framed movie ones ranged from *About Time* and *Seven Brides for Seven Brothers* to *Notting Hill* and *My Fair Lady*.

Sparkly scarves and chains of multi-coloured, glassy beads were suspended from the mirror of her bedside table over in the corner. Beside that was a bookcase, on which were propped copies of biographies from everyone from Marilyn Monroe to Dame Maggie Smith.

It was at that moment that Gillian took her cue. 'Tell you what, why don't I leave you two to have a chat, and I'll bring up some tea for you both?'

Without waiting for Cayla to reply, I dumped my bag down by my feet. 'I'd love a cup of tea. Thanks, Gillian. Just milk for me.'

Gillian looked fit to burst with delight. 'Wonderful.'

She clicked the door shut behind her, leaving me and Cayla.

'Sorry about that,' she whispered shyly, her cheeks crimson. 'I love my Mum, but she can be a bit cringe.'

'I think most parents are, but they don't mean to be.' I shrugged off my pink jacket and set it down on the bed.

'What are you doing here?'

'Is it ok if I sit down?' I asked, gesturing to the white chair at her dressing table and not answering her question.

'Sure.'

Cayla eyed me. "How did you find out where I lived?'

'Mrs Hazelwood told me.'

I could see her turning this over in her head. 'You were amazing in *Sinister*. It was such a cool series.'

'Thank you. I appreciate that. Pity some of the reviews weren't as positive.'

'You got bad reviews?'

'Fox. I don't know if you've heard of him?'

Cayla rolled her eyes. 'Isn't he the prick who has his own column in that newspaper? He doesn't praise anyone.'

I laughed. 'Yes, he's the one.'

Cayla shuffled closer on her bed. 'So, what's next for you? What role have you got lined up now? Oh wait. Maybe you can't tell me! Is it a secret?'

Now it was my turn to adjust my position on the

dressing table chair. 'Taking a bit of a break at the moment.' I paused. 'Your Mum said you've wanted to get into acting ever since you were younger.'

Cayla fiddled with the corner of her duvet. 'I did.' Her words picked up speed. 'To be honest, the more I think about it, the more I think I'm not good enough.'

'What makes you say that?'

She didn't answer.

'Who told you that?'

'No one. I just decided.'

My jaw gritted with temper. Bloody bullies! If only they could see what negative effect their spiteful actions had. But then again, would they even care?

I pointed to the copy of *Twelfth Night* lying beside her. 'I understand why you love it so much. You did Olivia's monologue justice today, and then some.'

Cayla flicked her fringe out of her eyes. 'Thanks.' She jammed her lips together. 'Some of the other kids think I'm weird.'

'Why?'

Her freckled complexion pinked even more. 'Because I like reading Shakespeare and acting. They say I think I'm better than them, but I don't.'

It sounded like history repeating itself. I shook my head. 'There's nothing wrong with not running with the crowd. It's good to be different.'

She didn't say anything.

I twisted round further in my chair. 'I had the same sort of thing at school. I got bullied too for a while because I wanted to be an actor. And some of the other kids teased me because I was raised by my grandparents.'

Cayla toyed with the ends of her hair. 'What happened to your mum and dad? Oh, sorry, maybe I shouldn't have asked.'

'No. Don't worry, it's ok.' I sat back on the dressing table chair as I told her the short and sorry story.

'Wow.' Cayla digested this. 'That's pretty shit.'

I buried a smile. 'It was at the time, I suppose. Look, Cayla, don't let anyone tell you that you can't do something. Go for what you want.'

At that moment there was a rap on the door, and Gillian entered clutching a tray laden with two cups of tea and a plate of shortbread fingers. 'Hope you're having a good talk.' She smiled before leaving again. I picked up on her hopeful smile as she eased the bedroom door closed behind her.

'You're seriously talented. I'm not just saying that. Don't turn your back on what you want to do and then regret it later.'

She twitched her nose and looked thoughtful.

'My Dad wanted to become an actor,' I remarked.

'Did he?' Her ears pricked up with curiosity.

'Oh yes. But he ended up not fulfilling his dream and became an estate agent.'

Cayla resumed picking at her duvet. 'Maybe he was like me. Not good enough.'

I sighed and reached for my cup of tea. I took a

considered sip and set it down again on the saucer. Cayla picked up her tea next and cradled it in her hands.

'Cayla, you can let the bullies define who you are and prevent you from doing something special with your life. Or you can decide to take a chance and go for it.'

She took a mouthful of tea.

I hesitated before I spoke again. 'Their behaviour says everything about them and nothing about you. They'll have been jealous because you have a talent and a chance to do something with it.' I retrieved my cup of tea beside me and took another mouthful. 'Mrs Hazelwood told me what a terrible time you've had.'

Cayla made me jump by clattering her teacup back down on its saucer. 'It's got nothing to do with any of that.' I wasn't fooled for a moment. She was struggling to look at me.

'And my mum had no right letting you in here.' Her cheeks were popping with red. 'Maybe she's just frustrated and wants to live out her dreams through me. She shouldn't have been talking about me, anyway.'

'Cayla...'

She shook her head, sending her fringe tumbling further into her spangly, green eyes. 'I know you're only trying to be nice and I appreciate it. But I've decided I don't want to act anymore, so you're just wasting your time.'

'Cayla, if you tell yourself that often enough, you might start to believe it. But I don't.'

Ignoring me, she jumped up from the bed in a flurry of

loose hair and cotton T-shirt. Her voice wobbled. 'I think you should go now. Thanks anyway.'

'But Cayla…'

Her eyes were shining with tears. 'Please.'

I slipped on my jacket, bundled up my bag and closed the bedroom door behind me, almost crashing into Gillian.

I encouraged her back down the stairs so we could talk without Cayla overhearing.

'How did you get on, Daisy?'

I pulled a pained expression. 'Not very well, I'm afraid. She said she's decided she doesn't want to act anymore.'

Her mother's optimistic expression collapsed. 'If I could get my bloody hands on that little witch Carina Whitelaw! It's a good job she's no longer a pupil at the school.'

I listened sympathetically. 'Cayla's got it into her head that she doesn't have what it takes, but from what I've seen, she definitely does.'

Gillian folded her arms. 'Thank you for trying to talk to her anyway, Daisy. I really do appreciate it.'

'You're welcome. She might change her mind if you leave the subject be. You know what teenagers can be like.' I offered a brief smile. 'And if she does want to talk to me again, you have my number.'

Gillian thanked me and stood at the front door.

I reached the end of their garden path. Something made me want to turn around and look up. Cayla's pair of lavender curtains twitched. Her forlorn, freckled face was peeking out.

When I looked up again, she'd gone.

Chapter Thirteen

On the drive back to The Ramblings, I kept thinking about Cayla.

She reminded me so much of myself at her age; full of spiralling hormones and the burning, all-encompassing desire to become an actor, intermingled with the creeping doubt that she might not be good enough and the aftermath of the bullying she too had been through.

I thumped the heel of my hand on the top of my steering wheel in frustration. I hadn't handled the talk with Cayla at all well. I'd ended up upsetting her and making her think her mum, Josie Hazelwood and I had been gossiping about her. The whole point of me chatting to Cayla had been to encourage her to rethink ditching her acting. Instead I'd made her dig her heels in even more.

I seemed to have a knack for stuffing things up these days. Just look at my own floundering career. Then there was the complication of Evan.

I shoved a stray lock of hair away from my face.

Not that Evan mattered in the long term, I reassured myself. It was just that I'd thought we'd come to some sort of understanding after the Fox incident.

I reached across and clicked on the car radio, which I'd tuned into the local news station, Forrest Bank Today.

As I drove past the shops with their lights twinkling in the late afternoon sunshine, the presenter mentioned the local farmers market taking place at the weekend. 'And in the meantime, bomb disposal experts are working to finish the sandpit construction in order to be able to safely detonate the two World War Two bombs, which were discovered on Sunday. It's hoped that this will be completed by the end of the week.'

I groaned at the radio. The end of the week? All I wanted was to get away from Forrest Bank and The Ramblings and get home to Strath Ross and Grandpa before I caused any more damage.

I needed the familiarity; I needed the rugged hillsides, the scattered farmland and the tranquillity.

I switched on Marlene's engine again and headed further down the lane, sweeping right into The Ramblings. I admired the way the sun splashed against its windows.

I parked, fetched my bag from the passenger seat and locked up.

I was heading towards the entrance when Evan appeared. It looked like he was heading towards his dad's car.

He spotted me and drew up. 'Hi.'

'Hi.'

His gaze melted over me. 'You had a good day? Thanks for helping Mum with dropping off those fabrics.'

'No problem.' Why did he have to be nice? It was worse when he was nice.

Since Leon, I'd been able to shut down that side of my life; ignore it; push it to one side and make my acting take precedence. It had taken time and a lot of soul searching, but I'd got there. At the beginning, I'd thought Leon and I had been destined to be together forever. I'd devoted so much time and energy to our relationship. Underneath it all, I'd known it was me who was putting in the lion's share of the effort and striving to please him rather than myself. I'd ignored the red flags: Leon's childish jealousy whenever my acting received a good review; his passive-aggressive comments whenever I was called back for a second audition and he wasn't.

I swore I'd never repeat that same mistake again, and that relationships and I weren't compatible.

But now … whenever I saw Evan, or he looked at me, I got all twisted up inside, and it was infuriating. I tried to think about something else or refocus, but I couldn't untangle myself.

'What else have you been up to?' he asked, his T-shirt sleeves rippling in the breeze.

'Trying to persuade a teenage girl to persist with her acting dreams.'

'Oh? How did that go?'

'Don't ask. Not great.'

Evan's mouth flipped into a smile. 'I'm sure you handled it better than you think you did.'

Oh, you're doing it again, yelled a frustrated voice in my head. *You're being so nice to me. Just stop right now. It isn't helping. It's making it worse.* I pulled an embarrassed face. 'I tried to make her see that she shouldn't give up on what she wants to do just because some spiteful, nasty school bully had tried to convince her she was useless.' I shook my head in exasperation. 'And she's anything but. She's terrific. She's got real potential.'

Evan held my gaze with a smile. My chest fluttered.

'Remember what we were like at that age, Daisy. Tell them to do something, and they'll do the opposite just for the hell of it.'

I got a waft of his delicious, woody aftershave. 'Off somewhere nice?'

'Just catching up with an old friend. Won't be long.'

I clocked Evan's polished, pointed brogues. He must be all dressed up for Sacha.

I took a couple of involuntary steps backwards, as though doing that would make my festering Evan attraction dissolve in an instant. I wished it would!

God, those dark, bitter eyes of his were lethal.

My stomach did a weird plummet to the floor as he stalked away and then drove off.

It was for the best, keeping Evan at arm's length. The last thing I should do was start stoking a fire that could very easily and very quickly get out of control. Evan must still have feelings for Sacha, so even if I had been tempted to get closer to him, it was a disaster waiting to happen.

I recalled the scent of his expensive aftershave and what he was wearing. He'd been secretive too about where he was going. He'd said he was off to visit an old friend. Yeah, right. An old friend with blonde, wavy tresses and a self-satisfied smile.

The sensation of his touch on my skin replayed itself.

I picked up speed as I headed into The Ramblings in an attempt to block it out.

'Hi,' I called out, as I shut the kitchen door behind me. Everything was pristine but empty. The copper pots and pans shone on their hooks, the marble breakfast bar gleamed and there was just the very faint hum from the huge Smeg fridge-freezer.

I tapped across the polished wooden floor and out into the cool, tiled, sun-spilt hallway.

'Anyone here?' I called out, my voice bouncing off the staircase and the opulent vases of dry reeds and flowers.

Hmmm.

Everybody else must've gone out.

I decided to go and dump my bag in my room and then take a stroll around the grounds. I'd give Grandpa a call too to see how he was.

At that moment, my phone buzzed in my bag. I fetched it out.

It was from Jade. She'd sent me a selfie. She was pouting at the camera. Her long, candy floss-coloured hair was styled in waves over one shoulder, and she looked dazzling in winged eye makeup and a glittery, slash-necked top.

Hoping to slay Jasper with my knowledge of sonnets and free verse, as well as my mermaid look! Hope all ok with the dashing lord!
Speak soon,
J xx

Jasper didn't stand a chance tonight. I almost felt sorry for him.

I fired off a reply:

You look stunning! I want all the details – well, not all of them, but you know what I mean.
Lots of love,
D xx

I didn't make any comment about Evan, but I did add in a purple heart and pressed send.

I plopped my phone back in my bag and started to make my way upstairs, my trainers slapping on the white marble, when I thought I heard faint voices travelling out of the dining room. The door wasn't quite closed.

I drew up and listened. It sounded like it might be Alison and Bennett. They couldn't have heard me arrive back.

I turned around on the staircase and tapped back down again and across the hallway to go and say hello. I reached the dining room door and was about to knock when I snatched my hand away again.

They were talking about The Ramblings and its financial situation.

'We need more income for this place,' said Alison, her voice carrying a desperate edge. 'Evan's monthly contributions are wonderful, but they're being swallowed up by maintenance bills.' I heard her sigh from the depths of her chest and recalled her similar comments to me when I'd accompanied her to the high school.

'Pity Dane wasn't as thoughtful as his older brother,' muttered Bennett.

I felt guilty standing there, but this conversation was firing up my curiosity – and my concern.

I glanced around to make sure there was no one else about.

'Och, you know how different our boys are, Bennett. Evan would give most folks the shirt off his back if they asked.'

My chest gave a flutter at this hot image.

'And as for Dane, well, I know he can be self-centred, but if he knew the extent of the issues we're having to deal with, he'd be concerned.' Alison tutted and continued speaking. 'And he is doing his bit with trying to keep on top of the gardens now that we've had to let Freddie go. I just don't feel comfortable taking money from Evan,' Alison carried on. 'It's too much, and he has to think about himself. The cost of living in the London area isn't cheap.'

'I know that,' agreed Benett on the other side of the door. 'He's a good lad.'

'Yes, he is, but he should be securing his own future.'

I turned over everything as I hovered there. It was such an altruistic thing for him to do for his family. Then again, if Dane knew the extent to which The Ramblings was struggling, which it sounded like he didn't, maybe he'd step up and try to help more, too. I was sure he would, even if he did tend to give the impression at times that he thought the world should revolve around him.

'Daisy? What are you doing?'

I leapt at the voice coming from behind me and spun round, guilt riven on my face.

It was Louise.

Chapter Fourteen

Embarrassment shook me.

Alison and Bennett were still talking, oblivious.

Louise jerked her head and encouraged me to follow her back across to the kitchen.

'I wasn't eavesdropping,' I protested as I scurried after her. My voice was a panicked hush. 'I thought there was no one home as I headed upstairs. Then I happened to hear Alison and Bennett.'

Louise drew up at the kitchen door and hitched one cynical brow at me.

'I didn't mean to overhear anything, but they were just talking about how much money The Ramblings costs to maintain.'

Louise listened before beckoning me inside the kitchen and easing the door closed behind us.

'I was making my way to my room, and then I heard voices coming from the study.' I dumped my bag by my feet. 'I know what it looks like, but it wasn't like that.' I rubbed at my face. 'But there was no way I was interrupting their conversation, especially when they were discussing financial matters.'

Louise nodded. 'I believe you. You're a good young woman. Anyone can see that. But aye, you're right. The Ramblings is beautiful, but it demands a lot of money to keep it going.' She gestured around at the huge, stylish, farmhouse-style kitchen. 'These stately homes are a money pit. This house needs a new heating system, the roof is starting to give cause for concern and then there's the stonemasonry issues.'

Oh dear. It sounded like Alison and Bennett really had their work cut out to keep The Ramblings in full working order. I flicked Louise a loaded look. 'Alison told me earlier about Evan donating a monthly amount from his earnings to put towards maintenance costs.'

Louise's expression dissolved into an affectionate smile. 'That's right. He's such a caring young man. Every month without fail, he sends a contribution to his parents to put towards this place.'

The sunshine bounced off the copper pots and pans suspended behind Louise.

Her lined eyes carried a sudden, faraway look to them. 'Do you know, I've worked here as the housekeeper and cook for over thirty-five years now? I've known Evan since he was a toddler and remember when Dane was born. He was always yelling his head off, and it's continued.' She chuckled. 'They'd come over here with Alison and Bennett to visit Bennett's parents, God bless them. They were both gorgeous boys, even then, but Dane was always a handful.'

'I get the impression he still is,' I joked.

Louise smiled and rolled her eyes. 'You're not wrong there. The number of times I've heard girls giggling in his room whenever he stays here.'

I found myself wondering about Evan. As though anticipating what I wanted to ask, Louise answered my silent question. 'His older brother isn't like that. Evan's always been far more serious.' She folded her arms as she spoke. 'Don't get me wrong. Evan attracts the ladies, too. Always has done. But whereas Dane's always playing the charmer, Evan is more career-focused.' She frowned. 'The only time I've ever seen him crushed by a girl was with that Sacha one.'

'What about Sacha? What happened?'

But Louise moved the subject back to The Ramblings and ignored my question. 'This house could tell a few tales.'

'Oh? What about?' I asked, intrigued.

Louise flapped her hands about, panicked. 'Och, you know, characters from the past.'

'Like who?'

'There were stories about a young woman called Florence Menzies who used to work here in the early 1900s.' Louise's gaze darted around. 'Local girl. Keen to be an actress.'

My eyes widened with interest. 'Really? Wow. What happened?'

'She was very talented, by all accounts. Bright too. A

local piano teacher took her under her wing and taught young Florence to read and write.' Louise pursed her lips. 'But she got blamed for stealing something from this house, and she didn't do it.' She toyed with a tea towel. 'My dad was into his history and researched some local families and events. Very prolific journal writer. I've still got them all.'

My curiosity was pricked. 'Do you have a journal he wrote about this girl Florence?'

'I do indeed. Would you like to take a look at it?'

'Oh, that would be great,' I enthused.

Our conversation was cut short when Alison and Bennett entered the kitchen.

Louise snatched up the navy blue Denby teapot by the sink. 'Shall I make us all a brew?'

I exchanged small talk with Evan's parents as Louise busied herself with making the tea.

Hmmm.

I wondered what had happened between Sacha and Evan for Louise to make a comment like that. I was also curious about the reference she'd made to The Ramblings' mysterious history and this young woman Florence.

There seemed to be at least a couple of secrets that this grand old house was keeping to herself.

Once I'd spent some time with Alison, Bennett and Louise and enjoyed a cup of tea and one of the delicious almond macaroons Louise had baked earlier that day, I vanished up to my bedroom.

Alison and Bennett made no reference to Louise or me about the financial stresses and strains they were experiencing. Instead, they talked about the latest charity they were doing some volunteering for, the Forrest Bank Disabled Care Centre.

It just seemed so unfair to me, I'd concluded as I had traipsed back up the sweeping, spiral staircase. They were good people. Kind. It was clear they wanted to give something back to their local community, even though they had their own worries to contend with.

This house had been part of Bennett's life for so long.

Dropping my bag onto the dressing table chair, I flopped backwards onto the four-poster bed. I lay there for a few moments, thinking about Evan and Sacha, before I dismissed them from my mind, but they kept insisting on creeping back in.

In the end, I clambered off the bed and rummaged around in my bag for my mobile.

I nestled myself back against the pillows and typed *The Ramblings Forrest Bank* into the search engine. But if I'd hoped for something exciting or juicy to jump out at me, I was disappointed. All that appeared was a few photographs of the house and gardens and confirmation of its location.

I thought again about what Louise had said about the Lords' financial issues before she'd looked uncomfortable, as though she'd regretted saying anything.

Undeterred, I scrolled through the next few pages, but there were still only photographs of The Ramblings and its rolling lawns.

In one photo, everything was draped in snow. Tangerine lamps glowed through the windows, and gold fairy lights were strung around the branches of a couple of the trees. It would've made the perfect Christmas card.

At that moment, I was pulled out of my thoughts by a knock on my bedroom door. 'Yes? Who is it?'

'It's me. Evan.'

Evan?

I almost toppled off the bed as I fumbled my way towards the dressing table mirror.

I had a stain of rose-pink lipstick on, but most of it was gone, thanks to the recent cup of tea and Louise's macaroon. My hair was escaping out of its high ponytail too. Reaching for my makeup bag, I dashed on a fresh slick of lip colour.

I knew what I was doing and why, which in turn made me annoyed with myself, so I stopped titivating my hair.

I strode over to my bedroom door, took a breath and opened it.

Evan filled the doorway.

He cocked a brow at me. He must've noticed me staring at him. Dang!

I rearranged my features into what I hoped were indifferent ones. 'Can I help you?'

'I wondered if you'd seen Dane around?'

'No. Not since I got back.'

His hot, dark gaze stayed on my face. 'Oh. Ok.'

I hoped I didn't look mesmerised by his eyes. 'Why did you say it like that?'

'Like what?'

'Like I should have known where Dane was.'

Evan pushed both his hands into the pockets of his casual, cream trousers. 'Well, seeing as you two were being so chummy at the gig the other night, I assumed…'

'You shouldn't assume,' I bit back. 'You just make an ass out of you and me.' I remembered that from school, and although it wasn't the greatest retort, it was the best I could come up with at that moment.

'Very droll. Just make that up, did you?' Evan's expression was intense. 'I spotted my brother and you exchanging megawatt grins at the gig.'

Hold on. I could have been wrong, but if I didn't know any better, I might have thought Evan was jealous!

'Well, I'm sorry to burst your bubble, but no, there wasn't and isn't anything going on between your brother and me, and like I said, I haven't seen him all day.'

'Ok.' He lingered, shoving that stray lock of black hair away from his angular face. He made no move to leave. 'Thanks again for helping Mum. I know she appreciated it.'

His kind words made me pull myself up. 'Oh. Right. You're welcome. She's a lovely lady.'

We both remained rooted to the spot. What was it with him? One minute he was a sarcastic sod, and the next he was complimenting me. Not only did Evan have the ability to mangle my head, he was also able to churn up my insides as well.

It frustrated me to no end.

'Did you have a good time then?' I cursed myself for asking. I didn't want to mention Sacha.

'Yes, it was good.' No further information was forthcoming.

His attention drifted lazily from my hair and down to my mouth. 'Right. I'll be off then. More work to do.' He strode across the hallway towards his bedroom. What was happening here? Was anything happening?

I clattered my bedroom door shut. It would be best for everyone if it didn't, but that didn't stop me from imagining.

Chapter Fifteen

It was Wednesday morning, and as I entered the dining room for breakfast the sound of Louise's digital radio came from the kitchen. It was a local news bulletin:

'The two unexploded bombs located in the Loch Crawe area are to be detonated at lunchtime today. Bomb disposal experts attending the scene have confirmed that the devices are now safely contained inside the man-made sandpit construction. It has been confirmed that the bombs will be detonated at one o'clock this afternoon.'

Oh. Wow! That was great news. It surely meant I could go home later on today. I could return to Strath Ross. I'd see my grandpa.

There was no sign of Evan, Dane, Alison or Bennett at breakfast, so I drank my tea, crunched on my oat cereal and slapped apricot jam on my toast on my own.

Louise sidled up to the table out of nowhere. 'God, Louise! You made me jump!'

'Sorry.' She was carrying a small white paper bag. She handed it to me. 'Some reading for you,' she remarked cryptically before vanishing again.

I set down my slice of golden toast and wiped my buttery fingers on a napkin.

Inside the bag was a worn, brown leather notebook. When I opened it, I was confronted by reams of neat, looping black handwriting and the name *Montgomery Johnson* on the inside left page. I turned over a few more pages and saw Florence Menzies's name mentioned over and over. This must be the research notes Louise's Dad made about Florence.

I darted back up to my room to spirit it to safety before returning to finish my breakfast. I couldn't wait to dive in.

Outside the dining room window there had been spring rainfall, and now the sun was making the remaining raindrops shimmer on the tree branches and the top of the grass like dangling diamond earrings.

It was as I was about to clatter back up the staircase after breakfast so I could begin packing that I heard what sounded like frustrated sighs coming from inside the study. The door was ajar. I then heard a few annoyed murmurs. It sounded like Alison. I was certain of it.

I whirled round and down the few steps towards the partially closed study door.

This time, I resolved to knock like a normal person. I raised my hand and gave the door a light tap.

'Come in.'

I stepped inside.

I hadn't had the opportunity before to take a proper look around. Alison and Bennett's office consisted of a semi-circular glass desk with a caramel-coloured, leather swivel chair and views of the gardens.

Potted plants sat on the surrounding shelves in between family photographs of Evan and Dane; everything from the two of them as podgy, cute, gurning babies to gangly school kids and shaggy-haired students, and then more modern photos of them.

There was one of Evan in a rugby kit, his hair tousled as he grinned down the camera, and another of Dane on stage, his head flung back as he belted a song into the mic. Both pictures took pride of place on a shelf behind Alison.

Her eyes were glazed with tears as I looked at her. She was hunched over behind the desk.

'Oh, Alison. Are you alright?' Daft question. I could see she wasn't. She looked like she was carrying the world's problems.

She brushed her face with the back of her hand. 'Yes, yes, I'm fine.'

I hesitated before clicking the door closed behind me and tilting my head to one side. 'Really?'

Her mouth trembled. 'No.' She slumped back in her leather chair. She picked up a pen and tapped it on some papers littered on the desk in front of her. 'Invoices,' she croaked. 'Every year that passes we all get older, and so does The Ramblings. That means the maintenance and repairs become more serious and more frequent.'

I hauled up a chair that was stationed in the corner and sank down into it.

Alison continued to fiddle with her rose-gold pen. The sun shimmered down one side of her troubled expression. 'This house is part of Bennett. Who he is. It belonged to his parents, grandparents and great grandparents.'

I had grown fond of Alison in this short space of time. I wished my mother had been like her: caring and kind instead of the self-absorbed, unfeeling woman I'd had instead.

Alison blew out a cloud of frustrated air. 'We're like ducks at the moment: serene on top but paddling like hell beneath the water.'

'I'm sorry,' I said with genuine feeling. 'Isn't there some way that you could generate some extra income?'

'We need additional, regular funds,' answered Alison with the backdrop of the tree tops looming behind her out of the study window. 'I feel so guilty that Evan keeps contributing to this place. He should be thinking about his own future, not trying to save what is essentially in the past.' She gave a tiny nod. 'I know if I said that to him he'd dismiss it, but still, it's true.' She folded her arms on top of her desk. 'His father and I aren't prepared to keep accepting money from him like this. We need to think of something else, because in the scheme of things, it doesn't feel right taking it from him, and it isn't making a huge difference in the long run.' She let out a dry laugh. 'I know Dane would've offered to help too if he knew the extent of our problems, but he's always on the road with Disciple and doesn't make a massive amount of money with his music anyway.' She allowed herself a small smile. 'He's adamant that will change though. Oh, listen to me wittering on. I'm so sorry, Daisy.'

'No. There's no need to apologise.'

Alison tilted her chin onto one hand. 'I just heard on the news that those two bombs are being deactivated shortly.'

'That's right.'

'So, I take it that means you'll be heading home to Strath Ross soon?'

I nodded. 'Yes. Today.'

Alison leant forward. 'Please don't feel you have to dash off, Daisy. You're welcome to stay as long as you like.' She blushed a pretty pink. 'It's lovely having another woman around. No disrespect to Louise, but you're young and vibrant. You bring sunshine into this old house.'

I let out an embarrassed laugh. 'That's very kind of you to say, but I haven't felt very vibrant recently.' I smiled. 'And believe me, I appreciate your offer of allowing me to stay on, but I think I've availed myself of your hospitality for long enough. And I really do want to see my grandfather.'

'Oh, of course you do.'

I stood up and made my way back towards the closed study door. 'Can I bring you anything, Alison? A cup of tea or something stronger? A nip of whiskey perhaps?'

'How about a solution to our mounting money issues?'

'I wish I could.'

I slipped out of the study, feeling wretched on Alison's behalf, and looked up to see Evan striding across the hall. It looked like he'd had a later breakfast, as he was coming from the direction of the dining room.

He spotted me and gave me one of his dark, unfathomable looks.

My stomach performed an impersonation of a washing machine on full cycle.

He's a prat, remember? I told myself. A moody, stubborn one.

I gathered myself and brushed past him on my way towards the stairs. 'Morning,' I clipped.

'Morning. Off out anywhere?'

I set one hand down on the top of the ornate bannister. 'I'm just off to start packing.'

He blinked at me. 'Packing? Why?'

'Haven't you heard or seen the news this morning? Those two bombs are being safely detonated at lunchtime today, and then the road will be clear up to Strath Ross.'

A strange expression clouded his features. 'Oh. Right. I see. No, I didn't know.'

I took in his blue-black hair and the way his brows gathered like storm clouds.

'Anyway, if you'll excuse me, I've got things to do.'

I hurried up the stairs to my room, wishing that I wasn't feeling conflicted like this.

I had to get a grip. Yes, it was ok to fall for a pair of

irresistible dark brown eyes, but it was everything else that went along with it that I had to watch out for.

I was relieved to closet myself behind my bedroom door.

As I began to pack, fetching my toothbrush, toothpaste and body lotion from the en-suite bathroom, I thought again about Alison's pale, distracted expression. The Lords had made me feel so much at home here. I just wished I could do something to help them.

I returned to the bathroom and gathered up my packet of flossers, deodorant and moisturisers next. I slipped everything into my big, quilted toiletry bag, before placing it inside the front cover of my case and zipping it back up.

What a hectic and surprising few days these had been. If someone had said to me last week that I'd be sleeping in a grand, four-poster bed in a Highland mansion owned by a lovely couple and having my emotions put through the wringer by their gorgeous but moody eldest son … and then, of course, there was Cayla. I had hoped I'd be able to reignite her passion for acting with my pep talk, but instead I'd made her dig her trainers in.

Cayla.

Just like this poor Florence, whom Louise had mentioned. Also a keen actress, who had worked here at The Ramblings before being sacked for something she didn't do.

My hand stilled as I unzipped the main section of my case to start packing up my clothes. Montgomery Johnson's journal sat on my bed, enticing me over.

I stopped packing, flopped onto the bed and picked it up.

I eased it open with the utmost care and began to read. His words about Florence's vulnerability and her struggle to throw off the shackles of being a servant gnawed at me: the stigma of being blamed for stealing a vase from this very house and how that had overshadowed the rest of her brief life.

Her desire to be an actress.

Her tragic and untimely death at eighteen from pneumonia after having had to clean people's steps in the freezing, damp cold when she lost her position at The Ramblings.

I forgot I was supposed to be packing and got lost in the contents of the journal and the tragic recollections of Florence and her past. I was catapulted back in time to the draughty Ramblings, imagining Florence's raw hands as she cleaned and her love of the theatre with its mixture of jolly performers and the smartly dressed, moustached men of the orchestra.

I turned page after page, devouring the account Louise's father had put together in so much detail.

My mind drifted from Florence to Cayla again. If the two of them had met, I bet they'd have hit it off; two young women, keen to reach their theatrical potential, but finding themselves held back by injustice in Florence's case and jealous school bullies in Cayla's. I reckoned Florence would have had more luck talking Cayla round than I had.

I stopped reading the journal and fiddled with the

zipper of my case beside me on top of the bed. Even though I had no idea what she'd looked like, my imagination conjured up pictures of Florence with long, conker-coloured hair and a dash of freckles over her pert nose. She was dressed in an ankle length, grey, cotton dress overlaid with a white apron. Her hair was secured underneath it at the nape of her neck in a tight bun.

Beside her appeared Cayla looking pretty, young and trendy with her loose, strawberry blonde hair and cropped jeans, decked out in a sparkly T-shirt and platform trainers. Both young women from very different times, but both chasing the same dream.

I gazed down at my case and then back at the open journal in my lap, the pages fluttering in the spring breeze.

Wait a minute.

I had a thought; very much a fledgling of an idea, but what triggered it had been Florence. It would capture a time in The Ramblings past.

The more I turned it over in my head, the more it took flight. This could work and bring in some extra income for The Ramblings.

It could be a regular event.

With growing excitement bubbling inside me, I picked up the journal and made for my bedroom door.

I dashed back downstairs.

I needed to speak to Louise, Alison and Bennett right away.

Chapter Sixteen

Evan had dropped by the study and was talking to his mother and father. Louise had also appeared by the time I drew up in the open doorway.

After a moment, the four of them sensed me loitering there, and their conversation screeched to a halt.

I was determined to ignore Evan's muscles straining under his lemon T-shirt.

I drilled my attention on Alison, who was seated behind the desk, and Bennett, who was standing on her right. I pushed out a courteous but rather anxious smile.

Oh God. Was this idea crazy? Maybe it was. But surely it was worth a shot? I clutched the journal to my chest.

Louise spotted it, and her brows shot up.

'I'm sorry to interrupt.'

'No, it's fine, Daisy,' replied Alison.

I was aware of Evan's gaze on me.

'What can we do for you?' asked Bennett.

I took a couple of faltering steps into the study. 'I've been thinking about ways that you might be able to drum up some more financial support for The Ramblings.'

Evan's brows arched, but I carried on. 'Look, please tell me if this is none of my business, but this is such a gorgeous old house, and you might be able to draw on its history to your advantage.'

Bennett looked intrigued. 'In what way?'

'Well, have you heard the name Florence Menzies?'

Bennett's jaw grew tight. He looked like someone had just trodden over his grave. 'Someone's been busy with their research.'

'Who's Florence Menzies?' asked Evan, confused.

Alison and Bennett exchanged glances. 'This isn't something my family's proud of,' stated Bennett after a few moments. 'Even after all these years. What happened to poor Florence. We don't talk about it. Cowardly I know, but the shame of what happened never left us.'

Evan's expression darkened. 'I've no idea what you're talking about, Dad.'

Louise interjected. 'She was a young woman who worked here in the early 1900s and was blamed for stealing a vase. Poor girl was sacked, but she was innocent. She died just a few years later, aged just eighteen.'

Alison pushed some ash-coloured hair back behind one ear and swivelled her attention back on me. 'What happened to that poor young woman was tragic and avoidable, but the people round here don't seem to remember what happened, because the Menzies family left Forrest Bank not long after Florence passed away.'

'Well, can you blame them?' ground out Bennett. 'They'd lost one of their own at a tragically young age, and she'd been blamed by my great-grandparents for stealing something when she hadn't.' He puffed out some air. 'The law wouldn't have been on her side, no matter what. All that mattered in those times was how much money you had and who you were related to.'

Alison chewed her lip. 'She was a hard-working, innocent, young soul but she wasn't allowed her own voice.'

Bennett swung round to Louise. 'And you knew about Florence's story, but you never said anything?'

Louise coloured. 'I didn't think it was my place to. My father was a keen amateur historian and found out about it years ago.'

I eyed everyone. 'And that's what I was hoping to talk to you about.' I raised the journal. 'This is part of Louise's dad's research.'

A puzzled look settled on Alison's face. 'Oh?' She gestured to me. 'Please. Sit down.'

Evan and his father adopted similar poses either side of Alison and Louise as I settled myself in the chair. I kept the journal on my lap.

I flicked Evan a brief glance. Didn't he have some pressing article he had to write? Or a dodgy businessman to expose? It was rather off-putting, him looming there.

I took a little breath and returned my gaze to his parents.

'It sounds tragic what happened to Florence and the circumstances surrounding her.' I hesitated. I had to choose my words carefully, as this was a delicate subject for the family. 'And you said just now, Alison, about Florence not having her own voice.'

I straightened my back. 'So, I wondered whether that could be put right now? And it could mean financial help for The Ramblings.'

'In what way?' questioned Evan. His brows were even more intimidating than before.

I sat forward, pinning my attention back on his parents as I ran one hand over the top of the journal. 'I thought that perhaps you could have a tour of The Ramblings – stage it regularly, say, three times a week. You'd welcome in the general public and tell the story of Florence.'

The three of them exchanged glances. Louise's mouth popped open.

Bennett looked awkward. 'Forgive me, Daisy, but what happened to Florence Menzies became a stain on our family reputation. Like we just said, it's not something we tend to brag about.'

'Exactly,' I parried back, returning my attention to a thoughtful Alison. 'This way, you're acknowledging what happened all those years ago, and you're also giving a voice to Florence.'

'What do you mean?' asked Evan, studying me.

'She wanted to become an actress,' broke in Louise. 'I've read my father's notes. But because she didn't have the right connections, and because of being blamed for that theft, her life took a different and tragic path.' She hesitated. 'Turns out, years later, that the damned vase was accidentally broken by one of the gardeners, Ernest Pugh, but he wouldn't confess to it at the time in case he lost his job. So he concealed the broken pieces, and poor Florence got the blame for stealing it.' She glanced over at Bennett. 'Your late great-grandmother noticed Florence with a little extra money, which she'd earned from shining shoes in the market, but she put two and two together and came up with five.'

'That's terrible,' I said. 'Did this Ernest Pugh ever admit to it?'

'Aye. According to Dad's notes, he did years later in a drunken stupor in the pub, but by then poor Florence had passed away.' Her expression grew more determined. 'Maybe some people round here do know about her story and what happened to her. Others won't.'

I turned to Alison and Bennett again. Every so often, their attention drifted to the journal in my lap.

'If you were to hold a regular tour of The Ramblings and have someone portray Florence, you're telling her story and bringing everything out into the open.'

The Lords didn't look convinced.

Undeterred, Louise picked up the mantle. 'Florence lived and worked here for a few years before things took an unfortunate turn. The Ramblings was a big part of her life.'

'That's right.' I paused. 'In a way, this guided tour would be honouring her memory.'

'And profiting from it,' murmured Bennett, looking uncomfortable.

'Like I said, you could also make a donation from the tour profits, towards a charity of your choosing.' Another idea pinged in my head. 'Or you could establish a new charity in Florence's name.'

Evan let out a gruff snort, but there was no denying the sudden sparkle in his Bourneville eyes. His voice carried a hint of admiration. 'You've given this a lot of thought, Daisy. But who would pull her story together? I'm a journalist, not an author.'

I eyed him. 'I wouldn't have thought it would be so hard to do. If Louise can supply any more of her dad's notes, we can pull together a script. I'm not proclaiming to be Hollywood standard, but I did do a course in script writing.' I gave him a look. 'And you're a journalist. Together, we can pull a script together. Then we can start recruiting local actors to play the roles.'

Bravery nipped at me. 'Don't worry, Evan. I'll issue the orders, and you just have to do as you're told.'

Alison, Bennett and Louise swapped knowing smiles.

Evan angled one brow suggestively at me.

I concentrated again, reminding myself why I was having this conversation.

'We just have to use a little bit of creative licence if need be.' My mouth twitched. 'Like I said, you're a journalist. Surely you're used to doing that.'

Evan pulled a sarcastic face. 'Very funny.'

I knew I was trying to goad him, but I couldn't stop

myself. 'Or are you trying to find an excuse not to be involved in making this happen, Evan? Think you aren't up to it?'

Evan stared me down. 'If that's what you think, then you don't know me very well.'

The steely, hard look in his eyes made me whip my head away.

'Come on you two,' cajoled Alison. She steepled her hands together again on top of the desk. 'So, how would this tour work then, Daisy?'

I flicked Evan a brief look of triumph. 'I know someone – a teenage girl whom I met the other day when I accompanied you to the high school. She's an amazing little actor. I saw her perform some Shakespeare.'

Bennett listened. 'Go on.'

'If I could persuade Cayla to take on the role of Florence, we can try out the tour and see how it's received.'

I steadied the excitement rising again in my voice. 'And if it did prove popular amongst locals and tourists, you could recruit another couple of actors to play Florence, so there would be a rota.'

Evan flexed a brow.

'And we could advertise it locally, regionally, nationally, even internationally. Other countries love these stately homes and all the history swirling around them.'

I sunk back in the chair. This was agony. I didn't want to upset anyone – well, maybe irritate Evan a little – but I was struggling to read the room. Had I overstepped the mark? I just wanted to help.

Nobody said anything. They just blinked across at me before swapping more unreadable expressions.

I found myself fidgeting. I patted the journal. 'Like I said, it was only an idea.'

I proffered an awkward smile and jumped up and out of the chair, as though my backside had been singed with hot coals. 'Thank you for listening to me witter on. I'll go and finish off my packing now.'

I headed for the study door and then turned around. I pulled my phone from my pocket and dashed off a text to Alison containing my mobile number and email address. Her phone pinged on her desk. 'I've just sent you my contact details so you can let me know what you think.'

Bennett smiled. 'Thanks, Daisy. It does sound like an interesting suggestion. We'll give it serious consideration.' He eyed Alison, Louise and Evan. 'And thank you for trying to help. It's appreciated.'

'You're more than welcome. It's the least I can do after you've made me feel so much at home here.'

I turned to Evan. 'In the meantime, I'll leave the journal about Florence with you. You need to read it.' I offered it to him, and he came and took it from me, his charged gaze flicking between me and the journal.

'Daisy.'

'Yes?'

'Thank you. I mean it.' His kissable mouth made me tremble. 'Thank you for trying to help my family.'

A lump of emotion caught in my throat. I managed a nod and a flicker of a smile. 'Don't mention it.'

I spent the next half hour bustling around my room, making sure I hadn't left anything behind and folding up my clothes. I would be sorry to leave The Ramblings behind, but the thought of seeing my grandpa again made my mouth break into a wide grin.

I was just angling my case from the bed when a voice at the doorway made me start. 'Need a hand?'

It was Dane, blond locks streaming loose down his back, his wrists adorned in his trademark leather straps.

Before I could answer, he came in and swiftly lifted the case down and onto the floor.

'Thanks.'

'No worries.' He gave me a wink. 'Always at the ready to help a gorgeous girl.'

'Do you ever switch off?' I teased, yanking up the handle on my case.

'Not when someone like you is around.'

I shook my head, laughing, and checked the room to make sure I hadn't left anything behind. Maybe my heart with Evan, I thought before dismissing it.

Dane flicked his hair back. 'I hear you've been making suggestions to turn The Ramblings into a theme park.'

I grasped the handle of my wheelie case. 'Hardly. Just trying to help out your parents.' My voice faltered. 'And your brother.' I tugged the case along the bedroom floor and made for the door.

'This place wouldn't be in such a state if Ma and Pa weren't such dogged do-gooders.'

Dane's harsh words made me draw up, my right hand hovering above the door handle.

'Charity starts at home and all that. They seem to forget that one day this place will go to me and my straight-laced big brother.' He cast his powder blue eyes around. 'If it carries on like this, there'll be nothing left to leave us.'

Dane meandered over to the bedroom window and gave the silky, wine-coloured curtains a dismissive flick. 'Angel Alison and Saint Bennett.'

My temper burned. He didn't know how fortunate he was to have two such wonderful parents.

'Don't talk about your mum and dad like that,' I ground out. I found myself abandoning my case by the door and stalking over to him. 'You take them for granted.'

Dane's eyes popped in his blond-stubbled face.

'You don't appreciate what terrific, supportive parents they are.'

Dane began to smirk, and that ignited my indignation even further. 'You should've been landed with the so-called mother and father I had.' I swallowed and eyed him. 'A mum who dumped me with my grandparents when I was three months old and never bothered with me, and a dad who, on finding out his girlfriend was up the duff, took off down to London and didn't want to know.'

Dane's smirk faltered, but I wasn't done.

'You just swan in and out of this place like it's some five-star hotel, only here for your convenience.' I shook my head. 'Do you have any idea what stress your Mum and Dad are going through right now? They're fighting to keep The Ramblings going.'

Dane tossed his hair back. 'I don't think things are that bad.'

The noise I made was a cross between a laugh and groan. 'You think?! The heating system, the stonemasonry; it all has to be attended to.'

I thrust my hands into the pockets of my jeans. 'Why do you think Evan has been contributing financially towards this place? He's been trying to help your parents out.'

Dane looked at me as though I'd just sprouted horns. 'Sorry?'

I eyed him. 'Evan giving your parents money every month. Didn't you know?'

Dane shook his mane so that it waggled like a blond flag down his back. His voice was smaller. 'No. No, I didn't.'

'Well, he has,' I rounded. 'Maybe your mum and dad didn't want to tell you because they didn't want to burden you with it.'

Dane rubbed at his blond stubbly chin. 'And what about Evan? Why didn't he say anything?'

'Maybe for the same reason. Perhaps he didn't want you to feel you had to do it too.' I marched over to where my case was standing to attention by the bedroom door. I grabbed the handle. 'Not everyone does something because they want something in return, Dane. Sometimes people do something for each other, just because they want to.'

He snorted, but I ignored him. 'Maybe you've been in

the music industry a little too long.' I yanked open the door and stepped out into the cool hallway with its scattered, heavy, woven rugs and portraits. 'It might be an idea if you took your head out of your arse for five minutes and gave a little more consideration to your family.' He followed me along the hall that smelled of beeswax, his cowboy boots tapping on the gleaming floor. His voice took on resentment. 'Now you listen here, Daisy…'

I swung round. 'No. You listen.' Frustration and a burning desire to stand up for Alison and Bennett took flight. 'You choose to let your family struggle on, yet you have no idea how many people would give their right arm to have a mother and father who think of others. They try to give something back, even though they have issues of their own to contend with.'

Dane's pale eyes locked with mine. He shifted on the spot.

'You're very lucky. You've no idea how lucky.' I swallowed at the thought of my own feckless, useless parents. Then pictures of my beloved grandparents replaced them in my head.

'You can be so charming and likeable. You saved me from choking, for pity's sake!' I studied him, standing there in front of me like a Nordic rock star. 'I can see why women find you attractive. But then you go and let yourself down by saying things like that about your mum and dad. Why don't you just grow up and realise that the world doesn't revolve around you? Sometimes you have to step up, Dane.'

'I'm sorry,' stuttered Dane, picking up speed behind me. 'Daisy. Wait.'

But I was already clattering down the staircase with my luggage bumping up and down in my hand.

I stashed my case in Marlene's boot and returned to where Evan, Alison, Bennett and Louise were standing in a row at the entrance to wave me off.

'Thank you for everything,' I managed as Alison bundled me into her arms. She smelled of Coco Chanel and strawberries.

Bennett gave me a fatherly hug next, followed by Louise, who presented me with Scottish salmon and cream cheese bagels wrapped up in silver foil, a flask of tea, a banana and a hefty slice of her homemade coconut and cherry sponge cake. 'That's to keep you going on the journey.'

I accepted them gratefully and laughed. 'But it's only a half hour drive.'

Louise shrugged. 'You never know if you'll get held up in traffic.'

'The worst she'll come across is being stuck behind a bloody tractor,' commented Evan.

Louise gave him a withering look.

When I reached Evan, I felt like I was a rag doll standing there, with him looking down at me. 'Thank you for giving me a lift that day.'

'Er. Yes. Of course. You're welcome.' My voice was thick. This could very well be the last time I saw him.

I tried to appear nonchalant. 'And once again, thank you for stopping me from getting sacked.'

Evan nodded his dark head. 'Don't mention it.' He stuffed his hands in his jean's pockets. 'I'll start reading the journal now.'

'Good. You'll find it's a sad but compelling read.'

We both stood there, eyes locked. It was as if the rest of the world had melted away.

I spun on my heel, my face stinging with pink, and jumped into Marlene's open driver side door. I clanged it shut and whirled the car around. It seemed like there were so many unexpressed emotions just now between us. It was as if both of us wanted to say something but didn't have the bravery to do it.

I was crunching over the gravel, heading towards the main road, when I caught sight in my rear-view mirror of Dane, who had come bounding out of The Ramblings and was performing some kind of frantic, weird semaphore. I pulled up.

What did he want?

I switched off the car engine and clambered out.

'What's he doing?' I heard Evan ask Alison. 'He's usually still in bed at this time.'

But Dane was striding towards me in his faded jeans and olive-green Iron Maiden T-shirt. 'Daisy.'

'Have I forgotten something?'

He shook his head. For the first time, he looked self-conscious; nervous even. The rocker swagger was gone. He studied his cowboy boots for a long time. 'I wanted to apologise for just now. I was an utter twat.'

I eyed him. 'Yes. You were.'

'I was out of order.'

'Yep. That too.'

His solemn face broke into a tiny echo of a smile, and I couldn't help but smile along with him.

I could see Evan watching us through narrowed eyes.

Dane shrugged and glanced up at the pearly clouds for a few moments, before looking back at me. 'Maybe I needed someone to tell me what was what. I've been walking around with my inflated ego for too long.'

I was about to say something, but the words evaporated as Dane reached out and took my right hand in his. What was he doing? With his gaze fixed on me, he lifted my hand and let his lips graze the top of it. 'Thank you. I mean it. That was what I needed. Some home truths. I just didn't realise it.'

Evan's face was blazing with something just a few feet behind us.

Talk about shocked. I was gobsmacked.

It took me a few moments to recover myself. Well, well. Maybe I had got through to Dane after all. I lowered my hand. 'You're welcome. And I'm sorry I was so rude.'

'Like I said, it's what I needed,' Dane assured me. 'Straight talking. I'm used to folks agreeing with me; sycophants going along with my suggestions all the time.' He continued to look down into my eyes, searching them.

Was he ok? A strange look travelled over his face, which I'd never seen before. I wasn't sure if Dane was going to say anything else. He continued to linger there. He pushed some hair back behind one ear, making the silver rings on his hand glint in the sunshine.

To try and lighten the moment, I teased him. 'Ok. This is weird. What have you done with the real Dane Lord?'

Dane's mouth drifted into a soft expression. 'You're something else, Daisy Madden, do you know that?'

I laughed and flapped one hand in the air. 'Yeah, yeah.'

Evan's unimpressed jaw clenched.

I returned to Marlene, turned the ignition and wound down my driver side window. 'Thank you again,' I called out over the throb of the engine. 'Take care, and do let me know what you think about my tour suggestion. I won't be offended if it's a no!'

Alison nodded and tucked her arm around Bennett's waist beside her. Meanwhile, Evan was firing black looks across at his younger brother, but Dane didn't notice; he was too busy gazing at me with a preoccupied expression as he watched me leave.

'We'll get back to you,' shouted Bennett. 'Drive safe now.'

I couldn't help it. As I edged towards the main road, my attention was drawn to my rear-view mirror again. My light grey eyes focused on Evan, who was splitting his attention between my car driving off and Dane.

When the next car slid past up the country lane, I began to ease out into the road and waved back.

222

More thoughts of Evan filled my head.

I put my foot down and headed right, down the rest of the lane towards the road signs that would take me past Loch Crawe and the bomb disruption of just days ago.

This could very well be the last time I set eyes on Evan Lord and The Ramblings, and if it was, I'd just have to accept it. It was fine. It was good. No problem.

My fingers dug into my steering wheel. Who was I kidding? It wasn't fine at all. I watched the lines and undulations of the hillsides flowing past outside my window.

I cajoled myself to think happier thoughts.

Strath Ross and Grandpa, here I come!

Chapter Seventeen

I was so frustrated with myself.

I should have been appreciating the strong, rugged scenery with Loch Crawe gliding past the driver side window like a shimmering, oval mirror. Trees were strung around it like jade jewels. Instead, my thoughts kept harking back to Evan.

The only hint now there had been two bombs was the outline of a sandpit in one of the nearby fields, which had several figures stationed around it, filling it in.

A few official-looking vehicles were stationed close by, but the traffic was moving both behind and in front of me, albeit a little more slowly than normal, directed by a couple of traffic police.

I pushed on.

Evan was fluttering at the corners of my mind again. Had I imagined there'd been a mutual feeling of attraction there?

I knew with flickers of embarrassment in my chest that I hadn't imagined my attraction for him, despite the protestations I kept making.

I could deny it all I wanted and pretend that it hadn't mattered, but it had.

Evan had managed to get under my skin.

I checked my rear-view mirror. The cars behind me were shining in the late afternoon sun, trailing behind each other like brightly coloured ants.

If I was being truthful, from the first moment I'd set eyes on him at the party lunch in his sharp suit and glittering cufflinks, he'd had an effect on me.

Maybe it was just some weird, temporary crush, I assured myself over and over as the shaggy Highland cattle and sloping mountains slithered past. I was grateful to him for stopping me making an utter tit of myself with Fox and losing my hospitality job. And yes, he was very, very handsome. But that was as far as it would go. A silly, momentary liking. He still had something going on with Sacha anyway, and no doubt he viewed me as an interfering busybody when it came to the tour.

I just wanted to get to my grandpa and Strath Ross so I could reset. And if Alison and Bennett did decide that my Florence tour suggestion was one they wanted to try, and I had to return to The Ramblings, then I could handle it. I could deal with Evan. I'd just have to throw all my energy into helping set up of the tour and remind myself why I was there. In the meantime, it was perfect timing for me to head home. It would allow me to clear my head and sort everything out.

It had been wonderful staying at The Ramblings. It was a charming, classy, stately home with mystery and history baked into every piece of stone, and Alison and Bennett were such a lovely, sweet couple.

Dane was … well, Dane. Charming and good-looking but self-absorbed. The way he'd acted when I left had thrown me, though. There had been a vulnerability there that I'd never seen before.

The only issue was Evan. No, he wasn't an issue, I corrected myself as I negotiated the traffic along the country roads. Oh God. I was doing it again! Stop dwelling on him, Daisy!

I rubbed at my face with one hand before returning it to the steering wheel.

My thoughts crossed to Cayla next. If Alison and Bennett went with my tour idea, would Cayla even consider playing Florence?

I guided Marlene around a corner and took us down a sun-dusted road, banked on either side by fluttering hedgerows.

Cayla would be great. I knew she would. If she did accept the role, it would be such a boost to her confidence. Just what she needed. Not only that, but it would look great on her CV too for when she began applying to acting school.

But I knew I shouldn't get too far ahead of myself. There was no guarantee the Lords would decide that my idea had legs. Maybe they'd consider it too gimmicky, or they wouldn't feel comfortable about dragging up the past. But if they did decide to run with it, surely the tour would put some extra money in the estate coffers? Raise the profile of The Ramblings? Open it up to the possibility of staging corporate events? Weddings, perhaps?

More visions about the tour tripped through my head. I could see it now: Cayla dressed in a frilly apron with her hair in a bun at the nape of her neck, a grey dress skirting her ankles; dashing here and there in front of intrigued tourists and locals; showing how Florence lived and worked so hard, whist keeping her acting dreams close to her heart like a burning secret.

We could reenact the vase being stolen and poor Florence's insistence she was innocent. We could show the aftermath of her having been blamed for the theft and how that impacted her.

It would capture moments in time and illustrate Florence's past.

The Ramblings still possessed that old, worldly aura with its sweep of grand staircase, tiled great hall and watercolour paintings decorating its walls.

Still, I reminded myself, glancing in my rear-view mirror as I drove along, I mustn't get too carried away. There was no guarantee Alison and Bennett would go with my tour idea anyway.

And even if they did, I'd still have to persuade Cayla to take the role of Florence.

I grimaced.

It sounded like even more of a monumental task the more I replayed everything over and over.

I turned the bend, and the sign for Strath Ross erupted out of the grass verge on the left-hand side.

My heart gave a little skip of delight. London seemed so far away with its hustle and bustle.

Instead of the Bohemian chic of Notting Hill and the endless streaks of red buses, I was confronted by the sight of the familiar, little, white, stippled cottages strung along the edges of the fields and forestry.

An osprey dangled above the hills, like a brown and gold kite bobbing in mid-air.

Strath Ross was a quaint little town, still stuck in the nineteenth century, but I loved it like that.

It had a small post office, a doctor and dentist, a newsagent and a sprinkling of independent shops. It was hemmed in on all sides by farms and banks of trees.

I drove on past a couple of old barns and grinning rickety fences, which reminded me of weathered teeth in the hazy afternoon sun.

Then I took a left down the snaking gravelled path towards my grandparents' house where I'd grown up.

I smiled as Marlene's wheels crunched on the crumbly stone path that led down to the house, remembering the times when I was a kid and I would roll down the lush, green banks of grass on the left-hand side, with my grandparents rolling their eyes and laughing at me through the kitchen window.

In the winter, the three of us would build a portly,

slightly off-kilter snowman, and he'd perch there on top of the hill, a sentry on duty in one of Grandpa's checked flat caps and Grandma's woollen scarves.

In autumn, I would kick the leaves and then help Grandpa to sweep them up. Our hard work would be rewarded by Grandma, who would present us with her delicious hot chocolate whipped up with fresh Scottish cream and drizzled with marshmallows.

They'd taken on the roles of my mum and dad with relish. Even now, my mother still wasn't a solid presence in my life. Even though she only lived in the next town, she was still absent, and that was fine. I'd accepted it, and although there was still a sliver of resentment that would sting me whenever I thought about what she and my dad had done, I knew I wouldn't have had the wonderful life I did if it weren't for my grandma and grandpa stepping up. I would never have been this happy.

Emotion clogged my throat as I stared out of the windscreen, Marlene's engine still purring.

I eased her to a stop just a few feet away from the tomato-red front door.

No sooner had I climbed out and savoured the familiar tang of earth and dry bark than my grandpa tugged open the door and burst out. 'Och, look at you, Daisy Dewdrop. You're a sight for sore eyes.'

I ran up to him and threw my arms around him in a fierce hug. There was a hint of woodsmoke in the air.

Grandpa took a step backwards in his tartan slippers and studied me out of his smoky grey eyes. His mouth melted under his white, pencil-thin moustache. His snowy hair was slicked back. 'You get bonnier every time I see you. Just like your grandma at that age.'

I laughed. 'And your patter never changes, Grandpa.'

I pulled my bag from the passenger seat and collected my case from the boot. Grandpa ushered me inside. It still smelled like home.

The cottage was the same. From its polished, hardwood beams to the amber, linoleum floor in the kitchen and the tall, glass cabinet in the sitting room, housing my grandma's treasured collection of porcelain wild birds, it reminded me a little of The Ramblings on a smaller scale, with its memories, characters and history imprinted on its heart.

The modest garden was brimming with paintbox-coloured potted flowers and shrubs, and the lawn looked like it had just been mowed. Grandpa had been flexing his gardening talents again.

Photos of the three of us, or The Three Musketeers as my grandma used to call us, were dotted all around the sitting room. Her serene smile shone out at me. My heart sagged in my chest. *Come on, Daisy. No bringing the mood down!*

'So,' I said in a bright voice. Grandpa was already filling the teapot at the kitchen sink. My grandma's two aprons still hung from the back of the door, and her favourite mug, imprinted with sunflowers, sat on the windowsill. 'What would you like me to make us for dinner?'

Grandpa turned around with a mischievous glint. 'You'll be pleased to know I've been shopping.'

'Ok.'

'And I got…'

'A chicken?' I supplied, folding my arms in a jokey manner. 'And let me guess, Maris Piper potatoes for roasting, sprouts, parsnips, carrots and Yorkshire puddings?'

'I might have done.'

I raised my brows at him.

'Aye. Alright. You guessed correctly.'

My grandpa had always adored my grandma's roast dinners, and although mine wouldn't be a patch on hers, I could rustle one up that wasn't half bad.

So while I sipped my mug of tea, I made a start on peeling the potatoes while Grandpa sat at the kitchen table nursing his.

'So come on then, lass. I bet you're taking that London acting world by storm.'

Oh, here it goes.

My hand stilled with the peeler in it. I couldn't tell him the truth. He'd worry for Scotland otherwise, and that was the last thing I wanted. 'It's going ok,' I said with a flash of a smile.

'Just ok?' he repeated, incredulous. 'You were amazing in that TV drama. Everybody around here watched it, you know. And I told all and sundry the lass with the blonde do was my granddaughter.'

I let out a playful groan. 'I bet you did. They will have tried to avoid you when they saw you coming.'

I resumed peeling another potato.

'So, come on then. What part have you got lined up next?'

'Oh, this and that,' I replied vaguely, busying myself with chopping the end off of a carrot.

I could feel Grandpa's eyes on me. 'Is everything alright, sweetheart?'

I whirled round, pinning a smile on my face. 'Yes, of course it is. Why?'

'You just seem a little distracted.'

I flapped my hand holding the carrot. 'No. I'm fine. I mean, I'm good. All good.'

Grandpa didn't look convinced, but he didn't push it. He took a considered sip of his tea and eyed me over the rim of his mug. 'This young man. Tell me about him then.'

'What young man?'

'This fella. The Lord. Ethan, is it?'

'You mean Evan?'

'Aye, that's the chappie.'

I picked up a second carrot and sliced the bottom of it with a sharp knife. 'What about him?'

'Jings,' sighed my grandpa. 'This is like pulling teeth. What's he like? Would I like him?'

I set down the knife on the chopping board. 'He's not a lord, Grandpa. Well, not in the way you mean.' I frowned at him. 'I think you would like him. But to be honest, I'm not sure where these questions are going.'

Grandpa winked at me.

I pulled an exasperated face and moved my attention out of the kitchen window to the grass, which was stirring in the early evening breeze. The sun was dancing behind the trees.

There was silence.

'What's the story with him, then?'

'There is no story.'

'Oh believe me, lass, there's always a story.' I heard him set his mug down on the table. 'What's he like? Good-looking, is he?'

I fiddled with the chopping board. Snapshots of Evan, like a film running in front of my eyes, played in slow motion. I steadied my voice. 'Yes, he's attractive.'

'Single?'

I turned round at the sink. 'I think his love life's complicated.'

'In what way?'

Letting out a playful sigh, I said, 'I see you're fishing again. You cast that rod any further, and you'll be catching a dolphin in the Moray Firth.'

Grandpa chuckled as he picked up his mug. 'Very funny.' Then his expression grew more serious. 'After that chancer Leon, I just want to see you happy and settled with someone. A decent young man.' He took a mouthful of his tea. 'You like this Evan, don't you?'

My mouth dropped open, and I clamped it shut again. 'What? No. No!'

I grabbed two parsnips from the draining board as though my life depended on it.

What was the matter with me? I couldn't shake Evan off.

My mind kept playing pictures of him on a continual loop, and it was driving me crazy.

'Well, you could've fooled me,' carried on Grandpa. 'The way your cheeks have lit up, they could power the National Grid.'

'It's warm in here,' I blustered. 'Have you got the heating on?' I didn't let him reply. 'Now, pass me those sprouts, will you please?'

Dinner was a success.

Grandpa exclaimed with delight at my fluffy roast potatoes, succulent, golden roast chicken and the buttered parsnips.

We also managed to force down a couple of scoops of clotted cream ice cream that Grandpa had stashed in his freezer.

We'd finished rinsing the cutlery, and I was stacking the dishwasher, when my mobile ring tone purred in the hall.

I hurried to my bag, which was hanging up on one of the coat pegs, and fetched it out.

'Hi? Daisy?'

'Yes?'

'I'm sorry to interrupt you. It's Alison. Alison Lord.'

'Oh. Hi!' I hooked some hair back behind one ear. 'How are you?'

'I'm fine, thanks. Did you have a good journey to your grandfather's?'

'Yes, I did, thanks. Nice, quiet journey, apart from getting past Loch Crawe. They're still clearing up around there.'

'I'm sure they are.'

I could see my grandfather hovering at the end of the hallway, pretending to tidy up his already neat mug cupboard in the kitchen.

'Good. Good,' she murmured down the line. 'I'm calling you because we've been mulling over your tour suggestion, and we've decided it's a wonderful idea!'

It took me a moment to realise what she'd said. 'Oh. Right. Well, that's great.'

'It is,' she enthused. 'It's just, we really want to get up and running with this as soon as we possibly can' She let out a nervous laugh. 'So, what I'm trying to say is, is there any chance you can speak to Layla? The talented young actor?'

'It's Cayla. And yes, of course.'

'Good.' Another pause. 'Look, Daisy, I know you've only just got back to your grandfather's, but is there any chance at all you could come back to The Ramblings and help us get this off the ground?'

I clutched my phone a little tighter to my ear. 'What? You mean, like, now?'

Embarrassment shot through Alison's voice. 'I'm sorry, and I know it's a lot to ask, but Evan said that if we could ask you to return immediately, it would be the best thing.'

I swallowed. 'Evan did?'

'Yes. He said we can't do it without you.'

What was he doing? Did he mean it? Was this some sort of game Evan was playing? Or had he come to his senses about the tour and simply wanted to get things up and running as soon as possible? I gathered myself. 'But like I just said, I've only just arrived at my grandpa's.'

'Och no! No!'

I turned around, to see my grandfather clutching a letter, which had just been slipped through the letterbox.

'Hold on a second please, Alison.' I lowered my mobile. 'What is it, Gramps?'

He waggled the letter this way and that. 'Bloody risk survey has been done after those two bombs, and the authorities have said this place is in the risk zone. They want me to temporarily relocate.' He looked like he wanted to stomp over the letter. 'They don't think there are any devices here, but they aren't prepared to take any chances.'

'Oh no.' This was just what we needed, poor Grandpa worrying about this cottage.

I returned my attention to Alison on the phone. Grandpa and his well-being came first. 'Look, Alison, I don't know if you heard any of that.'

'Indeed I did, Daisy. What a worry for him. But there's no problem. Bring your grandpa back with you. If he's ok with that, of course.'

'Sorry? You want me to bring my grandpa to The Ramblings?'

At this, my grandpa spun round, still gripping the council letter. 'Aye. I mean, yes. Absolutely.' He was nodding his white head so fast, he was giving me a migraine.

I lowered my phone and clamped my hand over it. 'Do you mind?! You don't even know what I'm talking about.'

Grandpa waggled his bristly brows. 'I may be old, but I'm not senile. They want you back to that big house where the dishy Lord fella is, and by the sounds of it, they've said this old git can go for the ride.' Grandpa tossed the letter down on the hall cabinet. 'Just let me go and pack.'

I shot him a look and raised the phone back to my ear. 'Er. Hello, Alison. Sorry about that.'

'No problem. I'm sorry to drop this on you, Daisy, but your idea is fantastic, and you would be doing us such an enormous favour. Would that be alright to bring your grandfather?'

This was sending me into a mental whirlwind. 'I mean, are you sure?'

Just as he was passing by me, Grandpa chirruped. 'Just off to get my things together for tomorrow.'

Alison laughed. 'He sounds adorable.'

'That's one word for him.'

'So, is that a yes?' Her voice rose with hopeful optimism.

A strange mix of emotions rattled through me at breakneck speed. This had all been my idea. I had to help, even if it meant it was happening rather faster than I'd anticipated. I just hoped I could talk Cayla round to playing Florence.

A loud clattering noise from behind me made me flinch.

I turned round to see the hall cupboard door open and my grandpa bent forward, staring in at its contents.

I lowered the phone to speak to him. 'Grandpa, what are you doing?' I hissed.

He pointed one finger at something in triumph. 'Ah. There it is.' He jerked his head up.

'What is it?'

He produced a battered, bottle-green suitcase that had seen better days. 'If I'm coming with you, then I'll need to start packing.'

I let out a groan. This was my fault. I was the one who'd come up with the Florence tour idea in the first place.

I shoved my mobile back up to my ear. 'Sorry about that Alison. My grandpa has already located his suitcase and is beginning to pack as we speak, so I think the answer to your question is yes.' I sighed. 'Are you sure about this? I hope we aren't inconveniencing you.'

'Of course you're not! Quite the opposite.' She hesitated down the line. 'I don't suppose you could return to The Ramblings tomorrow morning?'

'Tomorrow?'

'Yes. The sooner we hit the ground running with arrangements, the better.'

'Tomorrow morning?' I mouthed to my grandpa, who was back in the hall cupboard, rustling about for his best shoes.

He tugged his raincoat from one of the pegs and gave it a theatrical flourish over one arm. 'Sounds good to me.'

Ok, this was crazy, but there was no way I was prepared

to let them down. 'Alright. We'll set off tomorrow morning after breakfast.'

'Excellent. See you then. Thank you so much again, Daisy, and we really hope we haven't inconvenienced you.'

'Not at all,' I insisted. 'Thank you for saying my grandpa can come and stay. It'll help take his mind off this bomb risk survey and what's happening around the cottage.'

Alison was frothing with excitement. 'It's the least we can do. Goodnight.'

I hung up. Crikey. What had I let myself in for? Had I promised too much? Was my suggestion of the tour going to under-deliver? I still had to speak to Cayla.

'I bet that Evan will be pleased to see you again,' chimed Grandpa, giving his raincoat a playful swish.

'I'm not doing any of this for Evan,' I reddened, pretending to tap the screen of my mobile for something to do. 'I'm doing this for his parents.'

'Sure you are,' he replied, not convinced. 'Now stop dawdling, lass, and let's get sorted. You can help me choose a few of my best ties. I'm not letting the side down!'

Chapter Eighteen

After a tasty breakfast of porridge sprinkled with nutmeg, which Grandpa insisted on making, we stowed our cases in Marlene's boot and set off for the half hour journey back to Forrest Bank.

I always tended to overpack anyway and had added to my suitcase a few spare T-shirts, shorts and a couple of pairs of jeans that had still been hanging up in my old bedroom. Grandpa had tossed in a couple more short sleeve shirts and polo shirts for good measure.

Today, however, he'd adorned himself in his best milk chocolate pinstripe suit, buttermilk shirt and gold and beige tie. He looked like a dapper 1940s New York gangster.

I'd assured him he didn't have to stand on ceremony and dress up for Alison and Bennett, but he'd shaken his thick head of silvery blue hair. 'I want to set a good impression, lass. Not let you down.' His eyes creased with a sad smile. 'If your grandma were here, you know she'd be telling me to do the same thing.'

'Yes, she would,' I conceded. 'But you've never let me down before.'

As we made our way along the sun-drizzled country lanes back to Forrest Bank, Grandpa kept slipping me charged looks from the passenger seat. 'You look very pretty.'

'Do I?'

He flicked one hand towards my pale pink sundress sprigged with roses. I'd left my hair down, so it was tumbling in loose waves.

'Aye. You do. Any reason for the dress and the hair?'

'Sorry?'

'Evan?'

I tutted and clenched the steering wheel. 'It's a lovely day,' I blabbed. 'Just felt like making a bit more of an effort. Making the most of the weather.'

'Aye. Aye.'

He always said that when he was cynical about something, but I let it drop.

'You looking forward to going back then? To this big fancy house?'

'Yes. Why?'

Grandpa straightened his tie under his jacket. 'No reason.'

Now it was my turn to deliver him a look.

I clicked the indicator right, which led us further away from Strath Ross's stippled cottages and rippling fields.

'I don't know how long we'll end up having to stay at The Ramblings, Grandpa. Like I said to you before, it all depends on how fast we can get everything pulled together for the tour.'

Grandpa shrugged under his suit. 'I've got nothing to rush back home for, lass. And anyway, that risk survey thing will take a few days to complete as it is.'

The hedge-lined lanes twisted and curled like emerald satin ribbons.

The few tufts of clouds sailed overhead as Grandpa nestled back in his passenger seat and sang 'Caledonia' to himself.

And even though I'd protested like crazy that I hadn't been thinking about Evan, I was fighting not to register the fact that I'd made an extra effort with my outfit, hair and makeup today.

I glanced at my reflection in my rear-view mirror and saw my tousled hair and my floaty dress. From now on, I would be focusing on the tour.

I joined my grandpa in another rendition of 'Caledonia' and tried not to think about Evan for the time being.

The Ramblings opened out like a grand, sun-splashed image jumping out of a magical pop-up book.

'Bloody hell,' gasped Grandpa beside me. He sat up. 'Not exactly a two up, two down, is it?'

'It's hoovering up money,' I commented as Marlene's

wheels sent some gravel spinning. 'That's why I suggested Alison and Bennett stage a regular historical tour. They need the extra income.'

My voice vanished. Evan had appeared on the front steps, and I almost pushed my foot down on the accelerator by mistake.

I could feel Grandpa looking across at me with a knowing smile. I eased us to a stop down by the trees.

I was adamant I wasn't going to look over at Evan as I jumped out and dashed round to the passenger side to help Grandpa out of the car. 'You wait there, and I'll collect our cases from the boot.'

Still avoiding catching Evan's eye, I hurried to the back of Marlene and pressed the fob, and the boot opened with a noisy clunk. I'd only just stuck my head inside when a voice came up from behind me.

'Hi.'

My heart jumped.

Flattening the buttons on the front of my dress, I spun round. I could feel the hem fluttering against my knees in the sunshine.

Evan looked down at me like he was seeing me for the first time. I put my hands in front of me and twisted my fingers together. This bloody man! I hated that he had this effect on me.

I yanked my case and Grandpa's out of the boot and had just set them down on the gravel when Evan insisted on taking charge of them for me. Our eyes sought out the other's. 'Thanks for coming back here so quickly. I hope it wasn't an inconvenience.'

I opened and closed my mouth. I wanted to tell him I wasn't doing this for him. But right now, captivated by his dark eyes, ringed with a tinge of amber, I knew I couldn't. I managed a curt, 'No problem.' I flicked my hair back. 'Alison and I agreed that we should get things moving as fast as we can.'

He nodded. 'Well, it's appreciated, and not just by my parents.' His eyes lingered. 'You look amazing in that dress, by the way.'

There were more loaded looks between us, so much so that I almost forgot my important passenger until Grandpa performed a forced cough.

Evan dragged his attention away from me to stare at my grandfather across the car roof. 'Oh, let me help you there, sir.'

Evan transferred our cases inside, and he and my grandpa swapped pleasantries.

When they'd finished talking, and Louise was chatting to Grandpa, I sidled up to Evan. 'I got the impression you weren't keen on the Florence Menzies tour idea.'

He shrugged his sculpted shoulders under his navy V-neck T-shirt. 'It's like you said before. How passionate you were about it. Your enthusiasm is infectious.' He zipped a hand over the top of his hair.

Wait a minute. No. I must be imagining it. Was that a hint of a blush on his cheekbones?

Louise escorted Grandpa into the drawing room while Evan lingered. 'Mum told me all about your student and how you've tried to help her get her acting mojo back again. How much you've tried to help this girl.'

Now it was my turn to flush raspberry. 'I'm sure anyone else would've done the same thing.'

Evan regarded me. 'No, Daisy. I don't think they would. And even though you've only been gone from here a night, this place wasn't the same without you.'

The birds skipped through the treetops in the garden, but Evan and I were oblivious to everything else swirling around us as we walked together into the drawing room. Bennett was laughing and joking with Grandpa, Alison was asking after Strath Ross and Louise was addressing everyone to see if they wanted a slice of her freshly baked lemon sponge.

It was only when Alison called Evan over to ask him something about her mobile phone that Grandpa materialised at my elbow. 'Handsome young fella. Your grandma would approve.'

'Sssh! He'll hear you. Not that there's nothing to approve anyway.'

'Hey.'

I looked around to see Dane strolling towards my grandpa and me. His hair was gleaming blond down his back. My eyes popped with surprise. But wait, where were the faded rock T-shirts and patched up jeans? Instead of his usual garb, he was wearing a smart, slim-fitting, black and white shirt, teamed with light trousers. He drew up beside me, blatantly checking out my summer dress. 'Mum and Dad said you were coming back today.' He gave a soft smile. 'You look lovely.'

I blushed at him. 'Thank you. And you look very suave.'

Grandpa coughed under his breath, and I did the introductions. Dane shook Grandpa's hand, calling him Sir like Evan had just done, and then meandered further into the drawing room.

'Who's he?' whispered Grandpa with interest.

'That's Dane, Evan's younger brother. Bit of a wild child. He has his own rock band, who are trying to break into the big time.'

'He's a good-looking boy, too,' murmured Grandpa. 'Would look even more handsome with a haircut though.'

I tutted. 'Don't you dare go round upsetting anyone.'

'Who? Me?'

'No, Brad Pitt. Of course you!'

Grandpa looked affronted. 'I'm the personification of tact.'

He leant in towards me as Louise clattered the tea set behind us and prepared to come back out to go and collect her cake. Grandpa gave me a wink. 'Seems like you've made an impression on brother number two as well.'

Luckily I hadn't been drinking my tea yet, as I would've spluttered it everywhere otherwise. 'What? Don't be daft, Gramps.'

Grandpa arched his brows. 'Didn't you notice the way he was looking at you?'

I shuffled on the spot. Dane had been staring at me for a little longer than usual. And I had to admit, I did wonder why he'd made an effort with his clothes. I brushed it off. 'Oh, Grandpa, your imagination is in overdrive again.'

'I may be old, but there's nothing wrong with my eyesight.'

At that moment, Louise edged past us. 'You two go and make yourselves comfortable. I'll just bring the baking in from the kitchen.'

We did as we were told.

The Lords were sat in the squashy, pale armchairs, with Evan and Dane on the sofa. When Dane spotted us approaching, he leapt up. 'Come and sit over here, Daisy.'

Evan scowled at his brother.

'Do you think Cayla will agree to be Florence?' asked Alison, stretching over to the glass coffee table where the cups and teapot were set out.

Bennett insisted on guiding Grandpa over to the other vacant armchair, and I found myself sandwiched between Dane and Evan. 'I hope so,' I sighed. 'I'll do everything I can to persuade her.'

'If anyone can talk her round, you can,' grinned Dane.

Evan threw a dismissive look along the sofa at his brother. 'I thought you had rehearsals to go to?'

Dane looked unfazed. 'I'm sure the guys can manage without me for a little while longer.'

Louise re-entered with a huge tray, laden not just with red velvet cake but also fruit, plain, treacle and cinnamon scones.

'How many people have we got coming?' joked Dane, flashing Louise a charming smile.

She took a playful swipe at his arm.

I glanced along the sofa to where Evan was surveying Dane and me. His mouth flatlined. What was the matter with him? Only ten minutes ago, he'd been charm itself out by the car, insisting on helping with the luggage. Now his face was stormy, and he wasn't saying much.

We savoured the tea and cake over convivial chit-chat as the late morning sun caused a kaleidoscope of shapes to move over the gardens.

Grandpa and Dane chatted about plants, gardening and the Rolling Stones. 'If you need any help with potting some shrubs, I'm your man,' emphasised Grandpa.

'That would be great,' grinned Dane across at my grandpa. 'We've got a few honeysuckle and dwarf rhododendrons that'll need tending to.'

Once I'd finished my tea and cake, I started to make my way up to my room. Bennett had already assisted Grandpa up the staircase so he could take a nap.

'Where are you going?'

I turned to see Evan propping one arm on the bannister.

I felt my neck flush purple. 'I'm going to unpack.'

'Good plan,' he mused. 'But I also think we should get started on some brainstorming for this tour and how it's going to work.' Evan's eyes were charged. 'Work together.'

My mouth turned to sandpaper, but I managed a casual shrug. 'Er. Yes. Of course.' I eyed him. 'You started reading the journal yet?'

'Almost finished it. Couldn't put it down. Poor girl. What a life she had.' Evan drew a little closer. 'So now there's no excuse not to start pulling together this script between us straight away.'

'Yes, good idea.' I tried to compose myself. He stood there, holding me to the spot from under his lashes. His attention glided from the top of my head to rest on my mouth.

I'd been an idiot, I realised with a sudden, embarrassed jolt. I hadn't thought this through. The way he was looming over me, his jaw set like that. My frustration grew. What was with all the hot looks and the flirty voice? The sudden charm offensive? Was this some sort of game to him? Did he find it amusing, playing with people's feelings? Sacha one minute and me the next? Had he noticed Dane flirting with me and got annoyed?

If Evan thought for one minute that he could play me like a violin, he was mistaken! I'd had enough of that with Leon.

My emotions kicked in with such force I couldn't help myself. 'You're infuriating!' I burst out.

Evan didn't flinch. He just stayed where he was, his muscular, right arm propped on the bannister. 'What's the problem?'

I folded my arms. Heat seared in my cheeks. 'There isn't one.'

He raised his brows. 'You could've fooled me.'

I didn't want to be standing here, subjected to Evan's

penetrating attention. 'Well, you're mistaken,' I replied in a strange, croaky voice.

'Then why did you just tell me I'm infuriating?'

Another question shot out of me, before I could help myself. 'Aren't you preoccupied with Sacha? I would've thought you'd be too busy to work on the script.'

As soon as I'd said it, I wanted to shrivel away to dust on the staircase. What the hell had made me say that? I sounded petulant; jealous even. The thought pricked me over and over. This wasn't like me.

Evan offered me a slow, wolfish smile that made my legs tremble. 'Jealous?'

I hugged myself so tight it was like I was wearing a straitjacket. A weird laugh shot out of me. 'Me? Jealous? As if!' I pushed out my chin. 'Right, so, we need to get cracking on this script.'

'My thoughts exactly.'

'But I want to contact Cayla first.'

Evan shook his head. 'I've got other deadline commitments, so I suggest we make a start on the script now. You can tell her that things are in hand then. Looks more professional.'

I moved to disagree, but Evan was already striding towards the study.

'Well?' he called over. 'Care to join me? No time like the present.'

I bared my teeth at him and followed.

For the next few days, we toiled over a script outline. We began with Florence's young life, her being taught to read and write by the kind piano teacher; then we detailed her interactions with Evan's great-great-grandparents, the vase going missing and Florence being blamed; then her fledgling acting career floundering as a result; and finally her untimely death.

To my surprise, we worked well together. We bantered and joked, swapped ideas, disagreed politely and agreed with enthusiasm. I'd been sure the process would be a painful one, but instead Evan embraced the task, followed my lead and put forward some good ideas and suggestions.

It was still a relief, though, when the finished script was lying in front of us. But there it was nonetheless, all pulled together and telling Florence's life story.

'I'll type this lot up now,' volunteered Evan. 'I'm good with my hands.' He gave me a loaded look.

He was doing this deliberately.

I found myself hurrying off back up the stairs towards my room. My face was sizzling.

It was as if I wasn't in control anymore of what I was thinking and saying. What had happened to all the promises I'd made myself after Leon? I'd meant every word at the time, but now it was as though they'd vanished, and I couldn't even remember half of them anyway! 'I'll call Cayla now,' I shouted over the top of the stairs, hoping my voice didn't sound strangulated.

Waves of relief crashed over me as I clattered my guest

room door closed behind me. I took a few gulps of air. Had I made a gigantic mistake, suggesting the Florence tour in the first place? I hadn't thought of the ramifications of it. It was all well and good bringing in some extra revenue for The Ramblings and trying to restore Cayla's belief in her acting, but I hadn't thought about what that might mean for me where Evan was concerned.

And what if Cayla said no? I'd have to find someone else to play Florence, and I just couldn't imagine anyone else doing the part justice.

I dumped myself down on the edge of the bed and retrieved my mobile from my bag. It was approaching lunchtime, and the sun was sploshing across the silky, tangerine bedcovers.

I pulled up Gillian's number. After a few pleasantries, I asked her if Cayla was at school.

'Oh no, she's here. She's on study leave at the moment for her Advanced Highers. Hold on and I'll just get her for you.'

'Oh, please don't let me interrupt her revision.'

But Gillian was already letting out a throaty laugh. 'She'll be glad of the break.'

I rubbed one finger over the bedspread as I waited for Cayla to come to the phone.

'Hi, Daisy.' Cayla's voice swam into my ear. She sounded hesitant. I recalled what had happened the last time I'd tried to speak to her. It hadn't gone well.

'Hi, Cayla. How's things? Revision going ok?'

'Yeah, but I'll be glad when it's all over.'

'I bet. Still, all you can do is your best.'

'That's what Mum and Dad keep saying.'

'And they're right.'

Cayla paused. I could hear the hesitancy in her voice. 'Look, I'm sorry I was such a pain in the arse the other day.'

'Don't worry about it.' I took a breath. 'Look, there's something I'd like to speak to you about.'

Out of my bedroom window, a blackbird was playing hopscotch amongst the trees.

'What is it?'

'Well, do you know the big house, The Ramblings?' She did, so I explained about Florence, her age, working at The Ramblings, the vase going missing and her being blamed for it before her untimely death.

Cayla stayed silent until I finished. 'Whoa,' she breathed. 'That's so sad. She was almost the same age as me.'

'And that's why we want to tell her story, in the form of a tour of The Ramblings. The idea is that if it goes down well it would be a regular thing a few times a week.'

'Okay,' said Cayla, puzzlement in her voice.

I decided to take the plunge. 'So, the thing is, we've got a script, and we wondered if you would play the part of Florence, Cayla? I think you would be amazing.'

There was silence. I wasn't sure for a moment if she'd been cut off. Then Cayla's voice wobbled down the line. 'No. I'm sorry, Daisy. The answer's no. I'm flattered you asked me, but I'm not up to it.'

I shot off the top of the bed. 'Of course you're up to it, Cayla.'

But the girl wouldn't listen. 'I'm sorry to let you down, but I'm sure you'll find someone else who could do it.'

Then the line went dead.

Chapter Nineteen

I sighed and flopped back against the pillow.

Shit!

What now? What should I do?

I'd have to go back downstairs and tell Alison and Bennett that I hadn't managed to persuade Cayla to take on the role of Florence. A deep, sinking disappointment clutched at me.

And what about Evan when I told him? I'd look a right idiot. I felt like I'd let down the Lords big time. Even though I hadn't said it was a done deal with Cayla, a tiny part of me had assured myself that there wouldn't be a problem, and that she'd agree to do it.

So much for that.

I sank my upper teeth into my bottom lip.

We wanted to get moving on the tour; to start getting everything in place. But how could we do that if we didn't have Cayla as Florence?

I jumped up from the bed, pushed my phone into the pocket of my sundress and grabbed my straw bag from the nearby chair. My grandpa always used to say that you never gave up on anything until you'd exhausted every other avenue.

Maybe I should've gone and spoken to Cayla face to face rather than suggesting the idea over the phone? Although I'd done that the last time with no success.

I darted over to the oval mirror on the dressing table, rummaged around in my bag and located my rose-pink lipstick. I put on a fresh dash and gave my loose hair a ruffle.

Right. Time to try another avenue then.

Gillian's eyes widened at the sight of me hovering on her doorstep.

'Oh, hi there, Daisy. How are you?'

'I'm good, thanks.' In fact, I wasn't good. My insides were churning with worry that my tour was going to be blown out of the water before it had even started. I glanced over Gillian's shoulder. 'Is Cayla around?'

'Aye. She is. Come in.' She beckoned me inside and closed the door behind me. There was a vase of sunflowers on top of the nearby bureau. She lowered her voice. 'I'm so sorry about her attitude the other day. She was so rude!' Her cheeks lit up with embarrassment. 'She isn't normally like that.'

'Don't worry about it. I think I caught her off guard, and no doubt she was stressing over her exams.'

From upstairs, I could hear Sabrina Carpenter's vocals wafting our way.

Gillian tutted. 'Well, that's very understanding of you.' She moved to the bottom of the stairs. 'Cayla? Cayla!'

A bedroom door clicked open. 'What is it, Mum? You want me to turn it down?'

'No. Well, yes. That would be an idea.' Gillian fired me a loaded glance. 'There's someone here to see you. It's Daisy.'

At first, I didn't think Cayla was going to appear.

She didn't answer.

There was just the sound of Sabrina Carpenter, who'd finished singing about espresso and had moved on to tasting someone.

Gillian and I swapped awkward smiles.

After what seemed like ten minutes, there were a couple of creaks on the floorboards and the sound of feet padding down the carpeted staircase.

Cayla materialised wearing a pair of denim cutoff shorts and a cropped T-shirt with a silver heart on it. Her hair was piled up on top of her head in a messy topknot.

'Hi, Cayla,' I smiled at her.

Cayla picked at the frayed hem of her shorts. 'Hi.' She stared down at her bare, painted toes. They were sporting zesty green polish. Her eyes flicked up from the carpet to meet mine. 'If you've come to try and talk me round about acting again, you're wasting your time.'

'Cayla!" gasped Gillian. 'Don't be so rude. For pity's sake, Daisy is only trying to help.'

'It's alright,' I reassured her.

I made a move towards the front door. 'I'll go. Leave you to your revision.'

Then I turned around. 'I just thought you might be interested in telling the story of a young woman just like you, who wanted to be an actor as well. This is what I tried to talk to you about on the phone. Except her dreams were snatched away from her.' I eyed her tall, lean figure. 'She never had the opportunities you have.'

Gillian twisted the front door handle.

Cayla tried not to look interested. 'Was that Florence? The girl you mentioned on the phone?'

'Yes. She wanted to act, but in those days, it wasn't easy for someone like her.'

Cayla examined me from under her long fringe. She pushed it out of her eyes. 'When was this?'

'She started working at The Ramblings in 1905 as a scullery maid, but she was, by all accounts, a talented and driven young lady, just like you.'

One of Cayla's hands rested on top of the bannister. Her dolphin dress ring sparkled on her thumb. 'And you said she wanted to act?'

I nodded. 'Yes, she did. More than anything. She appeared in a few local productions, but she always dreamt of making it onto the West End stage.'

'But then she got blamed for stealing that vase?' Cayla's eyes were widening behind her fringe.

'Yes.'

'But she was innocent.' I tried not to smile at Cayla's entranced expression. I had already told her this, but it obviously didn't all register.

I nodded. 'That's right. But by the time it was revealed she didn't take the vase, poor Florence had passed away.'

Cayla pushed her hands into the pockets of her denim cutoffs. Gillian was stood beside me with her arms folded, riveted. 'I've never heard this story before, and that's saying something. You can't keep much a secret around here. The poor little thing.'

Cayla processed what I was telling her. 'So, she never made it to the West End?' Her eyes were soulful.

'No, she didn't. She passed away at the age of eighteen.'

'Oh, the poor lamb,' gasped Gillian, every bit as gripped by the tragic story as her daughter was.

Shock filled Cayla's pretty face.

'What did she die of?' asked Gillian.

'Pneumonia.'

Gillian gave her head a disbelieving shake. 'How did you find out about all this?'

I thought of Louise and the detailed journal that her late father compiled. 'Let's just say it was thanks to someone I know.'

Gillian widened her eyes. 'Like I said, I was born and raised in Forrest Bank, and I've never heard of her.'

I pulled a face. 'I get the impression that the Lords don't like to talk about it. It's not a part of The Ramblings past that they're proud of.'

Cayla frowned over at me. The late morning sun glided in through the pane of glass in the front door and slid down over her bare feet. 'It's terrible. What a tragic story.'

I took a step towards the teenager. 'It is, but that's why the Lords want to tell Florence's life story now. They want to stage a tour at The Ramblings regularly and show what actually happened.' I steeled myself again. 'And that's what I wanted to ask you, Cayla. I think you'd make the perfect Florence.'

The teenage girl's cheeks pinged bright red. Her eyes bored into the hall carpet.

'I wasn't just trying to boost your ego, Cayla. I meant what I said about you being a very talented actor. I think you'd do young Florence justice.'

Gillian broke into the conversation. 'And it's a tour of the house, you say?'

'Yes, and it'll tell the story of what happened. There will be an entrance fee, of course, and if it goes well it's hoped that the tour could be held two to three times a week with a rota of actors to play Florence, the piano teacher who teaches her to read and write, and the Lords.' I exchanged meaningful looks between the two of them, mentally willing Cayla to get on board with this. 'The script has just been written.'

'Did you write it?' asked Cayla.

'Yes.' I pushed out a smile. 'With the help of Evan Lord.'

'Alison and Bennett Lord's oldest son,' supplied Gillian to her daughter.

Cayla's eyebrows lifted under her fringe. 'Isn't he the dark-haired one? He's lush.'

Snapshots of lush Evan lodged themselves in front of me. I mentally batted them to one side. 'So, what do you say, Cayla? Will you help us? Will you be our Florence?'

Cayla looked agonised. She fidgeted at the foot of the stairs, looking everywhere but at me and her Mum. 'Thanks for thinking of me. Really. I am flattered.' She hesitated. 'But the answer is still no.'

My stomach plummeted to the floor and Gillian let out an audible groan. 'But why, sweetheart? Daisy wouldn't have asked you if she didn't have faith in you. She thinks you can do it.'

Cayla's eyes misted over.

'You've almost finished sitting your Advanced Highers now, and it would look great on your CV.'

'Don't you get it?!' erupted Cayla. 'I'm not an actor anymore. I'm not interested.'

'But why, love?'

Cayla turned and prepared to return back upstairs. She grabbed at her bun and wriggled it in frustration. 'It was a dream, that's all.'

'That's what it was for Florence, too,' I chipped in, unable to remain quiet. 'Except you've got far more chance of achieving your dreams than she ever did.'

Cayla gripped the bannister.

'I thought you might be interested in giving a voice to someone who was just like you all those years ago.' I offered a resigned smile to Gillian. 'Looks like I was wrong.

Anyway, I'll be off. Thank you again. Bye, Cayla. Good luck with your exams.'

Cayla didn't answer. She just remained on the stairs, all limbs and toenail polish.

'Thanks again for coming, Daisy. We really appreciate you thinking of Cayla. Don't we?'

The girl fiddled with her thumb ring.

I headed back off down their garden path, fringed either side with exploding, bright pansies. Now what? I'd have to have a word with the local amateur dramatics society and see if they could recommend anyone to portray Florence. I was sure Josie would be able to lend a hand too. She was bound to know a lot of the local acting fraternity. Or perhaps she could suggest another of her students who might be interested in the role? I just knew though that they wouldn't have this girl's star quality. Those bloody school bullies who'd drained Cayla's confidence. If they'd been stood in front of me right now…

'Daisy! Hold on! Wait!'

I turned around, startled.

Cayla was edging past her mum and heading towards me. She loped up on her long legs.

I could see Cayla turning over everything in her mind. Her hands pushed themselves back into her denim cutoff pockets. Then she shoved a stray hair back behind one ear. 'She passed away at eighteen you said?'

'Yes, she did.'

'That sucks.'

She glanced over at Gillian and then back at me. 'I guess you're right. She didn't have a voice.'

A kernel of hope started to grow. Was she going to change her mind? Had she had second thoughts? Maybe I'd been able to reach her after all? Make her see that she could make a difference with her acting talent?

I was holding my breath.

Cayla waggled her bare toes on the concrete path. Time seemed to stand still for a few moments. 'Ok. I'll do it. I'll be Florence.'

And as I let out a delighted whoop and bundled a laughing Cayla into my arms, Gillian, who looked fit to burst with relief, held back tears and mouthed a grateful, 'Thank you. Thank you so much.'

Chapter Twenty

Jade made a disbelieving laugh down the line.

I'd just got back to The Ramblings and had parked up.

The trees spiralled around me, and the crenelations could be seen in my rear-view mirror, dusted in golden sunlight. 'So, you're telling me that you're staying there? At Downton Abbey? With Mr Mean and Moody?'

'Yes. I mean, yes, I'm staying at The Ramblings for the time being to help get this tour off the ground.'

I didn't address Jade's mention of Evan. Whenever I thought about him, my whole body rippled like the sea on a windy day, which made me furious with myself, and then I got caught in this spiral of emotion.

'And Handsome Harry will be there?'

I didn't rise to the bait. I didn't answer.

'That's what I thought. Don't kid a kidder, Daisy chain.' I could hear her smile down the line into my ear.

'So, enough about me,' I jumped in. 'It's my turn to grill you now. How are things going in Somerset?'

She let out a dreamy sigh. 'It's been wonderful. Over all too quickly, if I'm being honest.' She paused for effect. 'But Jasper is keen to see me again, and we've arranged to meet up when he's next in London in two weeks' time.'

I grinned, delighted for her, and shuffled in my driver's seat. 'Hey. That's brilliant! You really like him, don't you?'

'Yes,' she whispered back, as though it were a state secret. 'I do. A lot. He's funny and charismatic and very well read. My parents would disapprove of course, which makes him even sexier. His elegies have to be read to be believed.'

I snorted. 'Nothing like an impressive elegy.'

'You may mock.'

I grinned out of the car windscreen as I sat there. 'I am. No may about it.'

'Yeah, I know!' Jade rounded off the call. 'I'd better go. There's a workshop in half an hour on acrostic poetry.'

'Ok. Have fun, and I'll see you soon, ok? I'll keep you posted, and safe journey back to London.'

'Thanks, Daisy. Oh, any more luck on the acting front?'

I wound my dress ring around on my right hand. 'No, nothing on the horizon at the moment. I'm going to take a break; get my head together.'

'I think that's a good idea,' responded Jade with a positive rise in her voice. 'But you're so talented. You'll get there. Wait and see.'

I promised to keep her informed on what was happening, blew a kiss down the line and hung up.

I reached across to the passenger side and fetched my bag.

I got out, locked up Marlene and studied The Ramblings again. Its windows twinkled like stars in the bright light, and the shadows playing off its balconied turrets and twists added to its majestic appearance.

Now to go and tell Alison and Bennett the good news; at least we had our Florence for the tour.

'Oh, that's wonderful, Daisy! Thank you so much!' Alison pulled me into her arms.

'That's alright,' I blushed. 'But it's not me you should be thanking. It was Cayla who agreed to take on the role.'

It was then Bennett's turn to give me a grateful hug. 'Please invite her and her parents over for dinner. We'd like to meet her before this tour gets underway.'

'Of course we should,' agreed Alison. 'That's a given.'

'What's going on here?'

Evan came striding into the study. His gaze flickered over me.

I hoped I looked nonplussed at his arrival. 'I spoke to Cayla, and she's agreed to play Florence for The Ramblings tour.'

'Isn't that great?' glowed Alison, clapping her hands together.

'Daisy tells us she wasn't overly keen, but she persuaded her.'

'Oh, I'm sure Daisy can be very persuasive.' His glittery, brown eyes teased me.

Was he flirting again? Or was he simply just being a smart arse and trying to make me feel awkward? Yes, that was more like it.

I pinned all my attention back on his parents. 'Just let me know how else I can help.'

'You're doing so much already,' said Alison with emotion. 'Now, if you'll excuse us, Bennett and I are going to speak to a couple of friends of ours who are involved in the Forrest Bank Theatrical Society. We have a few ideas about who could play his great-grandparents.'

'Yes,' mumbled Bennet with a hint of amusement. 'How about Eva Braun and Stalin?'

Alison laughed. 'Come on.'

And off they vanished.

Evan and I were left alone. The air prickled.

At that moment, there was a faint knock on the study door, and Grandpa popped his silver head around it. 'Hello, you two. Daisy, do you fancy a wander around the gardens? It's turning into a gorgeous day out there.'

Thank goodness. Bursting with gratitude, I reached for Grandpa's arm and linked it through mine. 'Good idea. Come on then.'

Evan and Grandpa exchanged smiles and nods.

I headed past Evan and got the distinct cloud of his bergamot aftershave. It was heavenly – drat him.

Evan dropped his voice as Grandpa was waxing lyrical about the explosions of heather and cherry blossom in the garden. 'We need to make sure we have publicity and marketing in place. I'll come looking for you around two o'clock this afternoon.'

A shiver of something raced down my back, but I just fired a terse look at him and hurried away to join Grandpa.

After we took in the kaleidoscope of colours, shapes and textures of the stunning gardens, together with the fountain of a small boy clutching a bucket, Louise made lunch for me, Evan and Grandpa.

Alison and Bennett were still out, and there was no sign of Dane, who Louise said was probably still in bed after another wild night of carousing.

Louise had made a delicious prawn salad. There were fat, glistening tomatoes, cucumber and slices of seeded bread.

Evan finished his and rose from the table. 'You can catch me in my room when you're finished,' he said as he edged past.

Colour flooded my neck.

I faffed around with my cutlery while Grandpa pointed his knife towards the dining room windows. 'It's just like Glasgow Botanic Gardens out there. Your grandma would've loved this.'

Once we'd finished our lunch, I helped Louise clear the

table while Grandpa shuffled off back to the drawing room for a post-lunch snooze. He was living his best life here and loving it!

Then I slipped upstairs and into my room. I found myself reapplying fresh lipstick and giving my hair a tousle.

I stopped. Why the hell was I doing this? Who was I trying to impress?

I decided not to dwell on the answers to those particular questions and fluffed the hem of my sundress. I headed out into the hall and closed my bedroom door behind me. My stomach swam.

I was playing with fire here. I knew it.

But I could resist Evan if I had to. I could, couldn't I? Of course I could. I would just have to remind myself what a low-life Leon had been and that I needed more heartbreak like I needed a toothache. Not to mention the Sacha-sized elephant in the room. Setting my back straight, I hooked my hair back behind my ears and knocked on his closed bedroom door.

'Come in,' rumbled his voice from the other side.

I opened the door.

Evan was seated at his writing desk, with his laptop open and glowing. The light from it was highlighting the planes of his face. He was wearing his spectacles again, and there was a faint dusting of dark stubble across his jawline. It suited him. It gave him a bit of a softer edge somehow.

My heart did a twisting motion in my chest, which made me grip the door handle tighter.

I closed the door behind me.

Evan removed his glasses and set them down by his laptop. 'Please sit down.'

He tugged over a spare chair, and I settled myself in it. I turned my attention to his laptop. 'What are you working on? Or aren't I allowed to know?'

'No, I can tell you. It's a piece about dating apps and whether they unintentionally kill the art of romance.'

'That's a bit of a diversion for you.'

'What is? Romance?'

I pushed out my chin, willing my cheeks not to light up. 'No, I was talking about the tone. More…'

'Light and fluffy?'

'Yes. I suppose so. I just get the impression you'd prefer to write the grittier stories.'

Evan stretched out his legs. 'Commission for a weekend newspaper supplement. Pays well.' The silence between us was stirring almost as much as his bedroom curtains in the May breeze.

I hoped I sounded and looked business-like. 'Right. So we need to ensure we spread the word about the tour; try to attract all ages, from locals to day trippers, tourists and everyone in between.'

He looked at me from under his dark, thoughtful brows.

I shifted, focusing my attention on everything from Evan's laptop to his black and silver bedding rather than him.

Evan sat back in his chair. His words caught me off guard. 'You don't have a very high opinion of me, do you Daisy?'

I flapped one hand around. 'Don't be ridiculous.'

'The other night at Dane's gig.'

I blinked at him 'What about it?'

He dropped his eyes for a moment before fixing his attention back on me again. 'He kept stealing all your attention.' He exhaled. He didn't speak for the longest time. 'Dane. I was jealous.'

His words rocked me. 'Jealous?!'

Our attention remained trained on one another like heat-seeking missiles. No. This was risky. I couldn't. I had to cling onto common sense. I wouldn't go through a rerun of what I'd had with Leon. I'd just put my heart back together again, and now I was contemplating putting it out there once more to be shattered by Evan? What was I? Some sort of emotional masochist? Yes, I thought he was gorgeous, but that didn't mean I should do anything about it. And where did Sacha feature in all of this?

I had to gather myself together first, before I said something I regretted.

I pinned on a cool smile. 'Well, no need to be jealous. Right, let's make a start on this publicity drive, shall we?'

Evan looked blindsided. Deflated, even. An odd look settled on his face. 'Yes. Ok. Sure. Good idea.'

I had to put some space between us. I had no choice. He was driving me to distraction. I didn't want to, but I had to. For my own sake.

The last thing I needed was losing my heart to him, which would be very, very easy.

'Are you ok?' asked Evan, catching me moving my chair away from him.

I hoped I could disguise the tremble in my voice. 'Yes. Why?'

'Is it my aftershave?'

'Don't be daft.' I forced out a laugh. 'So, I pulled together a scribbled list of newspapers and radio stations we could send press releases to. It's down on the desk in the study.'

I shot out of Evan's room and hurried towards the top of the staircase and started to make my way down, with Evan catching up behind me.

We'd reached halfway down the stairs when Louise emerged at the bottom, clutching some clean dish towels.

She frowned up at us. 'I don't suppose either of you have seen my white spectacles case? I had it in my apron pocket when I was giving the bannisters a dust earlier.'

I continued down the next couple of steps with Evan following behind. 'No. Sorry. I haven't seen it.'

I put my right foot down on the next step. It didn't connect. Instead, it caught on an object. I tried to keep upright, but it was no good. I could feel myself hurtling into the air.

I let out a stunned scream, preparing to land with an almighty bang. I was going to do myself some serious damage.

Oh bugger! These steps were beautiful, but steep…

Chapter Twenty-One

I could feel myself travelling, my terrified gaze staring up at the elaborately designed ceiling, which reminded me of a whipped meringue.

I couldn't brace. I couldn't do anything.

I waited for the inevitable pain to rock through my body when I landed.

But it didn't.

Hold on.

I hadn't tumbled down the staircase, nor had I appeared to have hurt myself.

Instead, I was staring up into the warm, deep-brown eyes of Evan. Again, just like when he'd carried me up these same stairs just days ago.

What?

I was being held in his arms, like a swooning Scarlett O' Hara being rescued by Rhett Butler.

'This seems to be becoming a bit of a habit,' grinned

Evan, his attention hovering on my mouth. 'Not that I'm complaining. Are you ok?'

No, I felt like saying. I'm far from ok. My heart was racing like mad in my chest as though caught in a crosswind. His arms were around me, his fingers gently pressing into my back. I couldn't stop looking at his mouth. *I'm so close to kissing you right now, you have no idea.*

'Yes,' I bleated. 'Thanks. I'm fine. Thank you. You can put me down now.'

The last thing I wanted was for Evan to let me go, but I knew I couldn't stay like that forever.

'Sure.'

Evan released me and set me down on both feet on the next step of the staircase.

Louise was charging up towards us, flapping her tea towels around. 'Oh God, Daisy! I'm so sorry. Are you alright?'

She bent down and snatched up a small, white, leather spectacles case. 'That's what almost made you come a cropper. My bloody glasses!'

'I'm ok, don't worry.' I turned and looked at Evan standing beside me. 'Thank you for catching me.'

'You're welcome.'

The air stilled between us. I didn't want to drag my eyes away from him.

After a few more charged moments, we set off together down the staircase.

Louise stuffed her retrieved spectacles case back inside the pocket of her apron. She was observing us with keen interest. 'Right,' she twinkled. 'I'll go and make you a cup of sweet tea to steady your nerves. I'm going to have one as well. Evan?'

He didn't answer. There was a preoccupied angle to his face as he looked across at me. We reached the bottom of the stairs. 'Evan? Earth calling?'

'Oh, sorry. Er, yes, a tea would be great, Lou. Thanks.'

She beckoned us to follow her into the kitchen. Strobes of sunshine were spilling in through the windows and over the tiled floor of the great hall.

We seated ourselves at the black marble breakfast bar while Louise fetched the teapot and proceeded to fill it at the sink. 'How are you feeling now, Daisy?'

'I'm fine, thanks,' I reassured her.

'You sure?'

'Yes.' I flicked Evan beside me the briefest glance. My blood pressure had rocketed, but for different reasons.

Evan waited until Louise had made the pot of tea and clattered over to the breakfast bar with it on a tray. She sat herself on a stool opposite both of us and poured it out.

'Florence Menzies,' said Evan abruptly.

Louise curled her fingers around her dainty, flower sprigged teacup. 'Yes, what about her?'

Evan pushed back a stray lock of hair. 'Do you know how your dad found out about Florence and what happened to her?'

'Aye, I do.' Louise took a sip of her tea. 'Like I said, he was always very into his local history.' She fiddled with the handle of her teacup in front of her. 'My dad, Montgomery, had always been a keen amateur historian. Some might say he was rather obsessed with the past, especially links to the local area.'

She considered her words. 'As I remember it, my dad had been for a pint or two at what used to be the most popular pub in Forrest Bank, The Fisherman's Tail. It's now that fancy scented candle shop.' Louise shook her head in wonder. 'Dearie me, this was about fifty years ago now. Where does the time go?' She pulled her attention back to her story. 'Anyway, my dad told my mother and me that your grandfather was in the pub and a few sheets to the wind.'

Evan's lips twitched and turned to me. 'If you'd met my grandfather, old Conrad, you'd understand. The stories I've heard about him and my grandma Betty.'

Louise picked up the story again. 'Conrad was bragging about The Ramblings and how wonderful his parents – your great-grandparents Blanche and Jeremy – were, and how much they'd brought to the local area, when someone sidled up to my father and muttered in his ear, "Aye. I bet Florence Menzies's relatives would have a different story to tell about old man Lord and his missus."'

Louise picked up her teacup again and took a considered sip. 'My father had no idea who this man was, but he was curious and tried to follow him out the pub, but the mystery man vanished. That was when my dad took it upon himself to do some digging.'

'And that was when he uncovered the story about Florence?' I asked, fascinated.

'Och, it took a long time, but my dad had so much patience and dedication for this sort of thing. He relished it. Unpicking the past, pulling back layers of history and revealing people who had been lost in the midst of time.'

Louise stared past us out the kitchen window. 'But yes, he did eventually uncover what had happened to poor wee Florence Menzies. He researched her family tree and managed to trace relatives who had once lived here but since moved to Inverness.' She gave a decisive nod. 'That was when he uncovered the fact that the vase had been stolen from here, and that Florence was blamed for taking it.' She sighed. 'The wee lass had protested her innocence right from the start.'

Evan tutted under his breath. 'Like my mum and dad said, I guess, as a family we buried it in the past and didn't want to talk about it. No wonder.'

I examined him next to me. His deep, dark, pensive stare shone back.

'It's a pity Florence's relatives couldn't have done more,' I chipped in, pulling my attention away from Evan.

'None of the Menzies family has lived here for donkey's years. And even if they had tried to say something, who would have believed them? A well-heeled couple who owned this house, or poor working-class members of the community?' Louise clicked her tongue. 'The Lords did a very impressive job of keeping everything hushed up. Apologies, Evan.'

'None taken. From what Dad has said about Blanche

and Jeremy Lord, they made Bellatrix and Voldemort look like Tom and Jerry.'

I laughed despite the seriousness of it.

Louise gestured around at the shiny copper saucepans, the vase of lavender heather on the windowsill and the woodland spread outside like an emerald sea. 'This is such a gorgeous house and has so many tales to tell. They should all be told, even the not-so-happy ones.'

She turned back to Evan and me. 'As you'll have seen from the journal I gave you about Florence, my father was a copious notetaker. When my mother passed away, I took ownership of all his journals. If there's any other information in them about Florence or your great-grandparents, I'll find it for you.'

'Thank you,' said Evan. He moved around the breakfast bar and gave her a fierce hug. She coloured up.

'When I go home tonight, I'll see what else I can find. I've stashed all his journals in boxes under my stairs.'

That night, I climbed the stairs and was about to crank open my bedroom door when I noticed across the hallway that Evan's door was ajar.

He was concentrating on his laptop with his spectacles perched on the end of his aquiline nose.

His mobile rang, making me jump.

He took the call and proceeded to murmur and nod, tapping his pen on the edge of his desk. 'We need some good and fast marketing and promo for this, Hal.' He listened as the person at the other end replied.

'Great! I appreciate it. It's a story that needs to be told, and I'm not going to lie, if the tour does grow legs and take off, the revenue will go a long way in helping to keep The Ramblings afloat.'

There was another pause as the caller at the end of the line said something else.

'Yeah, I've just fired you off an email with some background information. Mum and Dad have been amazing, but they can't be expected to do all this on their own. They're both always up to their eyes in their own charitable work. I've been doing my bit, but you know what these old houses are like. They eat money.'

Evan fell quiet and listened. 'OK, cheers, mate. Speak to you soon, and please say hi to Livvie and the kids for me.'

I waited until Evan had wrapped up the call and popped his mobile back down on his writing desk before I rapped on the door.

'Hey. Come in. Have you recovered from your staircase escapade from earlier?' He tugged off his spectacles and trained his attention on me.

I tried to pull my emotions together as I took a couple more steps into his bedroom. 'Yes, thanks to you.'

Evan winked. 'Not all heroes wear capes. It was just lucky I was in the right place at the right time.'

My breath caught. He even had a sexy wink.

Through a chink in Evan's curtains, I caught a sliver of milky crescent moon and a toss of blinking stars like pieces of broken glass. 'You busy?' I asked, noting how this man managed to turn my insides into knots for the hundredth time.

'Yes, just spoke to a friend who runs his own public relations and marketing company. He owes me a favour.' Evan stood up and stretched. His T-shirt tightened against his chest.

I averted my eyes.

'He can help us promote the tour. He's very innovative.'

'That's good. That's just what we need!'

I loitered, glancing at Evan's silver laptop.

There was a crackling silence. 'I just bumped into Louise downstairs, who said she hasn't forgotten about looking at more of her late father's journals to see if there's anything else that might help us.'

'That'd be great.'

I pushed both hands into my sundress pockets. 'Ok then, well, goodnight, Evan.'

I turned and started to make my way back towards Evan's half-open bedroom door.

'Daisy. Wait.'

I turned. 'Yes? What is it?'

Evan studied me. A myriad of emotions crossed his face. 'What's going on here? Between us, I mean?'

My heart spun. Had I heard him properly? 'I… I…'

He took a couple more strides towards me. Outside, I could hear an owl hooting through the trees in the darkness.

'You know what I'm talking about, don't you?' He let out an agonised sigh. 'We can't keep dodging it;

pretending it's not there. That there's no attraction between us.'

I could feel myself sinking into deep water. I was struggling to keep myself afloat. My feelings were drifting away from me, and as for my commonsense, well, it was as if that had already sailed off towards the horizon, and I'd waved it goodbye.

'And yes, I did deliberately drive up to the woodland that day when Dane took you out.'

'Why?' I asked in a hushed voice.

'Why do you think?'

My heart thumped harder. My thoughts drifted to Sacha. 'And where does Sacha fit into all this?'

Evan studied me. 'What about her?' A teasing smile hinted at his lips. 'Wait. Are you jealous?'

'Don't be so ridiculous!' I scrambled for something to say. 'It's nothing to do with me if you're seeing her or not.'

Evan gave me a steady look. 'Then why mention her if you're not bothered?'

I moved to speak, but Evan cut in. 'Oh, and I'm not, by the way. Seeing her, I mean.'

I hated this. I didn't feel like I was in control of my thoughts whenever Evan was around. Or in control of anything else, for that matter. His words pinged in my head. 'But the other day,' I struggled. 'When you went out, all dressed up.'

Evan screwed up his eyes in thought. His face cleared. 'I wasn't going out with Sacha. I was off to meet up with one of my old journalism lecturers, Martin Campbell. I wanted his advice on a piece about dementia that I'm pitching to one of the national newspapers.' Evan eyed me. 'I've kept in touch with him ever since I graduated.'

Shame gripped me. Why did this man have the ability to turn me into a green-eyed, emotional goblin?

'I insisted on taking Martin and his wife Polly out for dinner, as it was his sixty-fifth birthday last week.'

I'd assumed wrong. I wanted to disappear into the floor. 'Right. I see. But, like I said, none of my business.'

I was still in his bedroom. It was like I was juggling fire. His expression was focused; intense. It was like there was nothing else in the world right now except for me. I was fighting not to mention Sacha again, but I couldn't help it. 'But the gig? Dane's gig? You left with her.'

Without saying a word, Evan took a couple more deliberate steps closer. I could make out the brush of his dark stubble. 'I'm surprised you noticed. You seemed too preoccupied with my baby brother to see what I was doing.'

I let out a shaky laugh. 'Now who sounds jealous?'

When Evan didn't respond, I wrapped my arms around myself as though it might offer some protection.

Finally, he spoke. 'Yes, ok. I did leave the gig with Sacha, but not for the reasons you might think.'

I trained my attention everywhere in his room but at him. From his open, whirring laptop to the long, swishy drapes at his bedroom window, and then to the Brentford FC mug sat on his writing desk. It was half-filled with cold coffee.

This was excruciating. It was like I had this wound, and

I couldn't stop myself from prodding it and aggravating it. Part of me wished that Evan, in his sharp, sophisticated suit, had never interfered that day with my exchanges with Fox so I wouldn't be in this situation right now.

Evan's rumbly voice dragged me back. 'If you must know, Sacha told me that night that she had an interesting lead on a story which she wanted to run past me, but as soon as we left the pub, she confessed she'd lied and there was no story.'

I had my suspicions about her motives but still asked the question. 'Why?'

'She admitted that she'd used it as a ruse. She wanted to give our relationship another go.'

I swallowed a weird-shaped lump back in my throat. 'Oh, I see.'

'No, Daisy. You don't see.' Evan moved even closer to me. I couldn't help but notice the sweep of his nose and the way his full lips were parted ever-so-slightly. 'She said she'd quit her job at the local radio station and move down to London to be with me.'

Something was trapping the breath in my chest. My emotions were a snake coiled around me in a vice-like grip. 'And what did you say?'

Evan shrugged. 'I told her the truth. We split up two years ago, and I've moved on.' He considered what he was going to say next. 'Yes, I was in love with her, and I was heartbroken when we parted ways, but all that's in the past now.' His eyes levelled with mine. 'She's in my past.'

My skittering emotions were like marbles dropped all

over the floor. I'd promised myself that I could handle Evan. My acting career would be my sole focus. I didn't need to be left with my heart shattered into a million pieces again, desperately trying to patch it up. Securing the acting roles I wanted was my only aim in life. I almost laughed as I turned all this over and over in my addled head. *And how is that working out for you, Daisy?*

I couldn't prevent the next question from flying out of my mouth at a rate of knots. 'Do you mind if I ask what happened between you and Sacha? Why did you break up?'

Evan's mouth hardened. 'Dane.'

I gasped. 'Dane? Sacha didn't sleep with him, did she?'

'No, but it looked like it could've headed that way. There were lots of flirty smiles and banter between the two of them. She changed whenever she was around him.'

'In what way?' I asked, puzzled as to how any woman would be tempted to cheat on someone like Evan. Yes, Dane was attractive, but he didn't have his older brother's presence or witty personality.

Evan flipped back his hair. 'Oh, she'd suddenly turn showy and loud whenever he was around, which wasn't her at all. I think she thought she was impressing him.' He smiled. 'I think, compared to my rocker younger brother, Sacha came to the conclusion that I was rather boring.'

'You're not boring!' I erupted. 'Far from it. I'm sorry to say this about Dane, but he does come across as rather self-absorbed.'

Evan flashed his white teeth. I noticed he had pronounced canines, which added to his wolfish exterior.

'There's no "comes across" about it. He is self-absorbed. I love him. He's my brother. But he can be a right feckless knob a lot of the time.' He gave a resigned shrug. 'I think Sacha sees that now. She realises she made a right mess of everything, and that's why she wanted us to start over.'

Along the upstairs landing, I could hear my grandpa fiddling around in his bedroom with the digital radio.

'And is that why you broke up? Because of her attraction to Dane?'

'It was one of the reasons, yes, but mainly because she was so ambitious. She got shortlisted for a news desk post at one of the tabloids in London and was all set to drop everything; drop me; forget our future together if she got the job.' He let out a small laugh. 'She got interviewed for it and was convinced the position was hers. Told me that she hoped I'd understand that she had to move on.'

'But she didn't get the job.'

'Nope. By that time I realised all the genuine love and affection was on my side – or at least had been. Kind of ironic that she's now saying she'd follow me to London to be with me after all that.'

Evan gazed down at me, a knowing look in his eyes as the sunshine slid down the staircase ahead of us. 'Is that why you've been dancing around me, Daisy? Why you've been so prickly? Because you thought I was involved with Sacha?'

'I haven't been prickly,' I managed, imprinting his gorgeous features onto my mind.

Evan cocked his head to one side.

'Yes. Ok. Maybe a little.'

The only sound thrumming in my ears was my rattling heart.

'That day when I carried you upstairs,' he began. 'I've got to be honest. I didn't want to let you go.' Evan's eyes were like melting, dark chocolate. 'I'm sick of trying to hide my feelings for you. That first day at the cream tea, I thought you were the loveliest, most feisty and most principled woman I'd ever laid eyes on.'

What? Wait. Did I just imagine him saying that?

My stomach was a sea of knots. I sucked in some air. What now? What should I do? What did I want to do?

Downstairs, I could hear feet clipping on the tiles as Louise bustled around. Upstairs and just a matter of feet away, behind his closed bedroom door, Grandpa was humming along to Andy Williams.

Without waiting for my reply, Evan lifted one finger and tilted my chin up so I was staring into his face.

I knew I was ignoring my own advice. I was discarding everything I'd promised myself I wouldn't do: that I wouldn't fall for someone else. That I wouldn't put myself out there to be hurt again. That I'd protect myself; protect my heart.

But right now, in this glorious stately home with its creaking floorboards, gilt-framed portraits and shimmering woodland, I knew what I wanted right now without any shadow of a doubt.

I wanted Evan.

I didn't make any attempt to move away as Evan glided

one finger down the side of my face. The wait for him to kiss me was agonising. Every movement seemed considered and deliberate. It was as if he knew I was burning up inside with anticipation. His lips moved closer to mine. I wanted to snatch his face and taste him over and over.

'Don't keep trying to deny you feel the same way, Daisy. I can see it in your eyes whenever you look at me.' His hand caressed my hair.

'Evan,' I stumbled.

But I didn't say anything else. When our lips gently met, my legs performed a little tremble of anticipation.

His kisses were soft at first, like butterfly wings, searching me out and savouring me for the first time. But after a few more moments, our mouths wanted more.

Our kisses became greedier, with a growing ferocity. Urgency tore through us as Evan slid his hand up to my hair and laced his fingers in it.

I caressed his back as we pushed ourselves against each other. I could feel his muscles and sinews; the cuts and angles of him from every glorious direction. Our bodies moulded together as though they were one. Every contour of each of us, fitted together in perfect harmony. This was exhilarating. Leon had never made me feel like my world was tipping on its axis. I'd loved him. I'd been in love with him. But this rampaging feeling of wanting someone so badly was running amok in my chest. It was out of control. I'd never experienced this passionate urgency before.

I'd never known a kiss or feeling like it. Everything was

slipping away, twisting and dancing around me, and I couldn't get a grasp on reality.

A growl escaped from the base of Evan's throat. Our kisses were harder and more insistent.

'Evan? Son? You around at the moment?' Bennett's voice shot up from the great hall, tearing us apart.

'Oh, for Christ's sake!' groaned Evan against my mouth.

I stifled a laugh.

Evan smoothed his T-shirt. 'What is it, Dad? I'm upstairs.'

'What are you up to?'

'None of your business,' murmured Evan, reaching for me and planting another kiss on my tingling lips. I grinned against his mouth.

'It's just, I'm having problems with that bloody PC again. Could you come and take a quick look for your old man please?'

Evan contorted his face, which made me laugh. 'Dad, can't you switch it off and switch it back on again?'

Bennett's reply was brimming with frustration. 'I've already done that, and it didn't make any difference. The screen keeps freezing.'

Evan slid his arm around my waist and groaned into my hair. 'My father has immaculate timing.'

I reached up and delivered a slow, sensual kiss to Evan's mouth. Then I tapped the end of his nose. 'Go. He sounds desperate.'

Evan gave me a long look that caused my stomach to somersault like a circus act. 'He's not the only one.'

I playfully raised my hand and ushered him away. 'I'm sure you can contain yourself for now. Now go, please, and help your dad.'

'Ok. Ok. I'm going. But I promise you, Ms Madden, we will be continuing from where we left off, later.' He gave me a lingering look. 'Sacha made me wary of wanting to get involved with anyone again, and then you came along and turned my well-ordered world upside down.'

Me with Leon. Evan with Sacha. We both had relationship ghosts from our past who had been haunting us; holding us back from moving on. They'd made us apprehensive in case we made the same mistake again; loving someone who didn't deserve our love.

But now, both of us had been brave and taken that step towards the future.

Evan darted back, seized my face in his hands again and planted another passionate kiss on my lips before leaving.

I returned to my room, closed the door behind me and almost slid down against the wall in delirium.

Chapter Twenty-Two

The next couple of days were a blissful, heady blur of stealing kisses with Evan, having Cayla and her parents over for dinner to discuss her assuming the role of Florence for the tour and then following up with press and marketing for it.

The first tour would be taking place on the sixth of June, which was only a few days away now, meaning all loose ends had to be tied up and finalised; social media accounts updated, press coverage in place, costume fittings booked in with Mindy Dalziel, a dressmaker and long-time friend of Alison's, and the finalised script tweaked.

Louise had managed to lay her hands on a second journal that Montgomery had written about Florence and her family. From the extensive research he had undertaken, it was clear to see that Florence had come from a struggling but loving and hard-working family, and when she'd died, a part of them had died with her.

Her parents, Eliza and Hugh, had worked in service too, and that was how Florence had come by the piano tutor, Constance Miller, who had seen promise in Florence and had taken it upon herself to teach the young girl to read and write.

The more I read about Florence and her family, the more I was determined to show her for who she was, and I knew Cayla would do her justice.

Evan and I worked well together in between stolen, intimate moments.

We'd laugh, teasing each other about how we met, and Evan said he'd never been more grateful to a glass of champagne. I just wanted to savour every minute with him. We would both be heading back to London at some point soon, but I didn't want to get heavy and start mentioning the future.

What I did know was that misunderstandings and lack of communication could have torn us apart if we hadn't chosen to listen to one another.

Did we have a future together? I hoped so. Whenever his fingers glided over my skin and he pinned me to the spot with his serious, dark eyes, I knew I'd abandoned my common sense by falling for him, but I didn't care. We hadn't been able to take things further, and there always seemed to be someone around, but in a way, it added to the romance and thrill of it all.

I'd opened my heart to him – I'd banished my reservations over being hurt again and allowed myself to trust him – and it felt wonderful! It made my heart sing to know that I'd been the one to banish the pain Sacha had caused Evan from his life.

Leon's treatment of me and his deception had dissolved in my past. Evan wasn't Leon. He never would be, thank goodness. But this ... this felt like I'd finally managed to turn the page on what had happened with Leon and move on.

With Evan, I knew I was defenceless, and that was ok. In fact, it felt more than ok. It felt as though I was being spun around and around on some glorious fairground ride, and I never wanted to jump off.

Who would have thought that me almost soaking Fox with champagne would have led to this?

Alison and Bennett confirmed that the dressmaker, Mindy, was also an active member of the local theatrical group, The Forrest Bank Players. They put on frequent productions – everything from *Wuthering Heights* to *The Importance of Being Earnest* – and Mindy had confirmed that she and a couple of her staff at her dressmakers, Stitched Up, were making great progress on the tour costumes. Apparently they had a generous stash of outfits that would just require some tinkering and fitting.

Josie too had offered her services, saying she would be more than happy to provide assistance with rehearsals. Mindy even suggested a couple of other members of the theatrical group who she felt would be ideal to play Bennett's great-grandparents.

Then there was the piano teacher, Constance Miller, who

had taught Florence to read and write. Who could play that part?

When I'd knitted my eyebrows together over this conundrum, Evan had laughed and pointed right at me. Stage fright at the prospect had gripped me. Could I do it? Fox's review had bashed my confidence, and not having any other acting roles lined up at the moment wasn't helping. I'd been involved with writing the script, but could I perform in it too? I thought about what I had said to Cayla about feeling the fear and doing it. In the end, my love of acting overrode my apprehension, so not only was I assisting on the final details of the script and helping with any admin, I also had a role to play. I was loving the chaotic excitement of it all.

I think the creative mayhem was just what I needed.

Everything was beginning to slot together.

Alison and Bennett had discussed ticket prices for the tour and decided that eight pounds each seemed to be a reasonable amount. 'I think that's fair,' mused Alison.

Bennett had nodded his thatch of sideswept greying hair. 'We don't want to appear greedy, but we have to make a profit for this place. That's one of the reasons why we're doing it.'

Grandpa, meanwhile, while the rest of us were knee-deep in final arrangements, was hitting it off big time with Louise.

She kept plying him with endless cups of tea and slices of the latest cake she'd baked. I knew I'd have real problems getting him to leave The Ramblings when the time came, even though we'd been notified by the council that the area on which his cottage was built had now been assessed and was risk free!

In the meantime, Evan and I continued to push on with putting the finishing touches to the script.

We were out in the gardens, snuggled up together on a fringed, tartan rug. Evan had his laptop perched on his lap, and I was cosied up beside him, my face tilting upwards at the cloudless, baby blue sky.

The silvery waterfall tinkled in the background.

I leant across him and pointed my pen at the screen. I was about to make a comment about chasing up the local press, just to confirm that they were able to give it some coverage, as well as the local radio station (even though Sacha worked there) when I heard Evan breathe into my hair. 'You smell delicious. Like almonds and sunshine.'

I grinned. 'You need to keep your mind on the matter at hand.'

Evan broke into a mischievous grin. 'I like it when you're bossy. It's very sexy.'

I shivered with anticipation as Evan's hand moved to caress my thigh under my yellow printed sundress. 'You're driving me crazy,' groaned Evan, lifting one hand, balling it into a fist and pretending to bite it.

I slapped his hand and laughed. 'Stop that! Your mum and dad might see.'

'I can't help it. I want you.'

'Me too,' I answered, appreciating how delectable he

was. 'But I thought as it was early days, we agreed we'd keep us low-key for now.'

We'd been stealing precious moments together over the last couple of days – inflamed kisses, squeezing of hands when no one was looking, stroking the other's back when we walked past one another, hot looks across the upstairs hallway. But that was it. Any time we'd wanted to rip each other's clothes off, there was always a reason we couldn't.

'Yeah, I know, but you in that dress is doing nothing for my blood pressure,' complained Evan.

'Well, we can't exactly get down to it on the lawn.'

'Now there's an idea,' glinted Evan.

I shuffled to get more comfortable and stroked his bare arm in his T-shirt. 'We've always got company. If it's not Louise rattling her copper pans in the kitchen…'

'Is that a euphemism?' joked Evan.

I gave him a nudge in the ribs. 'Or it's my grandpa drinking endless cups of tea and inspecting your mum's flower beds.'

'And then there's my parents,' chipped in Evan, squinting at his laptop screen.

'Well, it is their house.' I tapped him on the nose.

At that moment, Alison, Bennett, Louise and Grandpa emerged from around the side of the house. 'Hello, you two!' called Bennet in his usual jovial manner.

We sprung apart like two guilty teenagers.

'Thought we'd pop up to the shops,' explained Alison, looking effervescent in her ankle-length, lilac, maxi dress and matching cardigan. 'Drop in and see Mindy in Stitched Up! Check out the costumes.'

'And then we thought we'd grab some lunch,' piped up Bennett from behind his sunglasses. 'Care to tag along, both of you?'

Evan muttered out of the corner of his mouth, 'We'll be alone. They're all going out.' He gave my hand a long, slow stroke, and I swallowed a gulp of excitement. 'No, it's ok, Mum. Thanks anyway, but Daisy and I want to push on with the tour stuff.'

'Are you sure?' asked Grandpa. 'You should both take a break.'

'We're fine,' I smiled back. 'Thanks anyway. You all go and enjoy yourselves.'

'There's some bits and pieces in the fridge you can use up for lunch,' said Louise. She smoothed down her blue and white, floral-print skirt. 'Pâté, fresh bread, cheese, some salad, cucumber…'

'Thanks,' nodded Evan. 'I'm sure we won't starve. Oh, where's Dane?'

'Just headed off to band practice,' said Alison. 'Said he won't be back till around dinner time.'

'Coast is clear,' whispered Evan to me. He mocked a salute to them all. 'See you guys later. Have fun.'

We watched Louise hook arms with my grandfather and vanish back around the corner, their cacophony of chatter and feet on the gravel heralding their leave.

As soon as Bennett's Mercedes disappeared out of The Ramblings gates, Evan took one hand and traced it along my jaw line. He lent in for a kiss, and I reciprocated, savouring the taste of him.

This still didn't seem real. My head was cartwheeling with happiness. Days ago, I'd been stressed over no acting jobs and chiding myself for falling for Evan.

Now, I was bursting with anticipation amongst these shiny, emerald lawns. Cayla had agreed to portray Florence on the tour, and I was falling for this wonderful, intelligent, handsome man. My life was turning a corner at last.

Without saying a word, Evan took my hand and pulled me to my feet. We stood there together in the sunshine. 'Come on.'

I could feel the sunlight glancing through the material of my dress as he led me across the lawns and back into his family home.

Every emotion sizzled through me.

The loaded glances Evan kept delivering over at me sent my stomach spiralling to the ground.

We clattered through the side door, into the kitchen and out into the great hall. My breath was ragged with excitement.

The grand, white staircase sat in front of us. Evan swept me off my feet and up into his arms. I let out a squeal of surprise and wrapped my arms around his neck.

'Bring back any memories?' he teased, cradling me in his arms as he strode upstairs towards his bedroom.

'Maybe,' I grinned, wanting to imprint every second onto my memory. The way Evan was holding me against his chest; the smell of his skin; the shine of his blueberry hair. He'd rescued me from myself and brought so much happiness and fun back into my life. At first, I'd thought he was a bit of a stuffed shirt, but he'd opened up to me and let me in. That had made me fall for him even more.

Was I imagining all of this? Perhaps I was dreaming it, and all this wonderful experience was happening to someone else?

I squeezed my eyes shut for a few seconds. Nope. I was still wrapped in this amazing man's arms, about to go to bed with him for the first time.

We reached the top of the stairs, and Evan proceeded to transport me past the portraits of his ancestors and the ornate wall lamps, along to his closed bedroom door.

The look he gave me as he delivered one bold kick to his bedroom door to open it made me gasp.

He laid me down on top of his queen-sized bed and grinned wolfishly. 'Don't you move.'

Evan closed his curtains, returned to his bedroom door and locked it. Then he turned and waggled his eyebrows.

I giggled and propped myself up on one elbow. 'Aren't we supposed to be working on the final arrangements for the tour?'

'Everybody needs a break now and again.'

Evan returned to the bed and playfully climbed on top of me. I was underneath him, wriggling with desire. My heart was skipping in my chest.

He leant down and kissed me. The serious fullness of his mouth was intoxicating. God, I wanted him so much it hurt.

I wanted to feel Evan's body against mine, fitting together like the pieces of a jigsaw.

The prospect of making love to Evan and appreciating every inch of him was making my belly ache with longing.

As I gazed up into Evan's chiselled face and ran a finger over his stubbly jaw, Leon didn't exist anymore. Nobody did. With just the birds chattering in the trees outside his bedroom window and the lunchtime sunshine lighting up the closed curtains, it was as if Evan and I were the only people in the world. I was falling in love with him. I trusted him.

We undressed each other slowly and deliberately, our fingers fumbling and brushing against each other.

And as we made love, tumbling around on the bed covers, I knew I couldn't feel any happier and more wanted than I did right now.

'A drink, Ms Madden?'

I nestled my head against Evan's bare chest with its irresistible, coarse dark hair.

His bedsheets were pooled around us, and the lazy afternoon sun was fighting to get through his closed curtains. He whispered into my hair. 'I think we should have champagne. After all, that's what brought us together.' Evan lifted a finger and traced it down my spine, making me shiver with delight.

'A glass would be lovely. Thank you.'

Evan dropped his head and delivered a slow, deliberate kiss to my mouth before getting up to tug his T-shirt and boxers back on. His naked body was sinewy and toned, just as I'd imagined it in my mind.

'Won't be long.'

I returned his dreamy, wide smile and sank back against the pillows. I found myself grinning like an idiot up at the corniced bedroom ceiling. Was it wrong to be so happy? Was I risking a major letdown feeling like this? Allowing my emotions to bubble and spill over? If it was, I couldn't help it. It was as if I were playing a part in some romantic drama, and at any moment the director would holler, 'Cut!' and I'd be dragged back to reality with a fierce bump.

From downstairs, I could hear him clinking champagne glasses in the kitchen and singing to himself. He sounded like I felt: lighter and bubbling with happiness.

I pushed myself upright in bed. It was as though this old house was savouring the moment too. Everything looked golden and brimming with promise. I strained my ears and beamed. Evan was belting out 'Universe' by Coldplay.

I heaved a contented sigh and swung my legs out of bed. Evan had tossed my yellow sundress over the chair in the far corner. I recalled the way his charged eyes had taken in the length of me, and how his fingers had dismissed my dress.

I padded over, scooped it up and slid it back over my head. My skin and lips still carried the delicious taste of him.

I caught sight of myself in his ensuite bathroom mirror

when I dived in there for a pee. My loose hair was tumbling around my face and down past my shoulders in dishevelled waves. My eyes shone back at me, knowing and silvery grey. Even my cheeks sang with a pretty, pink blush.

I washed my hands, tried to make myself look more presentable and returned back to the bedroom.

'Don't know about you, but I'm hungry,' called up Evan from the bottom of the stairs. 'I'll pop a couple of almond croissants in the oven.'

I twirled the hem of my dress as though I were some princess in a fairytale. 'Sounds good.'

It was as I returned to flop back down on top of the bed that I noticed Evan's laptop sitting on his writing desk. It was open and plugged in, making a soft whirring sound. It pinged, signalling the arrival of an email.

I tucked a couple of loose hairs back behind my ears, paying little attention to the screen at first. It was the mention of Fox that I noticed in the email which made me draw up, almost cricking my neck.

What? What was that?

My curiosity on fire, I approached the laptop as though it might take a bite out of me.

My eyes and brain struggled to process what I was reading.

Hi Evan.

Hope life is treating you well!

The old man is pushing for next week's copy for your Fox column. Not like you to be late turning it in!

Anyway, your trademark stinging, pithy comments and louche asides as usual, please, on the three TV shows as discussed.

Get that copy in sharpish! He's in one of his moods!

Hope to catch up soon when you're back in London for a pint or three.

Best,
Robin.

My insides froze.

What?

I'd misunderstood.

I forced myself to read over the email again, slower this time.

But it didn't change the meaning. It didn't change anything.

Was this some sort of twisted joke? A mistake?

No, it wasn't a mistake.

My eyes were locked onto the screen.

With my dress flapping around my knees and the noise of a jolly Evan clanging around in the kitchen, I grabbed onto the back of his leather chair in case my knees gave way.

My insides turned to concrete. Everything was shifting in front of my eyes.

That loud-mouth at the party; how he'd been talking

about *Sinister,* in the same way as Fox. How Evan had jumped in and stopped me from doing something I would have regretted later.

That bolshy ignoramus. I'd assumed he was Fox … I'd said that to Evan, and he hadn't contradicted me.

Oh God.

I stared at my stricken face in Evan's floor-to-ceiling mirror across the bedroom.

I'd got it all wrong. That man at the party hadn't been Fox.

Evan was.

Chapter Twenty-Three

My limbs were rigid; my feet stuck to the carpet like they were trapped in mud.

Just about to leave the kitchen and return upstairs with our champagne and croissants, Evan called up cheerily, 'I'm on my way.'

This was like some warped dream. Evan was Fox. Fox was Evan.

I rubbed at my bare arms so hard I was in danger of removing a layer of skin.

I'd fallen for him. Hard. The man who had criticised the high-profile TV drama I'd been in. The man who had all but sabotaged my chances of securing another significant role in the near future. And I'd just gone to bed with him.

Evan had played me. He'd kept his secrets tucked away. He'd let me think he was someone else. Was his story about Sacha just a ruse to get me into bed? Or had he asked me to stay here because he felt sorry about his scathing review of *Sinister*? Was he trying to assuage his guilt?

Pain and anger swirled through me. My wild eyes gawped back at me from the mirror. Part of my brain was telling me I'd misread the situation. Perhaps I'd got the gist of the email wrong?

But as my attention drilled into the email and I read it over yet again, the words blurring in front of my eyes, I knew I hadn't imagined it or misunderstood. The facts were glaring at me from the illuminated screen.

I stumbled away from Evan's laptop and sank onto the corner of the bed. What now? Had Evan been playing some twisted game with me? Making me think he had feelings for me?

My head was stuffed with questions. My fists balled in anger in my lap. I swallowed back tears. I wanted to scream and cry and throw that bloody laptop across the room. I wanted to watch it crash and splinter, just like my heart was doing right now.

What should I do?

I couldn't look him in the face. I didn't want to. Evan wasn't who I thought he was. Literally.

'Croissants and champagne, just for you!' Evan burst in, angling the tray in his arms. He'd even slipped a single red rose in a vase onto the tray. Talk about adding insult to injury.

I leapt up from the bed, clamping my arms around myself like a protective barrier.

He set down the loaded tray on top of his writing desk.

The golden champagne popped in two flutes, and the warm, almond scent of the croissants drifted towards me.

I watched as Evan reached for the long-stemmed red rose. 'This is for you.' He proffered it towards me, but I shrank away from it as though it were something hideous.

'You ok? What is it? You look pale.'

My heart was cracking in my chest. He was standing there, clutching the rose, looking irresistible. 'You just got an email,' I croaked. 'From someone called Robin.' I let my words hang there for a moment. 'Seems like you're late turning your Fox copy in for next week's column.'

He suddenly looked desperate. Evan's expression collapsed. 'Oh shit.' He lowered the rose. His troubled eyes never left me. 'Daisy. I wanted to tell you myself. Jesus, I didn't want you to find out like this.' He scratched his stubble. 'Nobody knows. I mean, not my family.'

So it was true. A tiny part of me had still been wishing I'd hallucinated it, or that the email had been sent to the wrong person. 'And that's supposed to make it ok?'

'Of course not.'

I flung a disgusted look at the champagne glasses, the buttery croissants and the rose Evan was still holding. In slow motion, he slid it back into the vase.

'So, what was that, Evan? Or do I call you Fox? Was it a sympathy shag?' I was fighting with every breath to speak.

'What? No! Of course not! You really think I'd do something like that?'

He took a couple of steps towards me, but I put up one hand. 'Don't.' My lips wobbled.

Evan swallowed.

'So, what was it then?' Tears sprung out of my eyes. 'Was it a joke to you? A bet maybe?'

'It wasn't any of those things.' His voice was imploring. 'I didn't recognise you at the party. I didn't know who you were until you told me. I mean, you wore that blonde bobbed wig in *Sinister*.'

'Yes, I know I did. You don't have to remind me.'

Evan hauled a frustrated hand down his stubbly face. 'Like I just told you, I thought you were gorgeous the first time I saw you at the birthday lunch. Then on our road trip back to Scotland I became more and more fascinated by you.' His face was pale and beseeching. 'When you told me who you were, yes, I admit I felt awful about what I'd written. I could see what effect it'd had on you, and I hated myself.' His voice was growing more and more impassioned. 'But that had nothing to do with what happened between us just now. As I got to know you more, I knew I was beginning to fall for you.'

I shook my head. 'If you keep telling yourself that often enough, you might start to believe it.'

'It's true.' He raised his eyes to his bedroom ceiling. 'You've been driving me to distraction, Daisy. When I realised who you were, I felt rotten about what I'd said – what Fox had said – about the TV series you were in. And then I got to know you, and by then...'

'By then what?'

'By then, I wanted to tell you who I really was, but I just couldn't do it.' He dropped his head to the carpet. 'I was on the brink a couple of times, but in the end, I didn't have the guts. I was terrified you'd hate me.'

I was struggling to stop the lump in my throat. 'I don't hate you.' My chest ached. 'I hate myself. I hate me for allowing myself to get used like this.'

'I didn't use you, Daisy. Please believe that.' Evan's voice was heavy and dark. 'You've got it wrong. You have no idea how I feel about you. When I thought you were interested in Dane, and I saw him flirting with you, it was like a punch to the gut.' He looked like his emotions were tumbling down around him, swamping him, and he couldn't get his head above water. Mine had already done that.

'That's why I seemed a bit distracted or off sometimes, and I didn't mean to be,' he said. 'I was carrying this guilt around with me about being Fox, and you were here, being so lovely, considerate and kind, and that made me feel like even more of a bastard.'

My voice was confused and strangulated. 'That idiot at the lunch; the one I thought was Fox.'

'I think he was trying to impress the girl in the red dress. I overheard her saying she wanted to be a film critic.' Evan looked pained. 'He kept trying to catch her eye, and I think he thought somehow that being a bullish, loud-mouthed sod and pretending to be Fox might work.'

My head was struggling to process any of this.

'Daisy, hear me out. Please. I know I've cocked everything up, but I know how I feel about you.'

But I wasn't listening. I was already pushing past him,

my sundress clinging to me and my mind reeling. 'I'll stay on just long enough to help get the first tour event up and running. I promised I would.' My head was spinning. 'Thank goodness it's only a few more days. Then Grandpa and I will be gone. And do you know what? I can't wait.'

I wheeled away and across the upstairs landing towards my bedroom. 'I'm not letting down your parents or Cayla. They don't deserve that, even though you've proven yourself to be an utter bastard.' I let out a dry laugh. 'And to think you have the audacity to call Dane self-absorbed.'

I dashed away a couple of tears with the back of my hand.

I wanted to let them course down my face and scream with frustration at how stupid I'd been. How could I have let things get to this point? I knew I should never have let my heart rule my head. Hadn't Leon taught me anything? I'd been so blinded by Evan that I didn't think for one second that he'd deceive me the way Leon had. I would never have imagined Evan capable. I bit my bottom lip to try and stop myself from dissolving into a torrent of tears.

Evan lingered a few feet away from me looking wretched.

All I wanted to do was lock the door, crawl under the bedcovers and mentally torture myself as to how I could have been so naïve. 'At least Dane doesn't try to pretend to be something he isn't.'

I grabbed the handle of my bedroom door, yanked it open and stepped inside. I banged it closed behind me. I could hear Evan calling my name from the other side, desperation in his voice. 'I deserve this and more, Daisy. But you have to believe me. I've fallen for you. Please. Open the door.'

I was emotionally spent. Hollowed out.

Evan had made me think he was someone else, when all the time he was Fox.

I threw myself on top of my bed.

Evan called out to me again. 'Daisy. Please. Let me in. Just hear me out.'

'Go away,' I choked. 'I don't want to speak to you.'

After a few more moments, I heard his dejected feet moving away back to his own room and him clicking the door closed.

That was when the torrent of tears broke through.

And as I lay on the bed, curled up with my fists bawled into my streaming eyes, I wished I had never met Evan.

———

'It's such a mess,' I sobbed down the phone to a stunned Jade an hour later.

'What is, Daisy? What's going on?'

I swallowed and wriggled upright on top of the bed. 'It's Evan.'

'What about him?'

My brain kept replaying us laughing together in bed. It was torture. My voice shook. 'He's not who I thought he was. I mean, he is Evan Lord, but...'

'Sweetheart, you're not making any sense.'

I could see the early June sunshine out of the bedroom window, casting its golden hue over the tops of the trees. Everything looked like it had been brushed with rose gold, from the leaves and breeze-whispered lawns to the towering hedgerows. It was such a beautiful late afternoon, and yet I felt like my insides had been shredded. I was so stupid.

'Daisy, talk to me.'

'Evan is Fox.'

The shocked silence from Jade down the line made me wonder if she'd been cut off. 'Are you kidding?'

'I wish I was.'

'But how do you know? I mean, did Evan tell you that?'

My insides twisted. 'No. I saw an email on his laptop from a colleague at the newspaper asking when their editor could expect his latest column – Fox's latest column – to be submitted.'

I flopped my head back against the pillows. 'So I asked him about it, and he confessed. Said he'd been planning to tell me, but he'd fallen for me and just couldn't bring himself to do it.'

Hurt swirled around inside me again. 'He's probably been laughing about this behind my back.'

'I don't think he would have been doing that,' said Jade. 'Didn't you just say he'd told you that he'd fallen for you?'

I rubbed my red nose. 'Yes, but I don't believe him. Well, I did, but not anymore. How can I after this? Jade, he publicly mauled the TV series I was in. His words have ruined acting careers.'

I was fighting to forget the way I felt when he grinned at me; how my body had responded to his. I wanted to banish the memories of the chocolate swirls in his dark eyes. I pushed my mobile closer to my ear. I cleared my throat. 'There's something else.'

'What?'

I didn't want to say the words aloud, because I knew it would make the bliss of earlier haunt me again. 'We slept together this afternoon. For the first time.'

Jade sighed. 'Oh, honey.'

My chest was rising and falling harder. 'It was wonderful. I was so happy. And then I saw that email, and everything came crashing down.'

Jade tutted. 'Right. So, when are you going to leave that house? Have you started packing your things?'

I pushed around my hair for something to do. I'd been mulling all this over for the past hour. The sensible thing to do would be to pack, tell Grandpa to do the same and drive us straight back to Strath Ross.

In all honesty, that was what my common sense was screaming at me to do.

But then there was Alison, Bennett and Cayla. I couldn't let them down. I couldn't just walk away. The Lords had been wonderful to me, and there was no way I could leave Cayla when I'd told her to return to her acting and not give up. I'd be such a hypocrite if I did.

Cayla had agreed to portray Florence and was putting herself out there because of what I'd said to her and my faith in her. How could I abandon her now when she was on the verge of making her debut?

No.

It wouldn't be for much longer. Just a few more days.

I could do it.

I'd acted opposite some right rude cretins in my time and been stuck with them for hours on end. The Ramblings was a big, old house. I would just make sure I avoided Evan and concentrated on what I had to do. 'I'm not leaving The Ramblings,' I blurted. 'At least not yet.'

'But how can you stay there after what you just told me?'

'Because I have to,' I said, trying not to think too much about what I was doing. 'It's only for a few more days. I'll just keep myself to myself where Evan is concerned, and as soon as the first Florence tour is over, Grandpa and I will be out that door.'

'But I thought you told me before that you and Evan had been working closely together on this.'

'Yes, we have been, but thank goodness most of the work is done now. It's just a case of tying up any loose ends and a few more rehearsals.'

'What are you going to tell your grandpa?' asked Jade.

Despite feeling like I'd been chewed and spat out a hundred times, I managed a short laugh. 'Grandpa would be challenging Evan to a duel at dawn tomorrow morning on The Ramblings lawns, so I'm not telling him anything until we leave.'

Cayla shimmered into my mind again. 'I'll stay and see

the first guided tour performance out.' A lump balled in my throat. 'Then I'm leaving here, and I won't be setting eyes on Evan – or Fox – ever again.'

I had dinner that evening in my room.

I couldn't face the prospect of sitting across the table from Evan.

Pretending to have a migraine, I stayed cocooned upstairs, and Louise insisted on bringing me up a tray of fish pie and vegetables while describing what a lovely afternoon she, Grandpa, Alison and Bennett had had at the pancake emporium. She was brimming with excitement too about the outfits that were having their final touches done by Mindy at Stitched Up! 'You're all going to look so authentic,' she gushed.

Once I'd thanked Louise for delivering my dinner to me, I made an attempt to eat some of the fluffy golden fish pie topped with potato and served with broccoli, but the food clogged up my throat. I pushed the tray away from me and took a sip of water.

Evan was Fox.

Every time I thought about it, my heart plummeted to the ground.

Feigning weariness after my migraine, I decided to have an early night.

I'd just finished brushing my teeth and had changed into

my dressing gown when I heard a soft knock on the door. 'Are you alright, lass?'

I opened the door and beckoned my grandpa in. 'Yes, I'm fine,' I lied. 'Don't worry. I think it's just overwork and a little too much sun today.'

He narrowed his eyes at me, but I just bent down and bestowed a kiss on his bristly cheek.

'An early night will do the trick.'

'Are you sure you're telling me everything, Daisy chain?'

Was I really that bad an actor after all? 'Of course I am. Now, stop worrying and go and relax. Sleep well, and see you in the morning.'

He loitered a few more moments, concern in his eyes. 'Och, ok, but you know you can talk to me. You always can.'

'I know.'

I hugged him and ushered him out of the bedroom.

I clicked the door closed behind him. I felt guilty for not being honest with him, but things would be awkward enough over the next three days without my grandpa throwing himself into the mix.

I stood by the bed and was about to remove my dressing gown and jump into bed when there was another rap on the door.

I tugged it open. 'Grandpa, I told you, I'm fine…'

It was Evan.

He examined me. 'Please, Daisy. Let me explain.'

I tightened my dressing gown around myself, covering

up my yellow, shorty short pyjamas. 'I've got nothing to say to you, Evan. Or should I say Fox. Or perhaps you have yet another identity I don't know about.'

He shook his head. 'No, I don't. Just that one.'

'Just that one?' I repeated with a stab of hurt. 'Just that one? The one that every actor fears? The one that mauled *Sinister* and my colleagues' performances? The one that's making me struggle to get another acting gig at the moment? Just that one?'

Evan looked wounded. 'Please, Daisy. I wanted to tell you. But it just got out of hand.'

'You mean I found you out.'

I gripped onto the edge of the door, willing myself not to get lost in his gaze. I dropped my voice. It was shaking with emotion. 'We made love this afternoon. You let me fall for you like an idiot, and all the time…'

Evan moved to speak, but I cut across him. 'I'm staying here with Grandpa until Saturday after the first tour performance is over, and then I'm gone.' I folded my arms. 'I'd really rather leave now and never set eyes on you again, but your parents have been amazing, and I'm supporting Cayla.'

'Daisy, this situation doesn't look good, I'll grant you, but me being Fox has nothing to do with us.'

'Of course it does,' I erupted. 'You didn't tell me. You let me rant on about him and the review, when all the time you were the one who'd written it!'

'Everything ok here?' Dane had appeared at the top of the staircase and was eyeing us both.

My eyes were glazed with temper and pain. 'Everything's fine,' I insisted.

'Didn't sound like it just now.'

'Evan was just going.'

Evan's jaw gritted.

'Goodnight,' I announced, closing my bedroom door with a decisive bang, leaving Dane and Evan on the landing.

Chapter Twenty-Four

I must have slipped into a tearful sleep, because a gentle knock on my bedroom door woke me from addled dreams.

Crumpled and disoriented, I squinted down at my watch.

I'd only been asleep for around half an hour, but it felt more like three days.

Tangerine light was pushing through my closed curtains, and the birdsong was lazy.

I rubbed my eyes and let out a groan. My head felt washed out.

There was another knock on the door.

Evan?

I lurched off the bed and recoiled at my appearance in the dressing table mirror. Evan's deception had squeezed the colour from me. My reflection reminded me of a gargoyle more at home jutting out from The Ramblings.

If it was Evan again, he could sod off, no matter how much he flashed those eyes at me or sweet-talked me in that husky rumble of his.

I yanked open the door, ready to hit Evan with a volley of home truths.

But it wasn't him.

It was Dane.

His Nordic good looks collapsed when he saw the state of me. 'Jesus.'

I sniffed and raked a hand through my hair. 'Thanks for the ego boost.'

'Sorry.' He hesitated. 'Can I come in?'

'I'm really not in the mood for company right now.'

'I can see that.'

'Look, Dane, I don't mean to be rude, but if you're just going to stand there and tell me what a fright I look, I already know.'

'I'm not.' His eyes softened. 'You look like you could be doing with a friend.'

My bottom lip trembled.

'I'm sorry I've behaved like a prize twat. You didn't deserve that.' His mouth broke into a gentle smile. 'Can I come in please, Daisy? Honestly, I'm a good listener when I'm not droning on about myself.'

'Ok. Thanks.'

I stood to one side, and Dane strode past me, all long blond hair and canvas trousers.

He sank into the chair at the dressing table and waited until I'd clicked the bedroom door shut and I'd dropped down on the edge of the bed. 'So, what's the beef between you and Captain America?'

I didn't want to dredge it all up again, and I certainly didn't want to cause a rift or any distrust in the Lord family. Evan told me none of them knew about him being Fox, and even though I was hurt and resentful, I wasn't malicious.

It wasn't up to me to tell his family. They should hear it from him.

I dropped my attention to the bedspread before looking back up at Dane's concerned face. 'I don't want to talk about it.'

'Look.' Dane leaned forward and twisted a couple of the ornate rings he wore around his fingers. I noticed that one was a Celtic cross and the other was of a thistle. 'I've never been known for my ability to read a room. I've tended to be more absorbed with myself than other people.'

I shuffled on top of the bed. I couldn't disagree with him on that one. From the moment I'd stepped into The Ramblings, Dane had reminded me of Narcissus: in love with himself, to the exclusion of everyone else, though charming and charismatic with it.

But as I watched him now, flashing me long looks and tapping his feet nervously in his canvas trainers, I realised he was a changed man to the one I'd met a few weeks ago.

He was pensive.

'Dane? What is it?' I asked.

He rubbed his peppering of blond stubble. 'I'm not known for being lost for words. I'm normally the mouthy, confident one. Hard to believe, I know.' Dane tossed back his hair and coughed. 'Christ, this is tough.'

'What is?'

He levelled his powder blue gaze at me. 'Like I said, I should've chosen a much better time, but now I'm here with you, I'm worried that if I don't seize the moment and say it now, I might not get another chance.'

He took a gulp of air. 'I like you, Daisy. I like you a lot.'

My eyes widened.

Grandpa had been right. He'd noticed Dane looking at me in a certain way and had commented on it, but I'd dismissed it.

Dane resumed talking. He was actually blushing. 'You aren't the usual sort of woman I meet. You're...' He flicked one ringed hand. 'You're special, Daisy. You made me look closely at myself. You think of other people. You're kind and caring, and you've got the most amazing eyes.'

I didn't know what to say or do. I looked everywhere around the room, finding the curtains swishing in the gentle evening breeze so fascinating. I was flattered. Very flattered. But...

The silence crackled.

'Can you say something?' joked Dane. 'You're giving me a complex.'

I shuffled forward on the bed, so that my feet were almost touching the carpet. 'I don't know what to say to you. I mean, I'm very flattered. You're a gorgeous guy, but...'

'But I'm not Evan.' His voice was resigned.

'No, that isn't what I was going to say. I was going to say that now is not the time.'

He appraised me with a sad but knowing look. 'You're in love with him, aren't you? My darling, big brother. The one who can do no wrong.'

If only you knew, I thought inwardly, my stomach clenching. I rubbed my arms. 'No. I'm not in love with him.' The words rang empty in my ears. If I was struggling to convince myself, how could I convince anyone else?

'Don't kid a kidder,' replied Dane with a resigned twinkle, stretching his legs out further. 'I hate to say it, but there's so much chemistry between you two, you could blow up an entire laboratory.'

Shame-faced at Dane pointing out the obvious, I watched him play around with a couple of his leather wristbands. He raised his eyes. 'You're something else, Daisy Madden, do you know that?'

I let out a self-conscious laugh. I was worried I'd burst into tears any moment now. Dane was being so lovely to me, and his kindness and attention were stirring up a huge pot of emotions. 'That's really sweet of you to say so.'

'It's true. You're selfless. Look at how you're trying to help Mum and Dad with this place. Not to mention that teenage girl who was having a crisis of confidence. Louise told me about that.'

He flicked me a toothy smile. 'When you first rocked up here, I thought you were just this cute little thing I could impress.' He paused. 'But then you gave me that mouthful –

and quite right, too – after our disastrous walk, and boy did you give me a verbal dressing down!'

'Sorry.'

'No, don't be, I needed them.' His mouth lifted. 'And then I saw first-hand you getting stuck into arrangements for the tour. Kind of ironic, really. I don't tend to have much trouble attracting the attention of women, and then the one girl I genuinely do like fancies my brother.'

He stood up. 'Like I said, you two definitely have the Romeo and Juliet vibe going on.'

He strode towards the door and opened it. He turned around and studied me from under his brows. 'Yep, karma I guess for the way I've treated girls over the years. Evan is one hell of a lucky guy.'

Then he was gone in a haze of streaming hair and rock T-shirt, leaving me feeling even more confused. Out of the two brothers, was Dane the good guy after all?

Chapter Twenty-Five

The next few days in the run-up to The Ramblings tour were a mad blur.

It was tiring, but throwing myself into assisting with final arrangements meant that I could temporarily forget about Evan being Fox.

Whenever my emotions crept up on me, promising to catch me off guard, I'd concentrate on helping Cayla learn her lines and practice mine again, or I'd involve myself in a final publicity push.

But even then, I'd keep thinking about the two of us in bed together, the whole situation and what I thought had been growing between us, which all now felt like a dream. It was as though I'd been duped.

Whenever I could, I found excuses to vanish up to my room or to leave The Ramblings for some solace.

Thankfully, Evan had been much busier with a couple of

new feature pitches and wasn't around anywhere near as much, which was a relief. I wasn't sure if that was deliberate or not, but it was for the best.

Dane, meanwhile, had made a few more attempts to get me to open up about what had happened between his brother and me, but I'd brushed him off.

'He's doing the same to me,' said Dane. 'I asked him what the score was between you two, but he told me it was none of my business and to butt out.'

I pinned on a strangulated smile. 'Don't waste your time. I'm not.'

The only good news was that sales of the tour tickets had been flying. Not only were intrigued locals snapping them up out of curiosity, but fascinated tourists were, too.

Dane had volunteered to deal with the online ticketing, as well as the social media side of things.

He'd set up impressive looking accounts on Facebook, Instagram, X and Tik-Tok, giving background details of The Ramblings history, including stunning photographs he'd taken of the estate, and then included a post I'd helped him write, giving an outline about Florence and her life.

Alison and Bennett had looked stunned when Dane had shown them what he'd been working on. 'Well, don't look so surprised,' he'd told their shocked expressions. 'This place is part of my life, too. It shouldn't just be up to you two to try and improve its future.'

Dane had offered me a conspiratorial smile.

Later that day, I'd been in the study, chatting to Alison

about the costumes and arrangements for final fittings ahead of the big day, when Evan had strolled in.

As soon as he saw me standing there, his expression changed.

I muttered to Alison that I'd forgotten to ring the local newspaper about coverage on the day and dashed out. It would be a relief when I could pack up and leave here with Grandpa.

Still, the momentum for the tour was rolling. We'd had a mention on the regional BBC Scottish News, Radio Scotland's Morning Show and the local radio station were being very supportive.

Not to be outdone, Grandpa had been delivering glossy posters designed by Dane to the local businesses to put in their shop windows, ably assisted by Louise.

The Ramblings was a cacophony of busy chatter, clattering laptop keys and ringing mobiles.

The older couple who were portraying Bennett's late great-grandparents, Mollie and Aubrey Fisher from the Forrest Bank Players, had been regular visitors, taking their roles very seriously and method acting for all they were worth. They would swan in, reciting their lines with Josie and drifting around the stately home like it had been theirs all along. They were driving Josie demented!

As for The Ramblings, she just remained her usual, glorious, majestic self.

Another costume fitting was underway in the drawing room, and I stood there while Mindy ensured the pinned waist of my button-up, high-collared gown was fitting properly. It was milk chocolate brown with a cameo brooch at the nape of my neck and fluttered down to the floor. Although it was very officious, it had an air of class about it which I loved.

I drew in a steadying breath and clasped one hand over my tummy.

Mindy looked up at me as she swooped this way and that, examining the dress from all angles. 'You've lost a little bit of weight, young lady. Please don't lose any more.'

It hadn't been intentional. It was just that, since finding out about Evan, I'd hardly been able to eat a thing.

'Still.' Maddie broke into an appreciative smile and stood back in her cropped jeans and capped sleeve T-shirt. Her sunglasses were still propped on top of her silver bobbed hair. 'You're the prettiest piano teacher I've ever seen. Most of them at that time were right hatchet-faced madams.'

I started to laugh, smoothing down the linen material of my dress.

Sensing someone's gaze, I stopped adjusting the cameo brooch at the base of my throat and looked up.

There was no one there.

I shook out the folds of my dress and strode over the tiled floor of the Great Hall in my lace-up ankle boots. It was as though I'd stepped back in time, and that I was indeed a strict but fair teacher, waiting for her students to arrive.

But instead of Edwardian children, I could see through the glass in the doors a long line of buzzing locals and tourists snaking away from The Ramblings front entrance, down the heavy stone steps and along the gravelled drive.

My stomach overflowed with a mixture of excitement and apprehension. This *had* to be a success.

The hem of my dress hissed across the floor as I moved.

Mindy, who'd trained as a hairdresser before becoming a dressmaker, had coiffed my hair into a classic Edwardian style. She'd put it into a half ponytail before pinning it up and backcombing it into a crown effect.

For Cayla, she'd combed her long, straight, strawberry blonde hair too before plaiting it into a French braid and securing it with a piece of cream satin ribbon.

As if on cue, Cayla clicked up behind me. She was decked out as Florence in a modest, fluted grey cotton dress down to the floor, with a starched white apron over the top of it. Even though the outfit was plain, she looked lovely; young and fresh-faced, with her shiny hair streaming down one side in its ribboned braid like a waterfall.

'Look at you,' I marvelled at her. 'How can you make such a plain dress look so wonderful?'

She blushed to the roots of her hair. 'Do I look stupid?'

'Of course you don't. This is what women wore then, and as you're playing Florence, you need to look the part.'

She laced and unlaced her fingers in front of her as the chatter from the public outside grew in volume. Cayla shot them a worried look. 'What if I forget my lines, Daisy? What if I freeze?'

I moved towards her and gave her a supportive hug. 'Then we'll help one another.'

She hugged me back. 'Thanks for being here for me.'

'I should be the one thanking you.'

She snorted. 'How do you work that one out?'

'I might have a bit more acting experience than you, but that Fox review...' My mind skittered to Evan and I blinked. 'It really drained my confidence, and I almost thought I'd never want to act again.' I flapped a hand. 'Ok, so this is hardly Broadway, but I'm getting back in the saddle, albeit slowly.'

Cayla glanced again towards The Ramblings main entrance doors, which were closed. Flashes of expectant faces could be seen through the glass.

She nodded at my dress. 'You really suit that colour. It looks great with your hair.' She paused. 'Where's Evan?'

I raised my chin. 'I've no idea. Why?'

'Oh, it's just I thought there might be something going on between you two.'

I fixed my attention on one of the urns of dry reeds in the corner of the hall. 'No. Not at all. What makes you say that?'

'Just a hunch,' she remarked lightly. 'Whenever I saw you two together, there was always this atmosphere. Like in a good, romantic way.'

Sadness and disappointment nipped at me, but I tried to disguise it.

'You've got a great imagination.'

Cayla offered me a gimlet, mature eye despite her teenage years. 'I didn't imagine any of it. You and Evan couldn't keep your eyes off one another.'

'You've been reading too many Ali Hazelwood novels.'

I steered the conversation away from Evan and towards how Alison and Bennett had transformed The Ramblings for the tour. Any hint of modern-day furniture or fittings had been stowed away, and in its place were reflections of the 1900s; walnut furniture and quilted chairs had been dotted around the hallway space.

'All set then?' grinned Grandpa, emerging from the direction of the kitchen and looking dapper in his best brown, checked suit.

'No,' half-joked Cayla, planting one nervous hand on her stomach.

'You'll be fine,' assured Grandpa. 'You've got my wonderful granddaughter here to keep you right.'

I rolled my eyes. 'Grandpa, Cayla doesn't need any help from me. She's got Florence nailed.'

He sighed in appreciation. 'Och, I'm sure she has. And you both look the part.'

The study door creaked open, and Alison, Bennett and Louise emerged next. They'd opted to wear their smart civvies, much to Bennett's relief. Alison was all floaty in a rose-printed dress, and Bennett adjusted his shirt collar.

He was wearing a dark suit with a lemon shirt and charcoal tie, while Louise looked very summery in an ankle-length dress studded with poppies.

'Well, well, well. Doesn't everyone scrub up well, or what?'

Dane was strolling towards us. He'd pulled his hair back into a low ponytail and was wearing a sharp suit of the finest pinstripe with an ice blue shirt and a silver, stripey tie.

I gawped in surprise while Cayla reddened and stared down at the tiled floor.

Outside, there was the impatient shuffling of feet from the tour attendees, who were eager to get inside.

'We're almost ready to open those doors,' gushed Alison, an excited wobble in her voice. 'We're just waiting for Mindy to put the finishing touches to Mollie and Aubrey's hair, and for Josie to do a final run-through with them.'

As if on cue, the study door opened wider, and Mindy and Josie emerged with Mollie and Aubrey bustling behind them. Josie caught my eye and pulled an agonised expression.

I clamped my lips together to stop myself from laughing.

Mindy had worked her expertise on the older couple, who were now modelling severe, centre-parted hairstyles and thorny expressions.

'We're method acting,' hissed Mollie to a startled-looking Cayla.

'Their resemblance to my miserable great-grandparents is uncanny,' joked Bennett out of the side of his mouth to Alison, whose lips quivered. He slapped a hand to his forehead. 'Oh, silly me. I nearly forgot.'

'Forgot what?' puzzled Alison, as her husband dived back into the study.

Moments later, he emerged cradling one of Alison's butter and gold Villeroy and Boch Mettlach vases. 'We don't have the original vase that was stolen,' pointed out Bennett. 'But this will more than suffice to tell the story.'

I nodded. 'It's very pretty, and it's just a prop anyway.'

Bennett offered it to Mollie, who clung onto it like it was from the Ming Dynasty and cast a suspicious look over at Cayla again. They really were taking their method acting to another level!

Alison surveyed us all. 'Right. It's almost time. Let's get started. I think the natives are getting restless.'

With her dress swishing about her knees, Alison started to make her way towards the crowd peering through the glass panes of the double door entrance.

I squeezed Cayla's arm, whispering, 'Break a leg,' and she managed to conjure up a preoccupied smile. I could hear her murmuring her lines under her breath.

'Even with that hair and in that dress, you still look amazing,' whispered Dane.

'Yeah, right.'

'You do. Kind of sexily repressed.'

I couldn't help but laugh. 'Trust you.'

Alison glanced down at her wristwatch and back at us

all, lingering in the hall. 'Hold on. Where's Evan got to? Has anyone seen him?'

A sliver of something raced down my back at the mention of his name.

'Haven't seen him since this morning,' answered Louise. 'He appeared much earlier than usual for breakfast and said he was going for a run. I heard him come back and go for a shower.'

Where had Evan gone then? Not that it was any of my concern. But still.

What a hypocrite, I told myself. He'd been making remarks about Dane not showing any interest in saving The Ramblings. Then, when it came to the day of the actual tour, when tensions were high and nerves jangling, he'd vanished.

No doubt he was off somewhere writing another poisonous Fox review.

It was still inconceivable that the Evan I'd got to know, my Evan as he'd almost become, was the acerbic TV and film critic who struck fear into the hearts of actors, producers and directors everywhere.

I gave myself a mental talking to and refocused.

Glances were being exchanged all round at Evan's conspicuous absence.

Dane straightened his suit jacket. 'Makes a change for it not to be me letting the side down.'

Alison clicked her tongue at her younger son, but Dane just flashed his mother a cheeky grin.

'I'll give him a ring,' said Alison, tugging her mobile out

of her pocket. She dialled Evan's number, but it went through to voicemail.

'Don't worry, my love,' assured Bennett. 'He'll be on a story or talking to some contact. He'll appear soon.'

Alison considered this. 'Oh, you're probably right. Come on then, folks. Let's get this show on the road.'

Observing Cayla perform as Florence was like being in the presence of the young woman herself: striving to change her life, vulnerable, but with a hint of steel running through her.

Cayla's parents, Gillian and Morris, were equally mesmerised by their teenage daughter's performance, and quite right, too.

Pride shone out of them.

Gillian kept dabbing at her eyes with a hankie.

Mollie and Aubrey, although very irritating, were compelling as Bennett's great-grandparents, but also infuriating and judgmental in equal measure.

The tour attendees gasped and muttered amongst themselves at the way the Lords were shown treating young Florence with disdain she didn't deserve.

Watching Cayla drift through The Ramblings, addressing the assembled locals and tourists and pleading her case, was a joy. Boy, did this girl have talent. If only she could believe that herself. I hoped the enchanted faces of the crowd in front of her would make her start to realise what a promising young actor she was.

As I delivered my lines, enjoying acting out our scenes together, I came to realise that it felt like I was home again, performing in front of a crowd and breathing life into a character whom I never met but could only imagine.

For just a short while, acting as the caring teacher who encouraged Florence to read and write meant I could park any thoughts about Evan and Fox and just lose myself in what I loved most.

But as Cayla began to deliver her moving epilogue, the realisation of what that meant struck me.

It was time for Grandpa and me to leave The Ramblings.

I'd kept my promise. I'd helped with getting the tour off the ground and making it a reality. This first performance looked to have been a big success, and my job was done. I'd carried out my promise.

I found myself glancing around at the assembled faces in the crowd, taking in the myriad of ages, expressions and accents and the rainbow of T-shirts and jackets.

The rapturous applause and exclamations at the end of the tour made me refocus on the present.

Alison and Bennett were doing their best to answer a volley of enthusiastic questions from the audience. 'How often are you going to hold these tours?' 'Are you looking for other actors?' 'Do you know if I can read up about poor Florence?'

Dane stepped into the breach to assist his parents, who were valiantly answering the questions the best they could.

'Please, can I take some photos of you gorgeous ladies and gentlemen to upload on our social media channels, and then we can respond to any questions you might have?'

He flashed his white teeth at two elderly ladies in the front of the semi-circle who grinned back and giggled.

Dane produced his phone from his suit pocket and took several pictures of the audience, as well as of Cayla, Mollie, Aubrey and me.

The crowd then dispersed back out of the front entrance, admiring the portraits and furniture as they went and thanking us for such a moving and wonderful performance.

'You did great, kid,' said Dane to Cayla, who blushed.

'And you weren't bad either, Daisy,' he added.

'Why, thank you.'

The sound of Dane's mobile ringtone, 'Thunderstruck' by ACDC, blasted out. 'Excuse me a second.' He put the phone to his ear. 'Hey, Dez, my man. How's life?'

'Well, that was something,' breathed Cayla.

But our conversation was interrupted by Dane's incredulous voice. 'What? Are you joking?' Dane lowered his phone and stared down in disbelief at the screen. He thrust the phone back up to his ear to resume his conversation. 'Yeah, I just looked. I'm getting texts and messages now.' He wrapped up the call.

'Everything ok?' I asked.

'I'll tell you in a minute.'

Alison, Bennett, Louise, Mindy, Josie and Grandpa, who'd been chatting to the departing audience, came wandering over. 'Alright, son?' asked Bennett.

But Dane didn't reply. He was too busy pulling up social media on his phone.

Intrigued, Cayla and I moved closer, trying to catch a glimpse of what was capturing Dane's attention.

He increased the volume on his mobile and did a double-take. 'What the hell...?! Evan, what are you doing?' he gasped.

Chapter Twenty-Six

We all clustered around Dane, who raised his phone horizontally, so we could see the screen.

Evan's image appeared.

Every fibre of me felt adrift at the sight of him.

'Evan's on your phone?' asked Alison.

'He sure is, Mum. Across social media, no less.'

Bennett frowned. 'Well, where is he? What's he doing?'

Dane squinted at the screen. 'Looks like he's standing in front of Loch Crawe.'

Louise glanced at Bennett. 'What's he doing there?'

'Broadcasting live by the look of things,' said Dane.

'Broadcasting?' repeated Alison. 'Broadcasting what?'

Dane shrugged. 'That's what I want to find out! Dez, one of my roadie friends was checking his social media and stumbled across Evan saying he was going to go live online and make some kind of announcement.'

An announcement? What announcement?

The Great Hall seemed to be holding her breath too.

Dane looked impressed. 'Looks like he's live on You Tube, Instagram, Facebook, Tik-Tok … I didn't realise my big brother was so tech savvy.'

'That's impressive,' piped up Cayla.

My attention jerked from Dane back to his phone. What was Evan doing up by Loch Crawe? What was he going to say?

But it was as if Evan could read my mind and didn't give me any more opportunity to mentally dissect this bizarre situation. Behind him was the silver splendour of Loch Crawe, lit up like a gilded mirror in the Scottish June sunshine.

His voice rang out around The Ramblings.

'You won't know me.' He appeared hesitant; even a little self-conscious. 'My name is Evan Lord, and I'm a journalist.' The sun, up by Loch Crawe, strobed through his dark hair.

I couldn't pull my attention away from the screen. What was he doing there? Was this some sort of surprise promotional thing he was doing on behalf of the tour?

Bennet shook his head. 'Can someone please tell me what the hell is going on here?'

'None of us know, Dad,' said Dane.

Evan cleared his throat. Behind him, Loch Crawe shimmied in the light. Puffs of cloud danced overhead. 'My family own The Ramblings, which is an old estate in the Scottish Highlands. It's full of character and has been in our family for generations.'

Evan's gaze bore down his phone camera.

'But, like many of these old houses, they eat up money. Now, I'm not looking for sympathy for me or my family.' He raised his square chin. 'We're very fortunate to have The Ramblings as the family home, but in recent years it began to fall into disrepair. It became one thing after the other.'

Evan raised a hand and counted off his fingers. 'If it wasn't the central heating, it was repairs to its stonework, or dry rot, or woodworm in the beams, or was electrical issues or leaks.' He paused, then proceeded to speak again. 'I could see how worried my parents were over the place and what would happen. They'd deny it to my brother and me so as not to worry us, but as I got older, I soon came to realise it was becoming a never-ending battle to keep the place going.'

Evan lifted his hands and let them fall by his sides again. 'I knew I couldn't stand by and watch them deal with this on their own. They needed some financial assistance, but I knew my brother and I couldn't help much on that score.'

Evan gave a sad, brief smile. 'And then something happened. At the time, it seemed like a blessing. We needed a financial injection, and this seemed like the answer.' He stared down his phone camera lens, as though he were looking right at me.

I found myself taking a deep, inward breath, oblivious to Dane noticing.

'I received this new job offer. It just seemed too good to be true.'

I glanced at the intrigued faces around me. Grandpa caught me looking over at him and arched a brow.

On the phone, Evan braced himself as Loch Crawe continued to shimmy behind him. 'A friend of mine, Dave Woodrow, worked as senior sports reporter on *The London Gazette*. He said that a new editor had taken over and wanted to shake things up a bit.' Evan hesitated. 'He'd had the idea of introducing a brash and controversial TV and film review column and asked Dave if he knew of anyone who could write sharp, controversial copy; pull new readers in and get people talking.'

My eyes widened.

'Where the hell is he going with this story?' puzzled Dane.

I swallowed, said nothing and returned my attention to Dane's mobile.

'Dave kindly recommended me to his editor; I got called in for an interview and was asked to produce some example column copy. The editor read it, liked it and said he'd give me a six-month freelance trial. He also said I'd have no byline; I'd be anonymous, and therefore I could say what I wanted, and it would stir up more interest about who was behind the column.'

Evan rubbed at his face. 'I created a monster. The nastier and more sarcastic I was about TV and movies, the more the editor loved it, and so did the readers.'

I swung my attention away from Dane holding up his phone and examined the bewildered faces around me.

Evan stopped scratching his dark, stubbly jaw. 'What I'm trying to say is.' He gathered himself. 'I'm Fox, the critic for *The London Gazette*.'

Even though I'd guessed the direction of travel Evan was taking, it was still a surprise to hear him utter Fox's name and confess that they were one and the same person.

Alison almost got whiplash, jerking her head at Dane and then Bennett.

Dane let out a, 'Shit! You're kidding!' and scrambled not to drop his phone on the tiled hall floor.

'What's he admitted this for?' I murmured to myself. 'Why did he have to go public like that?'

I froze.

Several sets of eyes swivelled in my direction.

'You knew?' asked Dane. 'You knew Evan was Fox?'

I struggled to think of something to say, but Evan picked up his monologue again, and the gasps around me fell quiet. 'But I'm not Fox. At least not anymore. I've come to realise that some things are more important than having people talk about you.'

His bright, deep, dark eyes seemed to lock with mine through the phone screen. 'Me becoming Britain's most talked-about TV critic doesn't matter to me anymore. I only did it in the first place for the paycheque to help out my parents and The Ramblings. But over time, Fox took over, and I guess my ego did, too.' He gave his head a brief shake. 'But it's taken one special young woman to make me realise that what I was doing wasn't me, even though I thought I was doing it for the right reasons.'

My stomach whooshed.

Evan blew out a cloud of air. 'Daisy,' he faltered, eliciting sets of eyes to switch back in my direction again.

'Daisy Madden. She's not only a wonderful actor, but a sweet, thoughtful and beautiful woman. I mauled the TV show she was in for my column, even though half of what I said, I never meant. Again, they were just words to pull in the readers and cause a stir.' Shame gripped his handsome face. 'But it wasn't until I met her and saw what effect my review had had on her and her belief in herself that I wondered what the hell I was doing.'

'I think a certain young man is in love,' piped up Grandpa beside Louise. 'He wouldn't be doing all this if he weren't.'

'I think you're right,' agreed Josie, giving me a soft smile.

My head was spinning. Evan was revealing who he was on social media. He was making his career implode. He was doing all this because of me?

Evan gazed down the phone screen. 'Daisy, I don't know if you're watching this. But I want you to know that I've fallen in love with you. You've made me realise what matters, and that if you don't like yourself, how the hell can you expect someone else to?' His generous mouth flickered. 'From the way you took care of Shaun on our road trip…'

'Who's Shaun?' puzzled Louise.

Cayla shrugged. 'Beats me.'

'The way you've done everything you can to help with The Ramblings financial situation; how you've thrown yourself into the arrangements for the Florence tour; how you got involved with Cayla to make her see what a great little actor she is…'

At this, Cayla grinned so hard she looked like she might explode.

'And I get now how reckless words hurt people and what impact my review of *Sinister* had on you. I got to see that first-hand. I didn't see the people behind what I was doing, because I was too preoccupied trying to keep Fox's reputation going.'

Evan gazed up at the cloud-scattered sky for a few moments before looking directly back down at the camera. 'I wanted to tell you, Daisy. I wanted to tell you too, Mum and Dad and Dane. But Daisy, I knew I was falling for you, and I also knew I couldn't do it. I was terrified of what you'd say.' He shuffled from foot to foot. 'I was in too deep by then.'

'All I can say is, I'm so sorry you had to find out through a random email. I love you, and you've made me look at everything differently.'

'You and me both,' uttered Dane.

Evan reset his expression. 'Anyway, I just had to do this and clear the air before I head back to London.'

His words made my blood freeze.

'I can't face the prospect of returning to The Ramblings without you being there, Daisy, so I've managed to book myself on a flight back down south later on today.' His face was still for a moment. 'I've messed up big time, but please know I never meant to deceive you. And as for my family, I'm sorry for not telling you the truth. Being Fox wasn't something I was very proud of, considering the effect my words had on people, but I did it to try and help secure the future of the family home.'

More gasps and murmurs rose up into the hall. 'It just turned out not to be the best idea, and it wasn't enough anyway.'

Evan lurched forward towards his phone and switched it off. The screen went dark.

Dane's phone proceeded to light up with more texts and messages from people who'd seen it. My phone then trilled. It was Jade, followed by Octavia.

Alison and Bennett were next to receive calls from friends who'd seen Evan's broadcast.

Cayla spun round. 'What're you going to do now, Daisy?'

I stared at her. 'You heard him. He's going back to London in a few hours.'

Cayla rolled her eyes. 'Duh. Yeah. Because he thinks you don't feel the same about him. He thinks Fox will always be in the way.'

I blushed under my backcombed, elaborate updo. 'He didn't tell me the truth. I can't see past that.'

'But it wasn't exactly a betrayal, was it?' piped up Dane, sounding serious and mature. He waggled his mobile. 'You heard him. He's in love with you.' There was a flicker of something sad in Dane's eyes. 'He didn't tell us about being Fox either. He thought he was doing this for all the right reasons.'

My head rattled.

Grandpa examined me. 'Daisy, I echo what Cayla just

asked you. What are you going to do now? Throw away a chance of being happy because of your hurt pride?'

Josie tutted as she approached. She patted me on the arm. 'I can't believe you're still standing there.'

One self-conscious hand shot up to prod my hair.

Cayla sighed with exasperation. 'What did you tell me when I said I was giving up on my acting? You told me to believe in myself and just go for it. Trying is better than not giving it a go in the first place. Don't live with regret, you said.'

God, she was so annoying when she was right.

'Do you love Evan?'

Dane's voice made me jerk my head away from Cayla to look at him standing next to me. There was an element of melancholy acceptance in his words.

What Evan just did, his standing there in front of Loch Crawe, washed over me. What he said and the flickers of emotion in the way he said it; what he'd just given up and sacrificed to tell the truth. 'Yes,' I managed. 'Yes, I am in love with him.'

'Then go!' ordered Alison, pointing towards the door to The Ramblings. 'Now!'

My heart galloped in my chest. I let out an odd sound – a mixture of a laugh and a sob – and started yanking out the pins in my hair. It fell down in a messy tumble of curls.

'Thank you,' I choked. 'All of you.'

'Here,' panted Cayla, reappearing and jangling my car keys and mobile phone in her hand. 'You'll need these. I got them from your handbag in your room.'

I hugged Cayla, planted a kiss on Dane's cheek and gathered up my skirts as I raced towards the imposing double doors.

'You're still wearing your gown!' pointed out Mindy.

'Don't have time to change,' I called back. 'I've got to get to Evan!'

I hitched up the hem of my dress, clattering down the stone steps in my ankle boots and towards Marlene, my hair flying loose behind me. God, it was a relief to get those hairgrips out and untighten my poor scalp.

I yanked open the driver side door, jumped in and fired up the engine.

I tried to call Evan on his mobile, but it was switched off.

I screeched away from The Ramblings, sending pink gravel spraying into the air, and headed for the main road.

I knew I had to get to Evan; to tell him I understood now why he'd done what he did, and how circumstances can overtake your plans. I had to tell him that I knew how exhilarating it was to become someone else, too, and that it was easy to lose your own identity.

He had become Fox for all the right reasons, and now I knew that. I also knew that we had a future together. I couldn't imagine him not being there in my plans.

Evan had thrived on Fox's anonymity, and now that he'd given that up, his life wouldn't be the same again. And the reason he'd done that? Me.

I concentrated through the sun-splashed windscreen and gripped the steering wheel.

On the seat beside me, my phone erupted again. Jade's name appeared. Moments later, Octavia tried to call me, too.

I fixed my attention on the road ahead, not taking any notice of the dusty country lanes and bustling hedgerows dotted with flowers. All I could focus on was getting to Loch Crawe. Thank goodness it wasn't far.

Evan was Fox.

Evan was in love with me.

I was in love with him.

Confessions were catching.

Leon and his tainted memories had held me back and made me cautious.

Not anymore.

Relieved to see very little traffic, I put my foot down on the accelerator.

Loch Crawe unfolded to my right like a huge, oval mirror in the sunshine.

'Please let him still be here,' I pleaded out loud, looking to the picnic area on the left. It was deserted.

I slowed down and looked around, but there was no sign of him. Surely he must still be here somewhere?

I parked up near the picnic area and jumped out, calling his name over and over, but there was no answer.

I yanked up the hem of my gown and darted this way and that, calling his number again. Still no reply.

I was almost hoarse by this time, weaving amongst the stately trees at the picnic area and then crunching down by the loch shore.

I couldn't see him anywhere.

I don't know how long I trailed around looking for him or hoping to catch a glimpse of him. The hem of my dress caught on the shingle by the loch shore. My hair clamped itself to my cheeks.

With dejected tears springing down my face, I trudged back to Marlene and sank into the driver side seat. I rested my head on top of the steering wheel.

Evan was gone.

I did love him, but he thought I didn't.

That hurt more than anything else in the world.

Chapter Twenty-Seven

Loch Crawe became a mist of glittery water through my tears.

The trees bled like a Monet painting.

After what seemed like an eternity, I raised my head from the steering wheel. I rubbed my eyes, clicked on my seatbelt and started up Marlene.

My phone lit up with texts and calls from Alison, Bennett and Dane asking if I'd located Evan.

I decided just to set off back to The Ramblings and tell them. It was over. I'd been deluding myself. Evan and I weren't meant to be. No matter how badly I wanted it, I had to face the fact that our love wouldn't be enough. I hadn't been enough for Leon. Perhaps this was Fate taking Evan and me in different directions?

The fields glided past in emeralds, ambers and jades.

Marlene slunk back into the grounds.

I parked up and tried to gather myself before confronting everyone.

My face was like an exploding tomato, and my hair was a sweaty tangle.

But I didn't care.

I just wanted to closet myself in my room, peel off this dress and wallow.

'You didn't find him?'

Dane came bounding down the steps. He'd changed out of his suit and had thrown on a pair of his old stone-washed jeans and a Metallica T-shirt. He'd let his hair out of its ponytail, and it was flapping in the breeze.

'He's gone.' I blundered past him.

Everyone was still milling around in the Great Hall, just as Dane and I entered. 'Evan's gone back to London,' I rasped, my throat clotted with emotion. 'Now, if you'll excuse me, I'll go and get ready, and then Grandpa and I will be off.'

Everyone exchanged forlorn glances.

'You're leaving?' piped up Dane. 'What, today?'

'Yes. I'm sorry. I can't stay here. Not anymore. And I did say we'd leave after the first tour anyway.'

Dane gently guided me to one side. 'Is there anything I can do?'

I gave him an appreciative, shaky smile. 'Thank you, but no.' I studied him through a mist of tears. 'You know, I can't believe how much you've changed.'

Dane blinked at me. 'In what way?'

'In every way. You're much more considerate of people

and more empathetic.' I sighed. 'Pity I hadn't been more like that with Evan.'

Dane coloured under his stubble.

'Don't tell me Dane Lord, rock god, is blushing.'

He grinned at me from under his fair brows. 'Like I said, that's down to you. You've made me more human.'

'Don't be daft.' I felt vulnerable and open right now, and I knew I'd evaporate into a puddle at any moment if anyone was nice to me.

'It's true,' said Dane. 'Your good qualities have rubbed off on me.' He hesitated. 'Look Daisy, I know I've said this before, but you know how I feel about you.' Then he erupted, 'Christ, my brother can be such a prick!'

He gathered himself and glanced up at the elaborate twirls and twists of the hall ceiling. He flicked his hair back like an agitated stallion. 'I like you. You know that.'

'Dane, I'm flattered, but now is not the right time.'

'I know. I know. But just please hear me out.' He lowered his voice as Louise drifted past on her way to the kitchen. 'I can be patient. I'm prepared to wait. For you, I mean. If there's any chance in the future that you could look at me like you did at Evan, then you just whistle, and I'll be there.'

I bit back more tears. 'Dane, please stop. I'm going to be crying all over you in a minute. You're a talented and very attractive guy.'

'But I'm not him,' concluded Dane with a ghost of a smile.

I gave my head the briefest shake.

'It's ok. I get it. You can't help who you fall for.'

I reached for Dane's ringed hand and took it in mine. Everybody had drifted off now in different directions, and it was just us alone in the hall. 'I'm sorry. I think the best thing for me right now is to try and lay low for a while until this whole Fox thing calms down. Spend time with Grandpa before heading back to London.'

'No, don't be sorry. You're being honest. That's what matters.'

I gave his hand a playful waggle. 'You'll meet some stunning rock chick.'

He returned the friendly squeeze of my hand. 'Nah. Not interested. I need to get over you first.'

I managed to laugh, but then a single tear slithered down my face.

'Oh, please don't cry. I'm useless when girls get upset. I always say the wrong thing.'

'You haven't this time.'

Dane stroked the tear from my cheek. 'You really are so special, Daisy. Evan's a dick.'

'Maybe I'm the dick for not letting him explain. I just saw red when I found out he was Fox. I thought I couldn't trust him. It reminded me so much of my ex, and I knew I couldn't – and wouldn't – go through all that again.'

I gathered my fists and rubbed my eyes. 'Anyway, I'm going to get out of this governess gown and pack, and then Grandpa and I will be off.

I rubbed his hand with affection and then made for the

staircase. My boots clicked up the first couple of steps before I turned around. Dane began to walk off.

'Dane?'

He spun round. 'Yep?'

'Thank you.'

'For what?'

'For everything,' I choked. 'For what you said just now. For being kind.'

'I was being truthful.'

I gulped. 'Well, thank you.'

I gazed up at the soaring hallway. 'I'm really going to miss this place.'

'It'll miss you.'

I clattered up a couple more steps of the staircase and looked around again at Dane standing below. I added, 'At least Evan knows who he is now, and everything is out in the open.'

And as I swished up the remaining steps to my room, closed the door, peeled off the dress and unlaced my ankle boots, all I wanted to do was escape from The Ramblings with Grandpa and head home to Strath Ross.

Yes, I'd miss this house, but without Evan here, knowing that he'd gone and taken a piece of my heart with him, it was no longer the house I remembered.

———

Alison suggested Grandpa and I stay for dinner before we set off for Strath Ross, but I politely declined; much to the irritation of Grandpa, who'd fallen in love with Louise's cooking. The fact that she was serving Scottish venison tonight, with her homemade mashed potatoes and vegetable medley, fresh from The Ramblings gardens, didn't make Grandpa's mood any better.

Evan's online revelations and him returning to London had made me feel stupid and wounded.

Still, I should have expected that. I hadn't given him a chance to explain his reasons about him becoming Fox and why he'd chosen not to tell me. I'd let my dislike of Fox colour my view, and I hadn't been able to see beyond that.

After throwing off the governess gown, I showered, pulled my hair into a ponytail and threw on one of my Mango T-shirts and a pair of wide-legged jeans.

Josie and Mindy had left to go home and relax after a hectic first tour day.

Josie had given me a prolonged hug and made me promise not to give up on my acting, and to not be a stranger, which had made me choke with more tears.

Once I'd assisted Grandpa with his packing, I took our cases downstairs to deposit them by the entrance.

As I got ready to make my way to the top of the Cinderella staircase, I tried to fight the temptation to look across at Evan's bedroom.

The door was ajar, and Louise had stripped his bed.

Snapshots of Evan and me rolling around, making love, laughing and kissing spilled in front of my eyes.

To try and block out the pictures, I gripped the handles

of our cases harder in each hand and thumped them down each of the stairs.

Louise, Alison, Bennett, Grandpa and Cayla were assembled in the hall. It looked like they'd gathered together to wave us off.

I noted that there was no Dane.

Had he taken offence at my rebuttal earlier?

Bennett noticed me frowning. 'Dane has a gig at that new music venue in Kingussie.'

'Oh, right.'

I plucked my phone out of my back pocket and glanced down at the screen. More missed calls and texts from people I'd acted with before, as well as more messages from Jade and Octavia about the Fox debacle. I'd speak to them when I felt up to it. There was nothing from Evan.

'The proverbial shit has really hit the fan now.' Bennett complained. 'We're getting calls and texts from the press about Evan. His Fox reveal even got a mention on the *Six O'clock News*.'

Alison attempted to brush off her husband's concern. 'It'll all blow over. Must be a quiet news day.' She let out an agitated sigh. 'But I still can't believe Evan was Fox in the first place.'

'He was playing a part of sorts,' I said, the meaning not lost on me. 'His alter ego took off, and he was struggling to control everything. I get that now.'

Grandpa gave my arm a supportive squeeze.

I lingered, taking in the proud old paintings, the glossy butterscotch and white tiled floor and the mullioned windows. I imprinted every crevice and crenelation of The Ramblings in my mind so in the future I could pull it out of my memory and remember.

There were emotional kisses and hugs all round.

'The Ramblings has a new lease of life now, thanks to you,' said Alison, delivering a kiss to my cheek.

'And we have plenty of volunteers to help with the future Florence tours, thanks to the Forrest Bank Players,' added Bennett, giving me a protective hug.

It was Louise's turn next to kiss Grandpa and me and show her affection. 'Please come back and see us again soon.'

Grandpa nodded and smiled, but I knew in my heart I wouldn't return here.

Cayla was next. She clung on to me and buried an emotional sob into my T-shirt, which made me fight more tears. She looked so different from earlier. She was back in her jeans and a strappy top. 'Thank you so much, Daisy, for everything.'

I also noticed G

randpa give Louise a look that lasted a few seconds longer than necessary. I didn't think it was just me who had lost my heart here at The Ramblings.

We all trooped out towards Marlene, and Bennett insisted on helping me stash our cases into the boot.

Once I'd got Grandpa comfy in the passenger side, I arranged my face into what I hoped was a winning smile and switched on Marlene. She purred into life.

I edged us out of the parking space.

The evening June sunshine was pushing through the trees and gliding across The Ramblings windows, serenaded by the birds.

It was a stunning, contented scene, and yet inside I was still torturing myself over what might have been.

It had been a mess, which we could have unscrambled together. But Evan had decided to return to London, and I'd realised too late that he had his reasons for being Fox and not divulging his secret in the first place.

Grandpa persisted with his concerned glances across at me as I edged up the driveway and towards the country lane.

Alison, Bennett, Cayla and Louise's pensive faces wavered in my rear-view mirror.

'You ok, Daisy chain?' Grandpa asked.

I nodded. 'I'll be fine.'

I clutched the steering wheel and watched a couple of cars flash past. 'It's ok. I mean, I'm ok.'

Grandpa shook his head. 'You don't have to pretend with me, sweetheart. I can see how much you're hurting over Evan … Jesus! Look out!'

I slammed on the brakes as Dane's bashed-up, white truck came swinging round the corner of the hedgerow, almost smashing into the front of Marlene.

'For goodness' sake, Dane!' I erupted. 'You took that corner far too fast…'

My voice petered to a stop.

Sitting beside Dane in the passenger seat and staring out at me, as though I were a ghost, was Evan.

The second Dane switched off his engine, Evan leapt out of his side of the truck.

He kept looking at me, oblivious to everyone and everything else.

I just gazed back at him through my sun-splashed windscreen trying to fathom what was going on.

'Well?' said Grandpa beside me. 'Are you just going to sit there and gawp at him, or are you going to speak to the poor lad?'

I blinked for several moments out at Evan, as though I couldn't move, before my fingers fumbled to unclip my seatbelt.

I clambered out.

My heart zoomed into my throat as I drew closer to him.

I was so preoccupied that I barely noticed Dane slipping out of his truck, too.

Evan walked to meet me halfway on the gravelly drive. The sun was brushing through his hair.

'What are you doing here?' I blurted. 'I mean, I thought you said you were returning to London.'

'I was. But I didn't want to. I thought you didn't want anything more to do with me after you found out I was Fox.' He motioned his head back, indicating Dane behind him. 'I'd switched my mobile off for a while because of all the texts and calls I was receiving after going online. But when I turned it back on, I saw Dane had messaged me repeatedly.'

Dane shrugged and delivered a bashful smile.

I was struggling to sort everything out in my head. 'I thought you had a gig tonight?' I asked him.

He coughed dramatically. 'Had to postpone it. Think I might be coming down with something.' Then he winked at me.

What was going on here?

Evan continued. 'I kept telling Dane to leave me alone, but he wouldn't take no for an answer. Then he showed up at the airport.'

Behind us were Alison, Bennett, Louise and Cayla, who had come spilling back out of The Ramblings on hearing the commotion.

'What's going on here?' asked Alison. Her gaze settled on Evan. 'Evan? What are you doing? I thought you said you were going back to London.'

'Mum. We'll tell you in a minute, ok?' said Dane. 'Just let Evan speak.'

The four of them fell into a hush.

Evan picked up the story again. 'Dane told me down the phone that I'd been a stupid prat, and that if I allowed Fox to ruin what I could have with you, then I was even more of a prat than he thought I was.' He let his toned arms rise and fall back down by his sides. 'Like I said online, I only took on the Fox column because I wanted to help my parents stop this place from going under, and then Fox and that column took on a life of their own.'

He sighed and looked down at me with his warm, dark eyes. 'But now I've come clean about everything, I feel free. Ok, so I've lost my work at *The London Gazette*, but I couldn't keep pretending to be someone I wasn't, especially when my words were damaging other people.' He paused, his handsome features focused on me. 'Most of all, what effect they'd had on you.'

I swallowed and took a couple of faltering steps even closer to him, my trainers crunching the gravel. 'I get how becoming someone else can be a compelling thing. I know only too well.' I fought to hold back tears. 'I did everything I could not to fall for you. I kept telling myself that you were a London townie, and that after my messy breakup, I needed another one like a hole in the head.'

I paused, appreciating every plane and angle of his face. 'I tried to pull back, but I couldn't.'

I folded my arms around myself. 'Then, when I saw that email and discovered you were Fox, my world felt like it was falling down around me again. I thought, "Here we go. More deception," and I was so angry at you for being like Leon. Or at least I tried to convince myself you were.'

Evan shook his head. 'Fox is in my past now. Sure, I'll have to deal with the fallout for a bit.' His brown eyes locked with mine. 'But that's a small price to pay.'

My stomach pirouetted. 'What are you going to do now?'

Evan broke into a smile. 'I've had offers already. Would you believe that a major publisher just called me and offered me a book deal to write about my time as Fox!'

'What?' I gasped.

'It's true,' interjected Dane behind Evan. 'The jammy sod took the call while I was driving him back here.'

But Evan was quick to swivel his attention back to me again. 'I don't care about any of that. All I care about is you, Daisy.' He let out a sexy, low laugh that made my skin tremble. 'How you were with Shaun during the road trip; what a terrific actor you are; how you've helped Mum and Dad with the tour; supporting Cayla; you do everything you can to make other people happy.'

He gazed down into my face. It was as if everyone and everything else was falling away: the past; Grandpa, Louise, Bennett, Alison, Cayla; The Ramblings with its golden brickwork glittering in the sunlight. 'You think about other people before you think about yourself.'

'I came up to Loch Crawe to look for you after you'd been on social media, but I couldn't find you.'

'I know. Dane told me.' He reached out one hand and stroked my cheek.

Dane dropped his eyes to the gravel, and behind me, our spectators tactfully turned their attention to the nearby shrubs and flowers and ambled off down the side of the gardens to give us some privacy.

I took his hand and pressed it against my cheek. I was worried that, if I closed my eyes and opened them again, he wouldn't be standing there. 'I didn't come to the airport to try and find you because I thought you might have done what you did for closure. You made that revelation on social media, and I came to the conclusion that it was an unofficial tying-up of loose ends.' I grimaced. 'I thought that really was it between us.'

Evan shook his head. 'You weren't the only one carrying

around baggage after a bad breakup. I was frightened, too,' he admitted. 'Frightened after what happened with Sacha that I'd end up feeling like an idiot and being let down all over again.'

'And now?'

'I'm not frightened of anything anymore, Daisy. I'm not frightened about having been Fox, and I'm not frightened of the future. Not if I have you.'

Evan lowered his lips to mine, and we kissed slowly, the promise of what was to come in the future spreading out ahead of us.

'Wait until I get you alone,' he murmured against my mouth. 'I can't do what I want to do with the oldies around.'

I grinned against his mouth.

And as Evan picked me up and swung me around, any doubts about who I was and who I wanted to be evaporated. It didn't matter who we'd been before or why.

All that mattered was the love we had for one another.

Epilogue

JUNE, TWO YEARS LATER

I t doesn't seem like two years since I almost sloshed a glass of champagne over that rude but innocent man.

Evan and I, along with Alison, Bennett, Louise, Grandpa, Dane and his new girlfriend (more about her in a moment!), have just returned from Loch Crawe, where the book launch of Evan's autobiography *For Fox's Sake* was held.

As its title suggests, it's all about his time as the eponymous newspaper critic: the pitfalls, the highs, the lows, the struggle to keep his identity secret and how it all came to a head when he met me.

Needless to say, Octavia has been delighted at the exposure I've received out of this. A couple of TV and film casting directors want me to audition for their rom-coms, and I've already filmed my part in an up-and-coming thriller miniseries set in Edinburgh for a well-known streaming channel.

But my life has taken another surprising and even more rewarding turn, because not only am I also helping out Josie by giving acting classes to her drama students at the high school, but Evan and I have also taken over the day-to-day running of The Ramblings!

We decided to move back to Scotland once all the Fox fuss had died down, and we're now living together in a cute apartment with Loch Crawe and the rolling hills on our doorstep. But a big shock was in store when Alison and Bennett confided in us on our return that they felt it was time The Ramblings was passed onto the next generation, leaving them to celebrate by taking a much-deserved round-the-world cruise. They had a ball!

We've turned this gorgeous manor into a romantic and much sought-after wedding venue, with its sweeping lawns and its guest rooms housing lavish four-poster beds. We've even organised a few film and theatre-themed weddings recently and have had more enquiries from interested couples keen to have a similarly themed wedding of their own now that word has spread. I'm in my element!

Table place settings were made to look like old-fashioned cinema tickets, and the tablecloths were printed with the musical notes of famous film scores. We also arranged for clapperboard-style bags of theatre-themed favours such as popcorn, 3D glasses and quotes from cult movies for the wedding guests. I also called on the services of a few actor friends of mine to mingle at the wedding receptions dressed as Marilyn Monroe, Charlie Chaplin, Darth Vader and Audrey Hepburn. Even the wedding reception music, supplied by musician friends of Dane's, ranged from instantly recognisable musical tunes to dramatic movie scores. It's such a thrill to see this beautiful old house providing the setting for so many newly married couples beginning their lives together.

Evan is still keeping his hand in freelance journalism from time to time, but he's more focused on The Ramblings these days and is loving every minute of it. We are in this together, and it feels wonderful.

Talking of loving what you do, Cayla was thrilled to secure a place at Glasgow's Royal Conservatoire of Scotland, my old alma mater, to study for a degree in drama after successfully completing her Advanced Highers. When she's able to come home for a visit, she more than happily reprises her role as Florence to give her fellow actors a break! Her confidence has soared, and she embraces acting again, as though her passion for it never went away.

I like to think that somewhere Florence is smiling and appreciative of what Cayla has done in portraying her story and showing her as the strong, determined and spirited young woman she was.

The tour has become such a success that Alison and Bennett had no problem recruiting keen volunteers from the Forrest Bank Players to play not only Florence but also Bennett's great-grandparents and Constance Miller in a rota system three times a week. And Josie is on hand to step into the breach whenever it is required, as well as assist with rehearsals.

We still stage the Florence tours regularly, and they

continue to attract fascinated people from the surrounding areas as well as other parts of Scotland, and even foreign tourists keen to witness first-hand a slice of Scottish history. I think the fact that what happened to Florence is a true story makes her tale resonate even more with the public.

Grandpa moved from Strath Ross last autumn and now lives in a sweet little cottage only ten minutes away from us here in Forrest Bank, but I'm delighted to say he isn't on his own. Louise has moved in with him.

They have become even closer over these past months, and both of them are a very treasured part of The Ramblings extended family. Louise is a godsend with her baking and organisational skills, playing a major part in the weddings we put on, and Grandpa heads for the gardens whenever he's here, keeping the flowerbeds neat, tidy and exploding with colour. Thankfully, due to the fortunes of The Ramblings turning around, Alison and Bennett were able to re-hire their former gardener, Freddie, and he and Grandpa are a horticultural force to be reckoned with!

Now, back to Dane and his new girlfriend, Erica.

He met her six months ago when he approached a new public relations company to get some advice about further promotion for Disciple.

Their following is growing, thanks in part to their great music and talented frontman, and also due to Dane being the brother of the famed Fox. Dane was the first to admit that the added publicity did him and the other guys in the band no harm at all! They lit up social media, and things are going from strength to strength for the band.

Erica is the complete opposite of a rock chick, all dark, chic, cheek-grazing hair and well-cut suits, but they're crazy about each other, and it's wonderful to see Dane evolving further into someone who his parents are so proud of.

But it's not just only the tour and other people's weddings that The Ramblings is playing host to; Evan and I are having our own summer wedding here in just three weeks' time!

We couldn't have considered holding it anywhere else. The Ramblings is in my heart now, too, and has given me so much: Evan and a new family.

Louise was thrilled when we asked her to make our wedding cake. After happy tears, she said she'd be honoured to make our three-tiered, lemon and buttercream affair, decorated with fresh flowers from The Ramblings gardens, which I think is a lovely touch.

We are continuing to keep it in the family, as Dane and Disciple are playing at our wedding reception, and Grandpa will be giving me away.

Jade is going to be my bridesmaid – well, her and her baby bump!

Yes, she and Jasper are expecting an autumn baby, and her aristocratic parents are thrilled, already spoiling 'Bug' (Jade's name for her bump) with assorted outfits and toys that are far too advanced for a newborn! I can't wait to become the little one's Auntie Daisy.

I've come to realise that you can't let what other people do and how they treat you define you as a person. It's up to you to try to move on and leave the past behind.

I know I'm loved and that I love the people around me. From Josie to Gillian and Cayla, Grandpa and I have a new family now, and both of us couldn't be any happier or more content than we are.

Just be yourself, because everybody else is taken … unless you're an actor, of course.

Acknowledgments

Thank you so much to my amazing editor extraordinaire, Jennie Rothwell, at One More Chapter. You never cease to amaze me with your talent and skill! Grateful thanks also to all the rest of the fabulous team at HarperCollins, including fabulous line editor Nicola Doherty, the fantastic copy editor Caroline Scott-Bowden and great proofreader Samantha Gale.

Thank you also to my friend and wonderful agent, Selwa Anthony, and to Linda Anthony. I'm very lucky to know you both.

Huge thanks and love as always to my boys.

And to anyone out there who has a dream: just go for it, and ignore the doubters. There's nothing worse than not trying and living with regret.

Like Daisy says, be yourself, because everybody else is taken.

ONE MORE CHAPTER

YOUR NUMBER ONE STOP
FOR PAGETURNING BOOKS

The author and One More Chapter would like to thank everyone
who contributed to the publication of this story...

Analytics
Imogen Wolstencroft

Audio
Fionnuala Barrett
Ciara Briggs

Design
Lucy Bennett
Fiona Greenway
Liane Payne
Dean Russell

Digital Sales
Laura Daley
Lydia Grainge
Hannah Lismore

eCommerce
Laura Carpenter
Madeline ODonovan
Charlotte Stevens
Christina Storey
Rachel Ward

Editorial
Rosie Best
Kara Daniel
Charlotte Ledger
Laura McCallen
Jennie Rothwell
Sofia Salazar Studer
Caroline Scott-Bowden
Helen Williams

Harper360
Emily Gerbner
Ariana Juarez
Jean Marie Kelly
emma sullivan
Sophia Wilhelm

International Sales
Ruth Burrow
Bethan Moore
Colleen Simpson

Inventory
Sarah Callaghan
Kirsty Norman

Marketing & Publicity
Chloe Cummings
Grace Edwards
Katie Sadler

Operations
Melissa Okusanya

Production
Denis Manson
Simon Moore
Francesca Tuzzeo

Rights
Ashton Mucha
Alisah Saghir
Zoe Shine
Aisling Smyth

Trade Marketing
Ben Hurd
Eleanor Slater

**The HarperCollins
Contracts Team**

**The HarperCollins
Distribution Team**

**The HarperCollins
Finance & Royalties
Team**

**The HarperCollins
Legal Team**

**The HarperCollins
Technology Team**

UK Sales
Isabel Coburn
Jay Cochrane
Leah Woods

**And every other
essential link in the
chain from delivery
drivers to booksellers
to librarians and
beyond!**

When romance author **Rosie Winters**'s own fairytale romance ends with a bang, she's determined to get away from everything. Rosie spent her summers at her late grandmother's coastal cottage in the Highlands and knows it'll be the perfect place to wallow for a while. Even better that there's a gorgeous lighthouse and dolphins in the bay.

What Rosie didn't expect was to bump into the new lighthouse keeper, **Mitch**. Despite her recent heartbreak, Rosie finds herself fascinated by the mysterious Mitch. As they spend more time together, is it possible that he needs Rosie every bit as as much as she needs him…

AVAILABLE IN PAPERBACK, EBOOK AND AUDIO!

When city girl **Darcie Freeman** is sent to the Isle of Skye to conduct research for a travel guide, she's horrified. The prospect of having to travel to a remote island in the Scottish Highlands leaves her wondering what she'll do. Step in **Logan Burns**. Gorgeous and adventurous, he lives and breathes the island and is going to show Darcie everything she needs to know about Skye.

As Darcie swaps her designer shoes for her walking boots, will she learn there's more to life than the picture-perfect presence she shares on social media, or will it be the case that Skye is the limit…

AVAILABLE NOW IN PAPERBACK AND EBOOK!

ONE MORE CHAPTER

One More Chapter is an
award-winning global
division of HarperCollins.

Subscribe to our newsletter to get our
latest eBook deals and stay up to date
with all our new releases!

signup.harpercollins.co.uk/
join/signup-omc

Meet the team at
www.onemorechapter.com

Follow us!

@onemorechapterhc

Do you write unputdownable fiction?
We love to hear from new voices.
Find out how to submit your novel at
www.onemorechapter.com/submissions